Oliver Optic

The Yankee Middy; or, the Adventures of a Naval Officer

A Story of the Great Rebellion

Oliver Optic

The Yankee Middy; or, the Adventures of a Naval Officer
A Story of the Great Rebellion

ISBN/EAN: 9783337212391

Printed in Europe, USA, Canada, Australia, Japan

Cover: Foto ©Andreas Hilbeck / pixelio.de

More available books at **www.hansebooks.com**

Latitude Forty-one: Longitude Sixty-two. Page 173.

THE YANKEE MIDDY

OLIVER OPTIC

LEE & SHEPARD.

BOSTON.

THE YANKEE MIDDY;

OR,

THE ADVENTURES OF A NAVAL OFFICER.

A Story of the Great Rebellion.

BY

OLIVER OPTIC,

AUTHOR OF "RICH AND HUMBLE," "IN SCHOOL AND OUT," "WATCH AND WAIT,
"THE BOAT CLUB," "ALL ABOARD," "NOW OR NEVER," "TRY AGAIN,"
"POOR AND PROUD," "LITTLE BY LITTLE," "THE RIVERDALE
STORY BOOKS," "THE SOLDIER BOY," "THE SAILOR
BOY," "THE YOUNG LIEUTENANT," ETC.

BOSTON:

LEE AND SHEPARD,

SUCCESSORS TO PHILLIPS, SAMPSON & CO.

1869

ELECTROTYPED AT THE

Boston Stereotype Foundry,

No. 4 Spring Lane.

TO

EDWIN FLEMING, ESQ.,

This Book

IS RESPECTFULLY DEDICATED,

BY HIS FRIEND

WILLIAM T. ADAMS.

PREFACE.

"THE YANKEE MIDDY" is a sequel to "THE SAILOR BOY," and traces the career of Jack Somers, as an officer, from the Naval Academy to his promotion to the rank of ensign. The hero is not an ideal being; he has hundreds of prototypes in our gallant navy. He is brave, but no braver than thousands of others, who have lived to see the Great Rebellion crushed out by their devoted efforts; he is true to God and himself, but he is only what hundreds of others have been who have passed through the fiery ordeal of temptation, and have come forth unscathed.

The incidents of the story are those which have occurred on the ocean, and on the bays, inlets, and rivers of the South, common in the experience of all our naval officers who have been actively employed during the war. As in its predecessors, so far as the work is historical, the best authorities have been consulted. The author is again indebted to his friend, Ensign Francis L. Harris, not only for verbal details, but for the use of charts, diagrams, and works relating to the navy. The text books of the Naval Academy have been constantly at hand during the preparation of the volume.

Again we submit Jack Somers — or rather Mr. Midshipman Somers — to our readers, young and old. We have intended to make him a noble and Christian young man : and we have left his daily life to teach the lesson of Christian fidelity and patriotism, without any attempt to enforce the moral by interweaving an occasional page of dry "deductions," which are very likely to be omitted in the reading. If the moral cannot readily be seen, it is not worth looking for.

The author, ever grateful for the kindness of his readers, submits the fourth volume of "THE ARMY AND NAVY SERIES," with the hope that it will be found worthy of the favor which has been bestowed upon its predecessors.

WILLIAM T. ADAMS.

HARRISON SQUARE, MASS., October 23, 1865.

CONTENTS.

THE YANKEE MIDDY.

THE YANKEE MIDDY;

OR,

THE ADVENTURES OF A NAVAL OFFICER.

CHAPTER· I.

MRS. COMMODORE PORTINGTON AND PARTY.

ANAGE the boat! Why, my dear madam, you forget that I served five years in the United States navy, and that I know every rope in the ship," said Mr. Philip Kennedy, steadying himself with the boat-hook he held in his hand.

"I know you are a good sailor, but — " And Mrs. Portington did not seem to be inclined to give further expression to the thought which was in her mind.

There had been a very pleasant party at the old fort on the Dumpling Rocks. It was a picnic, and the company had enjoyed themselves to the full extent that a sea-breeze in August, with choice eatables and cool drinkables, can produce enjoyment. Mrs. Commodore Portington and her fair daughter Kate were of the party,

and had attended under the escort of Mr. Philip Kennedy. An engagement in the evening obliged the lady
and her daughter to return to Newport in advance of the
rest of the company. She had come down to the
water's edge, where the gentleman had hauled up the
boat in readiness for her to embark.

The lady seemed to be perplexed with a serious doubt;
for though her husband was a commodore in the navy,
she had a womanly respect for salt water, especially, as
in the present instance, when the wind and the waves
were coquetting violently with each other, thereby wak-
ing up the sleepy tide, and creating a pretty heavy
in-shore sea. The lady did not like the looks of the
waves that beat upon the ragged rocks. They were
suggestive of wet dresses, and, more remotely, of an
involuntary bath, and still more remotely, of a commission to a fashionable undertaker.

The craft was a well and strongly built Newport boat,
with a single sail, worn on a cat-rig — the best in the
world for rapid movements. Mrs. Portington was the
wife of a sailor, and knew a safe and weatherly boat
when she saw one. It was by no means dangerous
weather; it did not yet blow even half a gale ; it was
only a jolly fresh breeze. Still, she was perplexed with
a doubt, and the longer she gazed upon the gentleman
in charge of the boat, the larger and more formidable
became the doubt,

If the picnic had been conducted on purely temperance principles, it is quite probable that the lady would not have been disturbed by a single doubt; for certainly it would not have been consistent for the wife of a commodore to be afraid of a fresh breeze and a sloppy sea. We are sorry to be obliged to say that a certain exhilarating fluid, wrung from the grapes on the plains of France, or from the apples on the plains of New Jersey, — we meddle not with intricate questions, — had been freely circulated among the ladies and gentlemen composing the party. At the same time we are happy to add, that most of those who imbibed used their worldly discretion to a degree which saved them from scandal. Mr. Philip Kennedy was not of this number. He boasted that he had " punished " an entire bottle of the sparkling beverage; and action and re-action being equal, as well in tippling as in mechanics, the bottle aforesaid, in its turn, was " punishing " him; and so far as the observation of the lady was concerned, the bottle was decidedly having the best of it.

Mr. Philip Kennedy could stand up, and could talk even more glibly than usual. The boat-hook in his hand was a convenience in preserving his equilibrium; but he was impatient to be in his seat in the stern-sheets of the boat. It was awkward to be obliged to stand up on the sharp rocks for an unreasonably long time. The rocks were slippery, and exhibited an inclination to fly up and

2

hit him in the forehead, though thus far they had behaved tolerably well.

"I don't think it is quite safe to go now," said Mrs.
Portington, after she had observed the young gentleman
for a moment in silence.

"Safe? Why, Mrs. Portington, you will be as safe
in this boat, with me at the helm, as though you were
at home in your own parlor. I pledge you my honor, as
a gentleman and a sailor, that I will land you safe on
the end of Long Wharf in just twenty-five minutes from
the present moment."

"I'm afraid you can't manage the boat," added the
lady.

"Really, my dear madam, a reflection upon a sailor's
seamanship would be an insult if it came from any other
person than a lady," replied Mr. Kennedy, throwing up
his head, with a display of dignity.

"I know you are a good sailor, Phil, — but — "

"But what, my dear madam? If you know I am a
good sailor, allow me to assist you into the boat;" and
he extended his hand to assist the lady in embarking.

"I am afraid to go with him," said Mrs. Portington,
in a whisper, to her daughter.

"What are you afraid of, mother?"

"Don't you see in what a condition he is?"

"I don't see that anything ails him," replied Kate,
whose knowledge of gentlemen in that condition was

happily very limited. "He is well enough, and I'm sure I'm not afraid to go with him."

"He has drank too much champagne, child. Don't you see that he can hardly stand up?"

"Let him get into the boat and sit down, then," added she, laughing merrily at the idea.

"Come, Mrs. Portington, let me help you into the boat."

"I am afraid to go with you, Phil."

"What are you afraid of, allow me to inquire?" demanded the gentleman, with a maudlin expression on his countenance, which, being interpreted, meant that he was hurt by the lady's doubts, and by her want of confidence in his skill as a boatman.

"I am afraid you can't manage the boat as well as usual, to-day."

"Why not to-day, madam?"

"Because you have drank too much champagne, Phil," said she, breaking the force of the harsh judgment by accompanying it with a merry laugh.

"Too much champagne! 'Pon my word, madam, you wrong me; you strike me in a very tender place. My capacity is two bottles; and I assure you, on the word and honor of a gentleman and a sailor, that I have drank but one bottle."

"Then it was the sea breeze; for you certainly are not in your usual sound and healthy condition."

"I beg your pardon, madam; but do you mean to insinuate that I am intoxicated?" demanded he, with another unsteady display of native dignity.

"O, dear, no, Phil! nothing of the kind — only that you have drank too much champagne," laughed the lady.

"Excuse me, madam, but I can't help saying that I am very much injured in my feelings by this unjust reflection."

"There, mother, you are making a mess of it," interposed Kate. "Phil is well enough. I don't see that anything ails him."

"Blessings on your sweet face, and sweeter words, Kate. You do me justice; and nothing more than justice. Your judgment is cool and unbiassed," added Phil, with enthusiasm.

"It ought to be, for I never drink champagne," replied the spirited girl, as, without any assistance from Phil, she leaped into the boat, and seated herself on a thwart amidships.

"You are a darling, Kate, and you shall be the figure-head of my ship as soon as I get one."

"I will thank you to be a little less familiar in your remarks, Mr. Phil Kennedy."

"Pardon me, Kate; it was but a momentary enthusiasm which prompted me to use the unseemly word."

"If you ever call me 'darling,' I will never speak to you again, if I should live to be two hundred years old.

Come, mother, we shall not get home any too soon if we start at once."

Mrs. Portington was still in doubt; but the words and the example of her daughter were not without their influence. She stepped into the boat no better satisfied than before, but with the hope that good fortune, rather than judgment and skill, would enable Kate and herself to reach the opposite shore in safety. She felt that she was tempting calamity to choose her for its victim; but Mr. Philip Kennedy would make himself intensely disagreeable, if he did not actually create a tempest, in the event of her refusal to accompany him. She disliked a scene, and against her better judgment she intrusted her life, and the more precious life of her daughter, in the keeping of an intoxicated man.

In the middle of the afternoon the wind had come round to the north-east, with the prospect of a storm. It was coming fresher and fresher every moment, and the longer the passage was delayed, the rougher it would be. Mr. Philip Kennedy, under ordinary circumstances, was a good boatman, and the boat got off into deep water without incident or accident. As she had to round the northern point of Goat Island, it was necessary to beat dead to windward. The gentlemanly skipper laid her course mechanically rather than with good judgment, and the weatherly little craft behaved herself exceedingly well for a time.

2 *

"We are doing very well, mother," said Kate, when they had made half a mile on their course.

"Very well indeed, Kate. Perhaps my fears were groundless," replied Mrs. Portington; though it was evident, from the troubled expression on her face, that she was ill at ease.

"There is not the slightest danger, I assure you, madam," added Phil. "I am troubled about the groundless charge you have made against me. If there is anything, madam, which is vile and despicable in a gentleman, it is intoxication — a condition, my dear madam, to which I have never been reduced. What will Commodore Portington say, what will my excellent foster-father say, when such an accusation is fastened upon me?"

"I don't propose to mention the matter, of course," replied Mrs. Portington. "Indeed, it was a mistake on my part, and I am sorry I uttered a word."

"Thank you, madam. You are very kind to acknowledge your error, and you remove a heavy load from my mind by your considerate words. Madam, if I could so far forget myself as to get intoxicated while taking charge of ladies, and especially of Mrs. Portington and her lovely daughter — "

"That will do in that direction, Phil," interposed Kate.

"If I had been guilty of such an impropriety, I could never forgive myself. I would jump overboard and drown myself the moment I realized the degrading fact."

" That is all very pretty, Mr. Phil Kennedy, but I will thank you to mind your helm," said Kate, as the boat fell off a little, and, under the impulse of a fresh gust of wind, careened till she took in a small quantity of water over her lee-rail.

" I'm all attention, Miss Kate. It is very rough out here in the channel; but I pledge you my word and honor, there is not a particle of danger," replied the boatman.

" I am not afraid, if you will only mind your helm."

" I am all attention, Kate ; " and the young man glanced ahead at the white-capped waves which dashed against the bows of the boat.

Mrs. Portington watched him, and watched the course of the boat with deep interest and anxiety. The condition of the tipsy boatman did not improve as the danger increased. He seemed to become more unsteady in his movements, and to pay less attention to the helm. She found it necessary to caution him frequently; and Kate declared if he did not keep a steadier hand at the helm she should steer herself.

" It's very rough out here in the channel," repeated he, when the boat was off Fort Adams, distant about a mile.

" Very rough indeed, Phil, and you cannot be too careful."

" No man can be more careful in a boat than I am,"

protested he. " I intended to go to the northward of Goat
Island, ladies, but I think I will go to the southward,
where she will be in smoother water, under the lee of
the land."

As he spoke, he let out the sheet and put the helm up,
taking the wind abeam. The ladies scrambled hastily
up to the weather side, for Phil had not let out the
sheet far enough to permit the boat to go easily on her
new course.

" You will certainly upset us, Phil," said Mrs. Portington, now actually alarmed by the uncertain movements
of the boat.

" 'Pon my word and honor, as a gentleman and a sail-
or, I will not ! " exclaimed Phil, as he unfastened the
sheet, and eased it off a little. " She is doing splendidly,
madam ; and I assure you again there is not a particle of
danger."

Mr. Philip Kennedy attempted to look easy, confident,
and unconcerned. He was trying with all his might to
disguise or conceal certain movements of his own, which
he was conscious were not entirely regular. The last
bumper of champagne he had taken seemed now to be
struggling for expression in his words and actions. His
estimate of lengths and distances was very uncertain ;
and when he intended to move the tiller a very little, he
threw the boat up into the wind, or put her before it.

Now, when he unfastened the sheet, — which, by the

way, ought not to have been fastened at all, in such a
gusty wind as that, — one of his miscalculations of distance caused him to lose his grasp upon the rope. He
thought he had hold of it, when it was a foot from his
hand ; consequently, he missed his grasp, and the strong
breeze acting on the sail jerked it out of his reach. Of
course the sail flapped violently, and the long boom beat
the water in the most savage manner. To the ladies it
looked very much like a desperate situation, especially
as the boat, having lost the steadying influence of the
sail, began to roll heavily in the trough of the sea. Still
there was no particular danger, as long as the little craft
was skilfully handled.

Mr. Philip Kennedy saw that his reputation for sobri-
ety and seamanship was in imminent peril, and his first
impulse was to save the bubble from a premature explosion. Unfortunately for him and the bubble, his judgment, impaired by the fumes of the champagne, was
not sharpened by the emergency ; and instead of putting
the helm down, and allowing the wind to carry the boom
aft, he leaped from his place in the stern, and sprang
forward to grasp the refractory spar. The boat was
very unsteady under him, and Mr. Phil Kennedy was
very unsteady over it ; and as he stepped upon the gunwale to catch the boom, a heavy roll pitched him into
the water, and he disappeared from the view of the
anxious ladies.

CHAPTER II.

A MIDSHIPMAN IN HIS ELEMENT.

HILE the scene described in the preceding chapter was taking place, a boat, similar in size and rig to that occupied by Mr. Philip Kennedy and party, put out from the pier at Fort Adams. It contained but two persons, one of whom was the boatman, and the other a young man dressed in the uniform of a midshipman of the United States navy. As the man in charge of this boat had drank no champagne, or other exhilarating fluid, he handled his craft with skill and good judgment.

The young gentleman with the four anchors on his coat collar had been sent down to deliver an important message to the officer in command at the fort, and having discharged this duty, he was now on his return to the Naval Academy. Though he was a midshipman, he had a conscience, and did not propose to waste a single moment of his time in skylarking about the bay; and therefore he requested the boatman to make his best time back to the landing-place at Newport. The boat made one short tack out into the channel to get au offing; but when she was ready to come about, the doubtful movements of Mr. Phil Kennedy's boat attracted the attention of the midshipman.

"There's some lubber in that boat; he don't know how to handle her," said the boatman.

"That's plain enough; and that's a pretty heavy sea out there for a fellow who don't know how to manage his craft. She has two ladies aboard," added the midshipman.

"Scared half out of their wits, no doubt."

"I don't blame them much. The boat yaws about as though she were half full of water."

"Shall I come about?" asked the boatman, mindful of the injunction which had been put upon him to lose no time.

"No, not just yet. I'm afraid there will be trouble out there, and the ladies may want some assistance."

"Just my sentiments exactly; and if you say so, I'll stand on towards the boat."

"Do so, if you please. We can go to the northward of the light without losing much time."

"Just as you say, sir."

"Do you know the people in that boat?"

"Can't make 'em out yet; but I know the boat, and there isn't a better one in the bay when she is well handled," replied the boatman, taking a careful survey of the craft, as she labored in the heavy sea.

"He has changed her course; he is going to the southward of the island. The lubber will swamp her!" exclaimed the midshipman, now much excited by the perilous situation of the little craft.

"That he will. There, now he has eased off the sheet, and she is all right again."

By this time the two boats were near enough to enable the boatman to see the faces of the parties in the other craft.

"I know who they are," said he, still gazing at the ladies.

"Who are they?"

"That's Mrs. Portington and her daughter. There has been a picnic over to the old fort, and they are just coming home."

"But who is the man in charge of her?"

"That's the fellow they call Phil Kennedy. They say he is courting the commodore's daughter; but I don't know anything about that. She is a desperate smart girl, and I reckon she is too good for such a fellow as he is."

"Well, he is no boatman, whatever else he may be," added the midshipman, with emphasis.

"No, but he ought to be, if he isn't. He's a passed midshipman in the navy; that is to say, he was a passed midshipman, and resigned when the war broke out."

"O, he is a secesh — is he?"

" They say not; somebody told me he resigned because they promoted some other fellow over his head."

" He was no great loss to the navy, if he can't handle a boat any better than that."

" I reckon you're more'n half right," said the boatman, laughing, as he watched the erratic movements of the craft.

" I don't exactly see how a man so loyal and true as Commodore Portington should permit an officer who resigned at the beginning of the war to hang round his daughter," continued the midshipman, musing on what seemed to him to be a very obvious inconsistency.

" There's a reason for that; and it so happens that I know all about it. I took him and another young buck down to Burnett's Cove the other day, and I heard him tell the whole story."

" I'm afraid he will swamp the boat and duck the ladies, before you can finish it."

" I'm afraid he will; but the story is a short one. Commodore Portington, you know, is a Maryland man. His father, old General Portington, is living now, and is worth a mint of money — the young chap says hard on to half a million. I don't know nothing about that, of course. The commodore's mother died some years ago, and the old general married a young widow by the name of Kennedy — in fact, this young chap's mother."

3

" Is the old general, the commodore's father, a loyal man now?" asked the midshipman.

" Well, as near as I could make it out from what this young chap said, the old fellow don't care a straw which side wins, so long as they don't take his money away from him."

" He is no such man as his son then?"

" That's a fact; the commodore goes in all over for the old flag."

" Go on with your story, if there is any more of it."

" The old general took a liking to his young wife's son, and treated him as if he had been his own. He got him into the navy, and it was generally understood that he intended to divide his money equally between young Kennedy and his granddaughter, Kate."

" He is a lucky fellow then," said the midshipman.

" Perhaps he would have been, if he had behaved himself well. The young chap owned up that he had been going it too fast, and rather got the old general's back up against him. Then, when he gave up his situation in the navy, the old fellow was as mad as Tophet, and said right up and down, that he wouldn't give him a sixpence."

" Then he has fooled away his chances."

" Well, he is kind of making it up with the old man now. That's about all I heard the young chap say; but I kind of guessed at the rest of it. I reckon the young buck means to marry one half of the old general's fortune, in case the other half should slip through his fingers."

The midshipman appeared to be deeply interested in the recital of Mr. Philip Kennedy's antecedents and prospects; but it was simply as a story, for he had no acquaintance with any of the persons mentioned, except that he knew Commodore Portington as a brave and loyal man, who had stood by the flag of his country without wavering, and without the shadow of turning, though he had many southern connections who were identified with the rebellion. But the interest of the story did not permit the midshipman to withdraw his gaze from the imperilled boat even for a single instant. At the conclusion of the narrative the two boats were within a hundred yards of each other, and the countenances of the ladies could be distinctly seen.

" There ! " shouted the boatman, jumping up in his seat, " the lubber has let go his sheet ! "

" Put your helm down ! " cried the midshipman, as he saw the gentleman leap out of his seat, and run forward to secure the truant rope.

But his voice was not heard above the dashing of the waves ; and probably it would not have been heeded if it had been heard.

" Steady ! " shouted the boatman again, as the neglected craft heeled over to leeward. " Steady, or you will swamp her!" he repeated, highly excited by the dangerous situation of the boat and her fair passengers.

Scarcely were the words uttered, when Mr. Philip Kennedy made his unfortunate misstep, and went over the side, disappearing beneath the angry waves.

" He is overboard, as sure as fate!" exclaimed the midshipman.

Mrs. Portington uttered a faint scream of terror as she saw the young man go down, and realized that she and her daughter were then at the mercy of the stormy waves, which were every moment increasing in fury.

" Port your helm a little, and run for the boat!" said the midshipman, in tones so full of energy and determination that the boatman did not venture to disregard his words.

" Will you let the poor fellow drown?" said he.

" No ; run down under the stern of that boat, and I will jump on board of her. You can save the man, and I will take charge of the boat with the ladies."

" All right," replied the boatman, deeply impressed by the vigor and energy of his young companion, and with a feeling that he was born to command.

The boat in which the ladies were seated, unsteadied by the sail, was rolling violently in the trough of the sea — so violently that at each motion she took in a large quantity of water. It was fully evident to the boatman and his passenger, that, without immediate assistance, she

Off the Dumpling Rocks.   Page 29.

would be swamped, and perhaps the worst fears of the mother realized.

" Now, steady as she is," said the energetic midshipman, as he placed himself in the bow of the boat.

In another instant — for the boat darted like a rocket — she was within six feet of the other craft.

" Up with your helm!" shouted the midshipman, as he gathered up his light and agile form, and sprang towards the stern-sheets of the storm-tossed bark.

It was a long leap to make from one unsteady object to another; and the enthusiasm of the leaper' had well nigh played him as ugly a trick as the champagne had played upon Mr. Phil Kennedy. But he had his wits about him, which the other had not, and when he realized that he had made a miscalculation, he did the next best thing; that is, when his feet failed him, he used his hands. He succeeded in grasping the rail of the boat, and though he was subjected to the discomfort of a complete ducking, his efficiency was not thereby diminished. He held on with his hands till the boat careened on the opposite side, and then, with surprising agility, scrambled over the rail into the boat.

The midshipman did not even stop to shake himself, but turned his attention at once to the safety of the boat. Seizing an oar, he heaved the boat's head up into the wind, which brought the boom in-board, and enabled him to recover the stray sheet. With this rope at com-

3 *

mand, the boat was soon brought under perfect control.
Having performed this work of necessity, he directed his
thoughts to the man who had fallen overboard. It was
his purpose to go about and assist in the rescue of the
unfortunate tippler ; but the boat had shipped so much
water that she was in no condition for such a service.

" Phil will be drowned ! " exclaimed Mrs. Portington,
when she saw that her own safety and that of her
daughter were provided for.

" I hope not, madam," replied the midshipman. "This
boat has so much water in her.that it would be hardly
safe to go about.

" The boatman has got hold of him, and is pulling
him out of the water," said Kate, with breathless eagerness. " He is safe, mother."

" Thank Heaven," gasped the lady. " If we only get
ashore, I will never trust myself in one of these boats
again."

. " I beg your pardon, ladies, but where do you wish to
land ? " asked the polite midshipman.

" Anywhere ! Anywhere, if you will only put me
on the dry land again," replied Mrs. Portington, with
emphasis.

" That shall be done very soon, madam, if you will
tell me where you wish to go on shore."

" I don't care where, if I only get on the land once'
more."

" I believe I have the honor of addressing Mrs. Commodore Portington," continued the young officer, as he touched his cap. " And I presume you wish to land in the vicinity of Long Wharf."

" I am Mrs. Portington, and you may land me anywhere you please. I am very grateful to you, young gentleman, for what you have done, and I shall never forget your gallant conduct."

" I thank you, madam, for your kind words, though I assure you I could not possibly have done any less. If you please, Mrs. Portington, I will bale out the boat, and then you will be more comfortable."

" What a nice young man!" said Kate, as she took the place assigned to her by the new skipper, who proceeded to bale out the boat with one hand, while he held both the helm and the sheet with the other.

The young man blushed up to his eyes as he listened to this gay remark from one who had so recently been in extreme peril. He could not determine what she meant; whether the words were intended as a compliment, or whether she was making fun of him. He cast a single furtive glance at her, but without solving the question. Though he did not solve that question, he did solve another, — one of no little importance to foolish young men, passing out of their teens, — that Miss Kate Portington was a very pretty girl. Perhaps this fact had something to do with the deep blush that mantled his cheek, as the novelists say ; for it is hard to be made the sport of any young lady, and doubly hard if she happens to be pretty.

"I said you were a nice young man," repeated Kate, apparently enjoying the confusion of the gallant fellow ; "and you are as speechless as an infant rhinoceros."

"I was paralyzed by the remark."

"Don't you think you are a nice young man?" persisted the fair tormentor.

"Really, Miss Portington, I have given the question so little consideration that I am not prepared to give a definite answer," replied the midshipman, rallying under the effect of what seemed to be the young lady's sarcasm.

"May I ask you to give the subject an earnest and patient examination, with the favor of a definite reply within three weeks?"

"I will endeavor to comply with so reasonable a demand."

"Thank you. I dare say you have been reading some vile, yellow-covered novel."

"Indeed, I have not. I have no time to squander as you suggest."

"Then you must be a natural born hero. No doubt you have been longing for years for an opportunity to rescue some forlorn damsel from a watery grave, or a fiery furnace. Your patience has at last been rewarded, and I am the victim."

" What an ungrateful girl you are, Kate ! I'm ashamed of you ! " exclaimed the mother.

" Isn't it ridiculous that I should become the heroine of a stupid melo-drama like this !   Pray, sir, may I ask your name ? "

" John Somers, at your service," promptly replied the midshipman.

CHAPTER III.

MR. MIDSHIPMAN SOMERS.

THE name and fame of Mr. Midshipman Somers had gone before him, for both Mrs. Portington and her daughter had heard of the distinguished young gentleman. His gallant conduct on the southern coast, and the exploits of which he was the hero, had been duly reported at Newport. He had been examined by the board of medical officers and by the Academic Board, and was not only pronounced physically fit to serve his country in the navy, but had been admitted to the second class in the institution.

It is true some wise and prudent people said that his admission was not altogether regular; but it was certain that he was admitted entirely on his own merits, whatever influence might have been used in breaking through arbitrary forms, that were invaluable in piping times of peace, but which the exigencies of the times could very properly vary. But we do not intend to discuss the "red tape" items in the career of our hero; and we can only say that he was a member of the Naval Academy, in high standing in his class, and in excellent repute with the officers and professors of the institution. We imagine his admission was no more irregular than the departure of the two upper classes when their services were needed in the active duties of their chosen profession. It was said that Commander Bankhead had more influence in Washington than some officers of equal rank; and this devoted and patriotic man was Somers's warm friend.

Our midshipman had studied with a zeal which was worthy of success. Before he entered the institution he had improved every moment of time, and even the greater portion of his thirty days' furlough had been spent in the solitude of his chamber over navigation, gunnery, and general mathematics. He had graduated with honor in the High School of Pinchbrook, and was therefore in condition to take advance rank in the Academy, after he had added to his early attainments the results of six months' earnest and devoted study.

Somers had not been satisfied to meet the requirements of the institution, but had used his spare hours to promote the great object of his present existence. His constitution was strong and his health vigorous, so that he did not break down under this pressure; and the result was evident to his teachers, though they were not clearly aware of the means by which he made such tremendous progress in his studies. At the June examination he had not a single demerit recorded against him, and his "general merit roll" placed him near the head of the class. He was trusted and respected, not only for what he had done, but for what he was.

When Somers entered the institution he was an able seaman, and had an excellent practical knowledge of gunnery and working a ship. While his classmates were studying and practising what he was competent to teach, Somers devoted himself to branches of study in which he had made less progress. Our young readers, therefore, must not suppose that he got his "learning" by instinct, for he obtained his position only by the severest labor and the most self-denying sacrifices. He knew nothing of the gay festivities of the brilliant watering-place in which he resided, and did not even witness the dissipation which abounds in that luxurious society during the fashionable season. His only visitor during the summer was Lieutenant Waldron, of the navy, whom he had saved from being washed overboard during a gale, on his passage home from Key West. This gentleman was fully alive to the merit of our midshipman, and freely expressed his desire to have him with him in the Rosalie, to which he had been appointed.

And now, having informed our readers who and what the midshipman was, we will return to the boat where we left him with the ladies.

" Mr. Midshipman Somers ! " exclaimed Mrs. Porting-ton, when the young gentleman had given his name ; " I have heard of you before."

" Mr. Midshipman Somers ! " repeated Kate. " *I* have heard of you before ; and you must know that I regard it as a very distinguished honor to be rescued from a watery grave by such a remarkable prodigy as Mr. Midshipman Somers."

" Don't you be so saucy, Kate," remonstrated her mother.

" I am not saucy, mother ; my heart overflows with gratitude to the distinguished young gentleman for the signal service he has rendered us," replied Kate, with a merry laugh.

The boat was now under the lee of Goat Island, where the water was comparatively smooth, and the confidence of both the ladies was completely restored. The other boat, with Mr. Philip Kennedy as a passenger, was about half a mile astern of her. Somers had baled out the water, and taken a reef in the sail. Miss Kate was comfortable, and could afford to be saucy. She was an enigma to the midshipman. It was not possible, after the good service he had rendered to her and to her mother, that the young lady intended to ridicule him. It was her humor ; and as she was very beautiful, she could afford to say and do almost anything, which would have been fatal to a less favored damsel.

4

"You are positively impudent, Kate," added her mother.

"On the contrary, my dear mother, I am using the strongest language I can find to express my admiration of the gentleman's gallant conduct, and my high appreciation of his efficient service to you and me."

"Spare me, Miss Portington," said Somers, with a blush and a smile.

"I will not spare you; you deserve praise, and praise you shall have, to the farthest verge of my capacity to commend you. I have heard my father say that you rescued Commander Bankhead from a watery grave."

"I beg you will not say watery grave again," replied Somers. "I am afraid you have been reading novels, Miss Portington."

"I was only trying to speak a language which you can understand. The only thing that vexes me is, that I should become one of your heroines — the victim of your insane desire to make a knight-errant of yourself. Pray, did you ever read Don Quixote?"

"I never did."

"Read it, by all means, at the first opportunity."

"I am afraid I have mortally offended you, Miss Portington," added Somers.

"Not mortally, only seriously. You knight-errants use provokingly strong language."

"I propose —

"Don't do it yet, young man. Even Don Quixote would not have been so hasty."

"Pray hear me out."

"I could not possibly listen to anything of that kind now," laughed the merry girl.

"I was only going to propose — "

"Don't do it, Mr. Somers. Spare me, if you please."

"I was only going to offer to correct the mistake I have made."

"What mistake, Mr. Somers?"

"I have been so unfortunate as to save you — in your own choice language — from a watery grave. It now appears that this was a grievous blunder on my part."

"Exactly so; you are infinitely more sensible than I supposed a prodigy could be."

"I propose to correct my mistake."

"Do, by all means. You will impose upon me a debt of gratitude which will last me the rest of my lifetime — "

"And which would soon be cancelled, then, if you were left to your own efforts in the heavy sea off the Dumplings."

"Really, that is quite smart."

"With your leave, I will endeavor to remedy the mischief I have done. After landing Mrs. Portington, I propose to return to the channel, and leave you exactly as I found you."

"Excellent idea. I will be your friend for life, then."

"Thank you for your kind consideration, — though our friendship would be short and sweet, like angels' visits."

"Positively, you are growing. brilliant, in spite of your wet jacket. But, seriously, Mr. Somers, don't you think I am to be pitied?"

"I do. I sympathize with you from the depths of my heart."

"Here I am, an unfortunate maiden of seventeen, who, without any fault of my own, and without the indulgence of a single sickly sentiment such as you find embodied in the novels, have been subjected to the peril of being drowned. Just at this moment, one of these little monkeys of midshipmen appears upon the stage, and saves me from my impending fate! Don't you think it is superlatively ridiculous?"

"Certainly it is; and I cannot express how deeply I regret my agency in the affair. Had I known your sentiments, it is possible that I might have saved your mother, without meddling with you."

"Kate, I will not listen to this impudence any longer," said Mrs. Portington.

"Excuse me, madam, but I assure you I enjoy it as much as she does," added Somers.

"You are determined to make yourself ridiculous, in

spite of all my exertions to save you from your own folly," continued Kate; and this time, for some reason which we cannot explain, there was a blush upon her cheek.

" She does not mean what she says," added Mrs. Portington. " She is really as grateful to you as I am; and I feel that I owe my life and hers to your gallant conduct."

" I should think you had been reading novels, too, mother. Of course I am grateful to Mr. Somers for wetting his jacket in my behalf. He has my thanks, and I shall ask father to make an admiral of him as soon as he comes back from New York."

" Thank you, Miss Portington; and for your sake I should probably accept the situation, if it were offered to me."

" For my sake! You are almost as impudent as our last boatman. Do you expect me to twine a chaplet for your lofty brow, Mr. Somers, and, like the heroines of romance, blush whenever your name is mentioned?"

" I should certainly wear the chaplet if your fair hands twined it; and it would afford me inexpressihle pleasure to learn that you blushed at the mention of my name."

" You are more impudent than Phil Kennedy."

" I haven't the pleasure of Mr. Kennedy's accquaint-

4 *

ance; but I believe I am indebted to him for the honor of this unexpected interview."

"The same accident that removed me from his protection placed me under yours. I did not submit to his impudence, and I shall not to yours. I am your victim; but I beg you will use your advantage as mildly as possible."

"I will. We are approaching the wharf; and as it is not probable that we shall ever meet again, permit me to say that the pleasure of my brief acquaintance with you amply compensates for the discomfort of a wet jacket."

"Dear me! I declare you are a philosopher as well as a prodigy."

"So my shipmates used to call me, which exhibits a remarkable unanimity of opinion between you and them."

"What tremendous long words you use, Mr. Somers!"

"They are all in the dictionary, Miss Portington, and all authorized by the best usage."

"Doubtless they are. I will look them out when I get home. If I remember rightly, you just now observed that we were about to part to meet no more, in the language of the sentimental songsters."

"Probably; by accident, possibly."

"I protest against any such conclusion, Mr. Somers," interposed Mrs. Portington. "I hope to meet you often, and to have an opportunity to express over and over again my gratitude to you for the kind service you have rendered."

"Mother has been reading novels, I declare! Well, it is perfectly safe for her; she isn't 'just seventeen.'"

"Now, Kate, if you don't join me in inviting Mr. Somers to spend the evening at our house, I shall be offended with you."

"Certainly, I will join you, mother. Mr. Somers, let not the hero and heroine of this ecstatic adventure be thus rudely sundered. Let not the cloud come between them on the very threshold of their acquaintance. Let not the dews of a genial friendship — "

"Take care the boom, Miss Portington," said Somers, as the boat rounded in at the landing-place.

"A plague upon the boom! You spoil a very flowery sentence, Mr. Somers."

"Pardon me, but I had to luff up, or stave the boat against the wharf."

The midshipman passed the painter through a ring, and secured the boat at the wharf. The sail was lowered, and the eventful voyage was ended; but the ladies preferred to remain in their seats till the arrival of the other boat with Mr. Phil Kennedy. In spite of the remarkable nature of the conversation, the young midshipman had enjoyed it to the utmost, and even forgot the discomforts of his wet clothing. In his estimation

Miss Kate Portington was positively fascinating ; and he regretted that the cruise should so soon be finished.

As they sat in the boat, Mrs. Portington tried in vain to have a little serious conversation with her deliverer ; but Kate's sarcasms spoiled her good inteutions. The conversation of the latter coutinued to be laden with merry impudence till the other boat touched the wharf, when Somers assisted Mrs. Portington to land. Kate, without waiting for any help, leaped lightly upon the wharf.

" After serious reflection, Mr. Somers," said she, as he stepped on the wharf, " I think we had better not part to meet no more, for in spite of your absurdities, I rather like you. Here is my hand, Mr. Somers. You will call and see us — won't you ? "

Somers took the offered hand, and felt a slight temptation to be silly. The fair girl was sincere and sensible now ; and as he pressed the little gloved hand, he experienced an emotion which was new to him, but decidedly pleasant to remember.

" You must excuse me, Miss Portington, but I am so constantly employed-that I find no time to go into company," replied Somers.

" Then you are angry with me because I have talked so lightly of the service you rendered me ? "

" Far from it. I have enjoyed your conversation more than I can describe."

" Then you will call at our house. If you do not, I shall believe you are offended, and shall never forgive myself for my idle words."

" I am not offended. It would be impossible for me to be offended with one — no matter ; I will not say it. You would accuse me of stealing the rest of the sentence from a novel."

" Promise that you will call, then."

" I will do so, if possible."

" I will content myself with that, for I know it will be .possible. Here is Phil."

The lady very gracefully introduced Mr. Phil Kennedy and Mr. Midshipman Somers. The former had completely recovered from the effect of his indiscretion, furnishing another proof that cold water is the best antidote for the malady with which he had been afflicted.

" Mr. Somers, I am happy to make your acquaintance," said Phil, as he grasped the young man's hand. " You are a brave fellow, and I shall cultivate your friendship, if you will permit me ; " and he proceeded to give, in minute detail, the particulars of the accident which had thrown him into the water, though he did not even remotely allude to the champagne which had been at the bottom of the mischief.

The party then separated, and Somers hastened up to the Academy to report on his mission to Fort Adams.

CHAPTER IV.

SOMERS ATTENDS AN EVENING PARTY.

ASS the word for Mr. Somers," said the captain
of the crew to which that young gentleman belonged, at the close of the recitation in the after-.
noon of a day about a week after the events
detailed in the last chapter.

Mr. Somers presented himself.

"You will report to the commandant forthwith,"
added the captain of the crew.

Somers repaired at once to the office of the commandant, much wondering for what he could be wanted
there. This was the way in which delinquents were
sometimes summoned for reprimand, and he tried to
think what wicked thing he had done for which he could
be called to the bar of the august executive of the institution. He had not failed in his studies; he had not been
late at any muster; he had not staid out after hours,
and he had not broken a leave of absence. He was not
conscious of being guilty of any real or constructive
enormity, and he therefore came to the conclusion that
he was to be detailed for some special duty.

Into the presence of the mighty man of the Academy he went, with some doubts but no fears, for a clear conscience is the best assurance which a young man can have in the hour of trial. There was an expression on the face of the commandant which he could not understand, as he removed his cap, and reported himself, as he had been ordered. There was an appearance of severity, but there was something else which modified it, and Somers could not tell whether he ought to expect a reprimand, or an order for special duty.

" Mr. Somers," began the commandant, " your conduct has been so uniformly exemplary, that I am very much surprised to find you under censure at the present time."

" Under censure ! " exclaimed Somers, his face turning as red as a blood beet. " I was not aware, sir, that I had transgressed any rule of the institution. If I have, I am very sorry for it."

" You have, sir," replied the commandant ; but there was something which looked very much like a smile on his fine countenance.

" I was not conscious of it, sir."

" Perhaps not ; but I must hold you responsible, nevertheless, and compel you to make all the reparation in your power."

" Will you be kind enough to inform me what rule I have disregarded ? " asked Somers, encouraged by the smile that still lurked about the mouth of the executive officer.

"Certaiuly, Mr. Somers. That rule which requires the naval cadets to conduct themselves according to the rules of politeness and good-breeding in all their relations with their fellow-beings, outside as well as inside of the institution."

"Really, sir, I was not conscious that I had been wanting in this respect in any duty I owe to my fellow-beings."

"You made the acquaintance of Mrs. Commodore Portington and her daughter under rather remarkable circumstances; and you partially promised to call upon the family. You have not done so, though a week has elapsed since the event."

"I have not yet abandoned the intention of calling upon the family."

"But your delay looks very much as though you intended to disregard the invitation. Mr. Somers, midshipmen cannot afford to slight the invitation of a commodore's lady."

"I did not mean to slight it."

"I suppose not. If it had been any other gentleman in the institution, I should have been applied to for leave of absence six times within that week. Why have you not beeu, Mr. Somers?"

"I wished to go very much indeed; nothing could

have afforded me more pleasure than to accept the invitation."

"Then, why under the sun didn't you go? You were sure of your leave of absence, for you have never asked a favor since you have been here."

"I am not exactly on an equality with the commodore's lady and daughter, and I concluded that my going to see them would look very much like an intention on my part to remind them of the trifling service I had the good fortune to render them."

"Somers, you are too modest by half; and you wrong the people of whom you speak. Now, I happen to know that the young lady is much grieved at your non-appearance, and fully believes that she has deeply offended you."

"That is far from the truth."

"I don't think we have any young gentlemen who can afford to be offended with the commodore's daughter. She is a little wild, and is sometimes rather erratic in her ways, but she is pure gold. I think you have not done quite right, and I feel compelled to give you leave of absence till ten this evening, with orders to report at Commodore Portington's house."

The playful manner of the commandant assured Somers that his disobedience was not very desperate, and he retired to put himself in order for obeying the mandate. We feel compelled to add, that his heart was all in a

flutter at the prospect of spending an evening in the presence of the commodore's beautiful daughter. He dressed
himself with the most extraordinary care, and laid every
lock of his fine curly hair in the best possible position.
We cannot say that he looked much better after he had
"fussed" for half an hour, than when he began; but
Nature had done so much for Mr. Midshipman Somers,
that it was hardly necessary to improve upon her handi-
work. It was no merit of his that he was an exceedingly good-looking fellow.

When he had completed his toilet, he hastened to the
residence of the commodore. The distance was short—
not half long enough to enable him to recover his self-
possession, of which sundry queer thoughts had completely
deprived him. His confusion was so great, that when
he reached the house, he had not the courage to ring the
bell. Somers was still a boy, and as bashful as a school-
girl. In spite of himself, he walked straight past the
door, stealing only a hasty glance at the front windows
through the corner of his eye. He walked half a mile
beyond the house, until he thought he had brought his
courage up to the sticking point, when he ventured to
turn around and retrace his steps.

Again he reached the house, and again the tremendous idea of standing in the presence of Miss Kate Portington so overawed him, that he passed the house with
a speed which must have led inquisitive people to think

he was after the doctor who lived a few squares beyond. Somers began to grow desperate ; and the more desperate he became, the more rapid was his pace. This time he actually walked down to the wharf where he had parted with the damsel a week before. The remembrance of her raillery almost blanched his cheek ; but it glowed again when he recalled the kind words with which they had parted, and the eagerness with which she attempted to extort from him a promise to call.

Under the influence of this last reflection, he retraced his steps again ; but when he reached the door of the fair one's home, his courage once more failed him. "She will call me a prodigy," thought he, "and I shall sink through the floor." It was true he had given some smart answers before, but he might not be able to do so again. He bolted past the door as though he had been a pro-jectile from a hundred pounder Parrott.

"What a fool I am !" said he, pettishly, to himself, after he had galloped off about a mile. I will either go in or give it up this time. I haven't any more pluck than a wooden man. Why should I be afraid of that girl's tongue? I can talk as big as she can, if I have a mind to do so ; and I will, too."

Thus thinking, and thus muttering his thoughts, he came about as squarely as though he had been on parade, and darted down the street again.

"I am going in this time," muttered he, as he approached the house. "I will charge on the battery, if I die for it."

Thus musing, he increased his pace; but when he reached the house, a stolen glance at the window disclosed to him the fair face of Kate. He looked down upon the sidewalk, doubled his speed, and passed the house for the fourth time.

"Avast there, Somers! Where bound?" said a familiar voice, hailing him as he bolted down the street towards the wharves. "I thought I saw you leave for Commodore Portington's an hour ago."

"You did, sir," candidly replied Somers, with a hasty glance at the quizzical face of the commandant of midshipmen, for he was the person who had hailed him.

"O, you have been there?"

"N—no, sir. I haven't been there yet."

"Indeed! Where have you been?"

"I have been taking a little walk."

"I should think you had. Why, I supposed, from your pace, that Miss Kate had a fit, and you were running for the doctor."

"No, sir, I haven't been there yet. Isn't it rather early, sir?"

"Early? No. They expect you, and will wait tea till you come."

"Expect me?"

"Certainly they do. I told them you would come, and

you have been wasting a whole hour of the most valuable time ever allotted to mortal man," laughed the commandant, for he ventured to smile occasionally on the
favorite of the Academy. "Come with me, for I am
bound there."

The die was cast now. He did not wish to abandon
the chase, and was rather pleased to find his "want of
pluck" had not defeated his good intentions. While
they walk up the hill at a more moderate pace than
Somers had descended it, we must pause to rescue our
little volume from the imputation of being a love story.
We solemnly assure our readers, old and young, that Mr.
Midshipman Somers had no more idea of falling in love
than he had of falling overboard. He was a youth of
eighteen, and of course there was no room in his head or
his heart for such a silly notion. If any stronger phe-
nomena than this appear to the experience of those versed
in such matters, we can only assure them that they were
simply "strokes of nature." A school-boy may be afraid
of the pretty girl who sits at the desk near his own, without having his common sense impugned; and we pledge
our word that Mr. Midshipman Somers's case was not a
whit more desperate.

The commandant rang the bell at Commodore Portington's house, with a firmness of purpose and a steadiness
of nerve which excited the envy of his young companion.
He would have given his prospect of prize-money for the

next year, if he could have jingled that bell without a trembling of the limbs and a sinking of the heart. The bell had been rung, and the Rubicon was passed. They were ushered into the drawing-room, where quite a large party were seated.

" Why, Mr. Somers, I am delighted to see you ! " ex claimed Kate Portington, rushing up to him, and extend- ing her hand, which Somers had the courage to take, though the floor beneath seemed for a moment to be composed of very unsubstantial material. " I was afraid you intended to deprive me of the romantic pleasure of being the heroine of an unwritten novel. I am delighted to see you."

" I thank you ; I called to invite you to sail with me on the first stormy day, that I may have an opportunity to undo the mischief done the other day,"

" I will not go. After careful reflection, I have de- cided to submit to the destiny in store for me, and be a willing victim. Being rescued by a prodigy of a midship- man ought to reconcile any lady to such a fate."

" Well, Miss Portington, whenever you are disposed to rebel at your destiny, I will cheerfully afford you an opportunity to join the mermaids, and sport in the cav. erns of the mighty deep."

" How poetical ! There is no limit to your attain- ments."

" I beg your pardon ; there is at least one limit."

" Pray, what is that ? "

" To look unmoved.upon one so fair, so witty, and so wise as Miss Portington."

" You are an impudent little middy, in spite of all your accomplishments."

" I am afraid impudence is contagious," laughed Somers.

" Worse and worse."

By this time Mr. Midshipman Somers had to be presented to the rest of the company. He had found his tongue now, and having faced the heaviest battery first, he was prepared for any other that could come athwart his hawse.

Mr. Philip Kennedy was there, and treated Mr. Somers with the most distinguished consideration. Commodore Portington was there, and with much emotion thanked him for what he had done for his wife and daughter. Mrs. Portington was as kind and motherly as though the tie of blood had connected her to the young gentleman. In spite of the courage and vigor with which Somers faced the sarcasm of Kate, he was reduced to the condition of blushing a dozen times before the party sat down to tea ; for, very much to the disgust of such a modest youth, he was the lion of the occasion.

Sarcastic as Miss Kate was disposed to be, she kept. Somers constantly at her side. O, they were excellent friends ! — nothing more, we again feel compelled to assure our readers. He sat by her side at the table, and if he ventured during the evening to wander from her chair, by some of those delicate arts best understood by young ladies, she contrived to bring him back. Entire candor compels us to say that Somers did not regard this imprisonment as a punishment; or if it was, he submitted with most exemplary patience to the infliction.

Kate continued to be sarcastic, and to make all manner of fun of " the prodigy of a midshipman;" but we are happy to inform our interested friends that Somers retorted with grace and spirit, always hitting, but never wounding. The commodore laughed till his sides ached, as he listened to this exciting badinage; and it is quite certain that Mr. Midshipman Somers lost nothing in his good opinion for the vigor and spirit with which he used his tongue.

At nine o'clock the party was prematurely broken up by the departure of a portion of the guests, and the others decided to follow their example. Somers, though urged to remain longer, did not deem it prudent to accept the invitation, but he promised, with the prompt indorsement of the commandant of midshipmen, to repeat the visit at an early date.

Somers left the house alone, for the commandant had another engagement. He had walked but a few steps towards the Academy, when he was joined by Mr. Phil Kennedy.

" Ah, Somers! Glad to meet you again. Whither now ?"

" Home," replied Somers.

" Is your leave out ?"

" No, not till ten."

"Walk up the street, then. You are a good fellow, and I should be happy to know you better."

" Thank you," replied Somers, as Phil took his arm, and they walked towards the Ocean House.

CHAPTER V.

SOMERS GOES ON NIGHT DUTY.

MR. PHILIP KENNEDY was a man of the world, and was perfectly familiar with all the phases of fashionable dissipation. His knowledge of the vices of society was profound and intricate. There was no game of cards, no turn of the dice, by which money changed ownership, in which he was not an adept.

Even Somers, simple as he was in worldly arts, did not for an instant suppose that Mr. Philip Kennedy and himself had met by accident. The brilliant young gentleman had probably waited for the midshipman, and thrown himself in his path in a careless manner, that no purpose or intention on his part might be apparent. He had an object in view, though Somers was too innocent to suspect him of any improper motives. The latter had been a lion in the party — had been treated with high favor by the commodore and other naval officers present; Mrs. Portington had been very kind to him; and Kate had artlessly monopolized his attentions during the entire evening. Very likely Mr. Somers's brain was turned by the consideration which had been awarded to him; very likely he considered himself a person of no little consequence. It was quite natural that Mr. Philip Kennedy should seek to cultivate his acquaintance.

We cannot positively say that Mr. Midshipman Somers passed all these things through his mind; but the notice of Phil Kennedy was only a continuation of what had been going on all the evening. It did not seem strange, therefore, that the " man of the world" should take his arm, and invite him to a stroll up the street. It is possible that the unsophisticated middy felt flattered by the notice of so brilliant a person as Mr. Phil Kennedy.

They walked up to the Ocean House, and Somers sauntered with him through the various halls and public apartments, and saw what of fashion and gayety the waning season had left behind. In the course of their peregrinations about the extensive establishment, they visited the billiard saloon; but Somers did not know the first thing about the game, and they finally came to a halt in front of the bar. With the nonchalance of a man of the world, Kennedy called for a sherry cobbler, and asked his young companion what he would have, in a tone which seemed to indicate that a refusal to drink was not to be expected.

Somers politely but firmly refused to " imbibe," and persisted to the last in declining to " join" his accomplished

friend, even to the extent of a glass of lemonade. Perhaps he was over-fastidious in refusing to partake of a
harmless beverage; but he had a perfect horror of a
public bar, and all Mr. Phil Kennedy's eloquence was
unavailing to change his purpose. If Phil had any
object in view he was utterly and signally defeated.

As they passed out of the bar-room, Somers made an
explanation; but it was not an apology — only an open,
straightforward statement that it was against his principles to taste intoxicating drinks. Phil took the explanation very kindly, and apologized for pressing the point as
far as he had done. He supposed all young men drank,
and nothing but a misapprehension could have induced
him to extend so offensive an invitation to one whose
principles were opposed to the practice.

At half past nine they separated, and Somers returned
to the Academy with a very high regard for Mr. Phil
Kennedy. That gentleman had treated him with the
most marked attention, and extended to him many cour-
tesies which a man of the world does not often bestow
upon a needy young middy. But, after all the kindness
and consideration of Phil, Somers did not employ many
of his leisure moments in thinking of him. His thoughts
dwelt more earnestly on the incidents of the evening at
the house of the commodore. Kate had made fun of
him for three hours, almost without cessation; but there
was something very pleasant to remember in her words,
her looks, and her manner.

Somers, though tolerably familiar with human nature among men, was profoundly ignorant of its developments in the opposite sex. It is a remarkable fact, deduced from long experience and close observation, that young ladies often make fun of those to whom they are the most strongly attached. They often call men monsters, even while they admire them, and rail at those to whom, at the fitting moment, they are willing to speak the kindest of words. Well, it is only an exhibition of that feminine tact by which ladies conceal, or attempt to conceal, their real sentiments. It is unfortunate for them that prejudice and public opinion compel them to hide their thoughts and feelings, their ·hopes and aspirations, till somebody has irrevocably committed himself. Whom she hates, she often loves ; aud whom she despises, she often takes to her heart.

This is worldly wisdom ; and Jack Somers, still a boy, knew nothing at all about it. But there were those present at that evening party who were not deceived by outward appearances ; and perhaps Mr. Philip Kennedy was deeply enough versed in the wiles of feminine ways to understand all about it. It was distinctly understood that he had aspirations in the direction of Miss Kate ; but, beyond a half concealed scowl, and an occasional impatient movement, he appeared to be utterly unconscious of the presence of Somers.

The dreams of our middy have not been reported, and

6

we have no means of knowing what vagaries occupied his sleeping hours that night; but we do know that the midnight bell had struck before he ceased to think of what had taken place at the hospitable mansion of Commodore Portington.

During the succeeding month Somers was an occasional visitor at the house of the commodore. Kate always railed at him, but her words, her look, and her manner were just as fascinating as on the first occasion. As they became more intimate, the raillery became more earnest; but everybody believed that Kate and the prodigy of a middy were excellent friends. Mr. Phil Kennedy was always present on these occasions, and always made himself as agreeable as the circumstances would permit. He continued to cultivate the acquaintance of Somers, who was rather pleased to be on intimate terms with such an elegant and accomplished young gentleman.

About this time, there was a brilliant party, for an out-of-season one, at the residence of Commodore Portington, who was on the point of departing for the South, where he had been ordered to a command. Of course Somers was invited, and obtained leave of absence till twelve o'clock, which is a very late hour for young men to be out of the house, and could only be tolerated at the Academy on the occasion of a commodore's party. Kate was unusually brilliant and fascinating, especially to Mr.

Midshipman Somers. It was observed that she danced only once during the evening; and some of the scandal-mongers were malicious enough to say that it was because the " prodigy of a midshipman " did not know how to dance, and therefore could not join with her in her favorite amusement. It was further whispered, that she had twice declined to dance with Mr. Phil Kennedy. Certainly this elegant man of the world was in very bad humor, which gave a color of truth to the scandal.

We have no intention of detailing the events of the evening, or of describing the beautiful dresses worn by the ladies on this interesting occasion; we pass on to more stirring events. About half past eleven o'clock a messenger brought a note to the commandant of midship-men, who, as a valued friend of the commodore, was never absent from his house on great occasions. The officer read the note, and his face wore a sad and troubled expression.

" Mr. Somers," said he, after he had read the note, " I am sorry to abridge your enjoyment, even for a moment; but I must ask the favor of your assistance in a matter of some importance. Pardon me for interrupt-ing you, Miss Portington."

" Mr. Somers cannot leave a moment before twelve," replied she, with well-made petulance. " I am teaching . him to box the compass, and he hasn't got half way round yet. He is the most stupid fellow for a prodigy that I ever met, and I wonder how he learns his mathematics."

"If you would shut your eyes he would be a better student; your glance distracts his attention. But you will excuse him, when I tell you that this is a work of mercy," replied the commandant, with a smile. "A transport steamer, from New Orleans, bound to Boston, has put in, short of coal. There is an officer, a friend of mine, on board of her, who is very low from the effects of a gunshot wound. The surgeon fears he will not live till morning, and has sent for me. I happen to know that the sufferer's sister is in Newport, and I wish Mr. Somers's assistance in conveying her on board."

Kate looked very sober and very sad, leaving no doubt in the mind of any one that she felt deeply for the poor invalid, who might die before the loved one could reach him to smooth his dying pillow. Of course she offered no further objection, and did not indulge in any unseemly remark.

"Mr. Somers, you will oblige me by going down to the wharf, and getting the school boat ready for us. If you can find a boatman, employ him; but I am afraid they are not to be had at this late hour. I will find the lady, but I may be delayed some little time," continued the lieutenant, as he departed from the house.

"Come to-morrow, if you can, Mr. Somers, and tell me about the sick man," said Kate, as they parted at the door.

" I will, if possible," replied Somers, as he took her offered hand, and was rather surprised to receive a gentle pressure, into which her interest in the suffering officer had probably surprised her.

" Confound that young puppy ! " muttered Mr. Philip Kennedy, as he witnessed this little incident. " Good night, Kate," he added, stepping forward and offering her his hand, perhaps with the intention of applying a test to the feelings of the young lady.

" Good night, Phil," replied she, apparently not seeing the hand he extended, at least not taking it.

He went his way, grinding his teeth with chagrin and disappointment. A few rods from the commodore's house, he was saluted by an elderly man, whose ill-favored visage even the darkness of the night could not wholly conceal.

" Well, Mr. Kennedy, I have been trotting up and down here for a full hour, waiting for you," said the man.

" It is not twelve yet," replied Phil.

" Business before pleasure is my motto," growled the stranger. " You must be off for Boston by the steamer at three o'clock, if you are going to do this job."

" Hush up, man ! Don't open your mouth here," said Phil, in low but earnest tones.

" We must have an hour's talk together before you go," added the hard-visaged man, in a more cautious tone.

5 *

" Not in the street."

" Anywhere you please; but don't lose any more time. Where shall it be — at your hotel?"

" No, the very walls have ears. Walk down to the wharf at the foot of the street, and I will meet you there in fifteen minutes."

" If you are not there in fifteen minutes I will not wait," said the stranger, gruffly.

" I will be there," replied Phil, as he turned and walked towards the house of Commodore Portington.

The company had not all left, and Kate was still in the hall, making her adieus to the departing guests.

" Kate," said he, stepping up to her with extended hand, " I am going away in the morning, and I may not see you again for weeks, perhaps months; and you refused to shake hands with me at parting."

" Refused? I protest that I did nothing of the kind! There is my hand, Phil, if you are going away," said she, suiting the act to the words.

" You seem to rejoice in my going, Kate," sighed he.

" Where are you going, Phil? You didn't say you were going."

" I was afraid the intelligence would be too welcome."

" What put such a thought as that into your silly head, Phil?" laughed the maiden, who seemed to be determined to repress any exhibition of sentiment on the part of the elegant young gentleman. " But you have not told me where you are going, Phil."

" I am going to Portland."

" You will return, some time, of course?"

" Possibly."

" Well, Phil, I shall see you if you do."

" Do you wish to see me again?"

" What a foolish question!"

Mr. Phil Kennedy used up his fifteen minutes in a vain attempt to win a word of regret at his going from Kate; but the obdurate girl, whatever she thought and felt, refused to gratify him. He took leave of the rest of the family, and hastened down the street in no enviable frame of mind.

" Confound that young puppy!" he muttered several times, and even interlarded his exclamations with some stronger expressions, which it would scandalize our page to write.

In the mean time Somers had gone down to the wharf, unmoored the school boat, hoisted the sail, and hauled her in by the landing steps. The commandant and the lady did not yet appear. Just as he had completed his preparations, it began to rain. We have before intimated that our middy was a philosopher. He did not believe in being uncomfortable, even for a single moment, when duty did not require the sacrifice. It was a mild evening, and the appearance was, that the rain was only a shower, which would soon be over. A wet jacket might keep him uncomfortable for several hours; and, true to his philosophy, he cast about him for the means of avoiding this unpleasant prospect.

The forward part of the school boat was decked over, though there was no bulk-head to separate the covered portion from the rest of the space. He crawled in beneath this deck, and stowed himself away on some old coats and pieces of sail-cloth, in such a position that he could see his passengers when they arrived.

He had scarcely coiled himself up in his narrow quarters before he heard voices on the wharf; but they were not those of the commandant and the lady, and he did not leave his covert. Two men stepped down the stairs into the boat next to the one occupied by Somers.

" Are we safe here?" asked one of the men.

" If any one comes we can push off from the wharf," replied the other. " I don't much like the idea of being out in the rain."

"The rain won't hurt you," said the first man; "it will soon be over."

" This thing is treason for me, but we must make a good job of it," continued the second speaker, in whom Somers recognized Mr. Phil Kennedy.

CHAPTER VI.

SOMERS LISTENS TO AN INTERESTING CONVERSATION.

OMERS was on the point of coming out from his concealment, for he was too high-spirited to play the part of a listener, when he heard Mr. Phil Kennedy acknowledge that the "thing" was tréason. He was not overburdened with curiosity, but when his elegant friend pleaded guilty of plotting against his government, he felt it to be his duty to hear more, and understand the "thing" better. He was shocked to find that Phil was not a loyal and true citizen; and he was quite sure that the family of Commodore Portington had no suspicion of his dangerous proclivities.

"Now, Mr. Kennedy, before we do any business, you must show me your commission as a lieutenant in the Confederate navy," said the stranger. "You know that all the business we have done thus far has been based upon the fact that you had one."

"Do you doubt my word?" demanded Phil.

"When I do business I want to know what I am about," added the stranger, stiffly. "I don't want anything left to chance which can be just as well reduced to a certainty."

"I told you I had a commission as a lieutenant in the Confederate navy; and that ought to satisfy you."

"But that does not satisfy me. I want to see the document. You young fellows talk a great deal of bosh."

"Don't insult me."

"Insult you? That kind of twaddle won't go down with me. We are talking about business, now, and you had better put your fine sentiment on the shelf."

"Of course I don't carry my commission in my pocket. It is in my trunk at the hotel."

"Very well; then I will see it before we part in the morning."

"I did not expect to have my word doubted," said Phil, sourly.

"Nobody doubts your word, Mr. Kennedy; but all our operations are based on that commission, and I must satisfy myself that everything is regular. I have fitted up the steamer at a cost of twelve thousand pounds, and she will be ready for you next Thursday. She has a good crew on board, who have an idea of the work in which they are to engage. When you get the vessel into Wilmington, you can select your own officers."

"Where is the armament?"

"All stowed under the cargo, where no one can find it."

" But I want to use the guns before we go into Wilmington."

" No, none of that; the parties of whom I purchased the vessel refused to sell her unless I would agree that she should go into a Confederate port before she was fitted up as a man-of-war."

" I may have a chance to capture a dozen vessels before I reach Wilmington," said the ambitious man of the world.

" You must not do it."

" Is the steamer fast? "

" She makes twelve knots, under favorable circumstances."

" She ought to make fourteen, for the business."

" Steamers that make fourteen knots are rather scarce. She is as fast as seven eighths of the Yankee gunboats."

" She will do. You are going with me — are you not, Coles? "

" No ; but I shall join you on the way."

" Join me on the way? " replied Kennedy, evidently much surprised at his answer.

" Yes, join you on the way ; that's possible — isn't it ? " answered Coles. " I have a venture on board of an old schooner in New York, which I intend to put into your vessel — something that will pay better than anything else we have."

" What is it? "

" Percussion caps. The bulk is small, but they aro worth their weight in gold in the Confederate States."

" But where will you board the steamer? "

" You will leave Halifax on Thursday. About Saturday morning you will be in latitude 41°, longitude 62°, where you will cruise till I join you."

" I don't like the plan very well," said Kennedy, after a momentary silence.

" Then some other man will carry it out. The first officer of the Snowden has orders to sail on Thursday morning, if you are not on board at that time. We can get along without you, Mr. Kennedy, if you don't choose to embark in the venture. I thought I was doing you a favor, instead of your doing me one."

" For which I am to pay half the expense," sneered Kennedy.

" If you ever have anything to pay with," added Coles.

" You have my bond for forty thousand dollars."

" To be paid when General Portington dies, and you come into possession of one half his property, which may never happen. A Jew wouldn't take such security."

" You are sure of your money."

" Not very sure, especially as the general has turned you out of the house, or done about the same thing."

" We are good friends now."

" How comes on the other speculation? When we

met last you were sure of marrying one half of the general's property, if you failed to get the other half. How does that speculation look just now?"

Somers did not hear Mr. Phil Kennedy grind his teeth at this question, but it was only because he was not near enough ; but he was appalled to hear that Kate was to be made the subject of a heartless speculation, and had no suspicion that he was himself regarded as an obstacle in the carrying out of the operation.

" You don't answer," said Coles, with a low chuckle.

" Everything is right there, or at least it will be in due time," answered Phil, carelessly.

" Then there is a hitch there?"

" Perhaps you can help me out a little."

, " Perhaps I can ; but I don't like to meddle with such matters."

" A young puppy of a midshipman stands directly in front of me, just now."

" O, ho !" laughed Coles. " Then the value of my bond is going-down in the market."

" Not at all. The young cub is the son of a poor man ; and when he is sent to sea, Kate will forget all about him, and I shall be all right again. If you could contrive some way to bring this fellow off to the Snowden in your schooner, perhaps it would add something to the value of your bond."

" Perhaps it would, and perhaps it wouldn't. In a

7

word, Mr. Kennedy, I don't attach much importance to your speculations in the matrimonial line. General Portington, I happen to know, has made a will in your favor. If he don't alter it, I am all right."

" So am I. But I am determined to marry the girl, if it is only to punish her for her impudence. I hate this young cub of a midshipman, and I would rather get him on board the Snowden than capture a thousand-ton ship. Couldn't you contrive some way to have him as a passenger in your schooner?"

" Perhaps I could, if it would accommodate you very much."

" I am very much obliged to you," thought Somers; " and I will hold you in affectionate remembrance for your kind intentions."

" I will give you ten thousand dollars for him."

" In bonds?" laughed Coles.

" From my first prize-money."

" That's worth thinking about."

" If we get the Snowden into Wilmington, the Confederate government will pay us more than she cost, and I shall be in funds then."

" I will look the matter over."

" Thank you," said Somers to himself. " When you get me, I shall be there."

Mr. Kennedy then proceeded to give Coles a very minute description of the " young puppy of a midshipman," with some particulars of his past history, and even ventured to suggest a plan by which he could lure the young gentleman on board of the schooner. But Coles was a practical man, and rejected the plan without a thought, indicating the point at which it would inevitably fail.

" I have a better method than that," said Coles.

" Hush ! " said Mr. Kennedy, as he seized the oars of the boat; " somebody is coming."

Somers saw a carriage stop on the wharf, from which a lady and gentleman alighted. Before they reached the landing-stairs Kennedy had pulled off out of sight in the darkness, and the listener was deprived of the satisfaction of hearing Coles's plan for getting him on board of the steamer. He was greatly disappointed, for his curiosity was deeply roused to learn the notable method by which the plot was to be carried out.

" Mr. Somers ! " called the commandant.

" Here, sir," replied he, springing from his place of concealment.

" Is your patience all gone ? " added the commandant, as he handed the lady into the boat.

" O, no, sir ; I have been well occupied all the time."

" I had some difficulty in finding the lady, which detained me longer than I expected. Shove off, Mr. Somers."

A distant church clock struck one as the boat gathered

way before a light breeze. As the reader will have no
difficulty in believing, Somers was intensely excited by
the treasonable plot to which he had listened. The conspiracy against himself personally caused him no uneasiness; but the mischief which an armed steamer might
do the cause of the country demanded prompt action.
The presence of the lady passenger on board the boat
prevented him from saying anything to the commandant;
but as soon as they had boarded the transport steamer he
related to him the conversation which he had overheard.

Mr. Revere was incredulous; and when Somers told
him he had crawled under the half deck to keep out of
the rain, he thought he must have been asleep, and
dreamed the whole story. Mr. Phil Kennedy was understood and believed to be a loyal man; and his relations to the family of Commodore Portington rendered it
necessary to proceed with the utmost caution. After the
commandant had seen the sick man, it was decided to
leave the sister with him, and return to the shore.

"I think you must have been asleep, Mr. Somers, and
dreamed this thing," said the commandant, as the boat
pushed off.

"I am very confident, sir, that I was wide awake. I
don't often go to sleep when on duty."

"Mr. Kennedy has been trying to get back into the
navy. He has offered his services, and would have
been accepted; but some question about his relative rank

interfered. He cannot be a traitor. He is on the best of terms with Miss Portington — is he not?"

"I believe he is."

"She would have spurned him if there had been any suspicion against him."

"I only know what I have heard, sir."

"I think there must be some mistake, though I cannot see where it is. I will call at the hotel and see Mr. Kennedy."

"I am certain you will find it as I have stated, sir," replied Somers, confidently.

They soon reached the wharf; and after the boat had been properly secured, Mr. Revere, attended by Somers, proceeded to the hotel where Phil Kennedy had a room. The night porter said the gentleman had retired.

"Was there any one with him when he came in?" asked the commandant.

"No, sir; he was alone."

Mr. Revere looked at Somers, and smiled significantly.

The young man was confused and confounded to find his statement of so little value in the eyes of the commandant, and was almost sorry that he had said anything about the affair. As it was, he had not mentioned that portion which related to himself. The incredulity of the commandant almost shook his own faith in the reality of the events which had transpired at the wharf.

Mr. Revere decided to visit the room of Phil Ken-

7 *

nedy, and they found that gentleman in bed, and appar
ently asleep.

"I heard you were going away in the morning, Mr.
Kennedy," said the commandant, after apologizing for
disturbing the sleeper.

"Indeed! Who told you so?" demanded Mr. Kennedy, rubbing his sleepy eyes.

"I heard so after we left the commodore's."

"Did Kate tell you so?"

"No; it was some other person. I only wanted to
ask you when you return, for there may be a commission
for you soon."

"It was only a joke I played off on Kate," said Mr.
Kennedy, laughing as though he enjoyed the recollection
of the jest. "I am not going away at present."

"I thought not; excuse me for breaking your slum-
bers, and I will see you in the morning," said Mr. Revere, as he retired from the chamber.

"Why don't you examine his trunk, sir?" asked
Somers, more confused than before.

"Examine his trunk?" laughed the commandant.
"That would be a serious matter. Now, Mr. Somers,
I don't doubt your sincerity, but I believe you have been
mistaken. If you didn't dream, you put a wrong construction on what you heard. If Mr. Phil Kennedy
plots treason, he don't do it in an open boat, within hail
of the wharf. I will look into the matter still further in

the morning. If you will show me Mr. Coles, that will be a point gained."

"I should not know him; it was pitch dark and raining hard when they came on board of the boat."

They returned to the Academy, where Somers, almost convinced that he had made a blunder, wrote down such particulars of the treasonable conversation as he could recall, particularly the name of the steamer which was to run the blockade, and then be sold to the Confederate government, and the latitude and longitude in which she was to be in waiting for the schooner.

In the morning it was found that Mr. Phil Kennedy had departed, bag and baggage; and Mr. Midshipman Somers's credit as a reliable witness rose high in the estimation of the commandant. He was given a day's leave of absence, to enable him to hunt up Coles, who would be another link in the chain of evidence. But it was almost a hopeless task, for he knew nothing about the man except the sound of his voice. Whether he was young or old, tall or short, spare or stout, he knew not. He visited all the hotels that were open, listened to the voice of every stranger, but without coming any nearer to the solution of the problem. Coles was an unsolved mystery, and was likely to remain so, unless, in attempting to carry out the benevolent wishes of Mr. Phil Kennedy, he should make himself known to our hero.

After dinner, Somers called at Commodore Portington's, not only to inform Kate that the wounded officer had died just before the transport sailed, but also to learn what he could about the sudden exit of Phil. Kate told him he had announced his intended departure to her; but beyond this, there was no information to be gained.

Somers left the house but little wiser than he entered it. It was patent to the commandant, as well as to him, that Phil had told a deliberate lie when he denied his intention to leave. Our midshipman had no particular qualifications as a detective, and he was tired of the job which he had been ordered to perform. Hopeless of success, he strolled up to the Redwood Institute, and sat down upon a seat in the grounds, to think over the events of the last twenty-four hours.

While he was musing, a gentleman seated himself at the other end of the bench.

"Fine day, after the rain," said the stranger, when they had sat there a short time.

"Splendid day," replied Somers.

"I see by your uniform that you are a naval cadet," continued the stranger. "Do you have a good time there?"

"Yes, very good, but plenty of hard work."

"I suppose so; but the country wants you as fast as you can get ready."

"We are ready now," laughed Somers.

" Very likely you all think so. I am a stranger here, and I should like — "

" Mr. Coles, if I am not mistaken," said Somers, when he was satisfied that the voice was a familiar one.

" That's my name ; but I do not remember to have met you before," replied the stranger, with no little confusion evident in his features.

" I cannot tell where I have met you ; but I have seen you before," added Somers.

CHAPTER VII.

SOMERS SENT UPON ACTIVE SERVICE.

AFTER some time spent in fruitless efforts to determine where they had met, Coles expressed his desire to visit the Naval Academy; and Somers told him how he could gain admission. All this, of course, was simply to make talk. The stranger, in his own estimation, was playing a deep game; and he certainly managed the affair with great adroitness, so that without the advantage which he had obtained the night before, Somers would have felt highly honored by the pleasant words which his companion so freely uttered. As it was, the midshipman was amused, and gave his polite friend " all the rope " he wanted.

The interview ended with an invitation on the part of Coles for Somers to visit him at his hotel, which the latter promised to do when his duty would permit. He had obtained the name of the stranger's hotel, which was all he had been waiting for; and taking leave of the inquiring gentleman, he hastened to report to Mr. Revere the result of his day's work. It was very satisfactory, and the midshipman obtained more credit for his diplomatic skill than he deserved, or would have been awarded to him, if he had told the part of the story which related to himself.

" Mr. Somers, I have what I suppose will be pleasant intelligence to you," said the commandant, with a smile, after he had listened to the young gentleman's report. " You have been ordered to sea, with your friend Mr. Waldron, who goes out in command of the Rosalie."

" It is indeed good news to me, sir, though my residence in Newport has been very pleasant," replied Somers.

" The Rosalie is a fine topsail schooner, of about two hundred tons, and a very fast sailer. Mr. Waldron is an excellent officer, and you will find yourself well situated on board of her. Of course you will not neglect your studies, for you will still be a midshipman, and a member of the Naval Academy."

" I certainly shall not neglect my studies. I have too great a dread of examinations to do that, sir."

" That's a very wholesome dread. I know all about it myself, from bitter experience. It drives one to be faithful to his duties. But, Somers, you must go to New York to-morrow night; for the Rosalie may be ordered off at any moment."

This was rather short notice, and Somers immediately wrote a letter to his family at home, informing them of the fact that he had been detailed for duty. Leave of absence was given to him during the remainder of his stay, and of course he did not neglect to make a final visit at the house of Commodore Portington. Kate received him with a smile, as she always did.

"I am glad you have come, Prodigy, for I have a skein of worsted for you to hold, while I wind it."

"I thank you for the honor you propose to confer on me," replied Somers, as he held out his hands to receive the skein.

"Truly it is an honor which is not conferred on every little midshipman that prinks himself like a bantam in the morning sun. Middies are useless beings as a general rule, and I feel that I am doing a benevolent act when I redeem one from idleness, even for a single moment."

"Your benevolence deserves a monument; but I am happy to inform you that I shall not much longer be a proper subject for the exercise of your beneficent genius."

"And why so, Prodigy?" asked she, looking up into his face.

"I am going to work — am saved from the miseries of idleness."

"Pray, what can such a useless fellow as you do?"

"Not much. I am ordered to duty."

"What?"

"I am going to sea immediately. I leave for New York to-morrow night."

Kate stopped winding the worsted, and looked Somers full in the face.

" Do you mean so ? "

" Certainly I do. I am ordered to the Rosalie, now ready for sea, at New York."

" I haven't the least idea that you can be of any use on board the Rosalie ; but I suppose the government wants to keep some of the middies out of mischief," said Kate. But even Somers could not help seeing the crimson on her cheek, and being aware, now that his eyes had been opened by the kindly revelations of Mr. Phil Kennedy, that she was not at all pleased with the idea of his departure.

She tried hard to conceal what was really passing in her mind and heart, but she did not wholly succeed. She was less flippant during the remainder of the evening, and even became quite sober and sedate before nine o'clock. She was a little absent-minded, and several times failed to answer the questions which her mother put to her.

" Well, Mr. Somers, I am really sorry that you are going, for I shall have no one to make fun of," said she, when the young gentleman rose to depart. " There are plenty of middies in Newport, but very few prodigies among them."

" I am sorry to go, but I am very thankful that I have had the grace to contribute, in a humble degree, to

8

your amusement. Perhaps Mr. Kennedy may return, and you can make fun of him."

" Perhaps he may," she replied, rather vacantly. " I am going to extort one more promise from you before you go."

" I promise in advance."

" Don't be rash — middies should never be rash."

" I know that I may safely promise anything which Miss Portington can ask."

" That's very gallant, even for a prodigy ; but I am not going to demand anything very serious."

" I knew you would not, and therefore I gave my promise in season."

" You are going to sea, and you are a prodigy. You have already done deeds fit to be put in school histories for little children to study, and very likely you will do something again."

" Possibly I may," laughed Somers, who had long since ceased to depreciate his own merit when she railed at him.

" Probably you will. I want you to promise, if you do any great things, that you will write me a letter, and tell me about them ; but mind, you are not to write unless you do something that is decidedly splendid," continued Kate ; but somehow, there seemed to be less heart in her raillery than usual.

" I promise ; but I can assure you, before I go, that

my investments in postage stamps on this account will be very small."

" How, sir ! do you mean to break your promise in the same breath that you make it?"

" I mean to keep my promise ; but you ordered me not to write unless I shall have done something that is decidedly splendid."

" You shall be your own judge of the quality of your great deeds."

" I do not expect to perform any great deeds, Miss Portington."

" I declare, the prodigy has some modesty, after all ! " said Kate, with a feeble laugh.

" Perhaps my ship may do something worthy of record. May I write to you when she distinguishes herself? "

" I don't care a straw for your ship ! "

" Then I am afraid I shall have no opportunity to write to you."

" What a silly dolt you are ! I thought you were a good scholar, and knew an elephant from a basket of chips," exclaimed Kate, provoked that he did not promise without making any reservations or exceptions.

" Thank you. I am always stupid in your presence, just as the stars are invisible when the sun shines."

" Well, upon my word, you need some refreshment after such an effort as that remark must have cost you. Let me bring you a glass of cold water."

" Thank you. I am not at all exhausted by it. I could do the same thing right over again."

" Then you will not write to me, Prodigy?"

" Certainly I will, with the greatest pleasure, if you will remove the restrictions you imposed upon me."

" What restrictions?"

" That I should write only when I had done some big thing."

" Well, you shall use your own judgment."

Somers departed almost with the belief that Phil Kennedy had good reason for his hatred. He was not conscious, however, of anything more than a very pleasant friendship, such as boys and girls sometimes get up among themselves, and was utterly unable to realize that he was the slightest obstacle in the way of Phil's matrimonial speculation.

The following day was spent in making his preparations for sea. He left the Academy with the kindest wishes of all the officers and professors, and with the good will of nearly all the young gentlemen; for there were a few who envied his fair fame, and resented his bright example. In the afternoon, as he was returning from Commodore Portington's, where he had been to take his final leave, — for these things have to be done over several times in particular cases, — he met Coles, who, it was apparent from his movements, had been on the lookout for him.

" Ah, Mr. Somers, I hear that you are ordered to duty," said the polite gentleman.

" Yes, sir, I go to New York to-night."

" How fortunate ! We shall be fellow-passengers ; for I had made my arrangements to leave to-night."

" Then I shall be happy to meet you on board of the steamer ; but you must excuse me now, for I am in a great hurry."

" You must be busy at this time ; excuse me for detaining you," replied Coles, as he turned and walked up the street.

A thin-faced man, on the other side of the street, turned round, and went up the hill at the same time. Whoever saw Coles that day, might have seen the sharp eyes of this man fixed upon him everywhere he went.

At eight o'clock Somers was on board of the Empire State, bound to New York. Coles was there, too ; and so was the thin-faced man, though no one knew him — least of all the object of his constant and keen scrutiny.

" Good evening, Mr. Somers ; I am glad to see you again," said Coles, as he seated himself by the side of the midshipman. " Did you secure a state-room ? "

" No, sir. I can sleep very well in the cabin."

" I always take a room ; it is so much more comfortable to be by yourself," continued Coles, his hard visage lighted up with an amiable smile. " There are two berths in my state-room; allow me to offer you one of them."

"Thank you; but you would not be by yourself if I accepted your polite invitation," laughed Somers.

"It is more pleasant to be with one's friends even than it is to be alone. I don't like to flatter young men, for it spoils them; but you must permit me to say, that I have learned some of the particulars of your history, and I feel a deep interest in you. My friend, Captain Bankhead, gave me a very interesting account of your exploits at the South, and I assure you I feel highly honored by being permitted to make your acquaintance."

"Thank you, sir; you are very complimentary," replied Somers, who knew that the other's statement must be a lie, made out of whole cloth.

Coles continued to say pleasant things, and Somers received them for what they were worth. As he listened to them, it occurred to him that he might serve his country by learning more about this traitor's schemes. He had been assured by Mr. Revere, that the information he had obtained on that eventful night would be used. Whether it had been or not, he was now in ignorance; he was not even aware of the presence of the thin-faced man who dogged the steps of Coles, whose slightest movement did not escape his notice. Perhaps the government was too busy, just then, to attend to small traitors; and Somers concluded that he might obtain more useful information by humoring his complimentary friend.

With this view he considered Coles's invitation to occupy one of the berths in his state-room. After supper they met again in the saloon, and the thin-faced man was within ear-shot of them. Coles said Captain Bankhead — *his* friend, Captain Bankhead — had told him Somers was a splendid boatman, and a fine judge of a good vessel. Somers acknowledged that a handsome craft was his especial delight.

"I have just been having a schooner yacht built for my private use. Nautical men say she is a beauty."

"Indeed! I should like to see her," added Somers, fully confident that this was the development of the plan, the details of which he had been disappointed in hearing while in the boat at Newport.

"I should be delighted to have you go on board of her," said the pleased owner of the fine yacht — which, of course, was a myth. "She lies in New York harbor, and if you have time, in the morning we will visit her."

"I am afraid I shall not have time. I must report on board my ship as early as possible."

"Ah, then I can arrange it for you, so that you will hardly lose a moment. Your ship, I presume, lies off the navy yard?"

"She does."

"We can take a shore-boat, visit the yacht, and then pull off to your ship."

Somers liked the plan, and readily assented to it. He had not the remotest fear of being personally injured by his polite companion. He had a loaded revolver in his pocket, and considered himself man enough for Coles, or even two or three like him. He wanted to see the vessel which was to convey the valuable venture out to the Snowden, so that he could report her to the proper authorities, and have her seized before she had a chance to depart upon her errand of mischief. At ten o'clock our travellers retired to the state-room; for Somers had accepted Coles's polite invitation in order to prevent him from indulging any suspicions. Both of them were exceedingly well satisfied with themselves, and each was confident that he was effectually carrying out his own cherished scheme.

They entered the state-room, and the thin-faced man made a note of the fact that they were fast friends, and that they were going off together in a boat in the morning.

The Empire State reached her pier at half past six the next morning. Coles with his valise, and Somers with his bag, took a carriage together, and were driven over to the navy yard ferry. The thin-faced man sat on the box of another carriage, and did not lose sight of them for a single instant. They crossed the ferry together; but the thin-faced man had on a mustache and a different colored coat as he stepped on board of the steamer. On the other side, Coles took a boat, and they pulled out from the pier into the stream.

"Yonder is my yacht," said Coles, pointing to a beautiful schooner, which lay a short distance from the shore.

"She's a beauty," replied Somers. "I should like to sail in such a craft as that."

"I should be happy to have you; but I suppose that would be impossible at the present time."

"Have you a crew on board?"

"No; and her cabins are locked up. The man in charge of her is on board of this old schooner," replied Coles, pointing to an old vessel near the yacht. "I shall have to go on board of her for the keys."

Somers concluded that this old schooner was to be the bearer of the rich venture to the Snowden. He could not understand how the keeper of the yacht should be on board of this schooner, and he did not think it worth his while to investigate the mystery. Coles directed the boatman to pull up alongside of the old vessel.

"This schooner belongs to me, too," said Coles, as he stepped over her rail. "I will not detain you above a minute."

He disappeared for a moment, but presently returned with an invitation to Somers to go on board and take a cup of coffee, which would not detain them five minutes. Somers, though fully aware that a plot for his capture had been matured by Kennedy and Coles, did not hesitate to step on the deck of the schooner. He had a perfect contempt for Coles as a physical power, and a boyish confidence in his own ability to take care of himself. Besides, he was so intent upon obtaining valuable information for the government, that he almost forgot that he was himself an object of Kennedy's scheming.

He stepped down into the cabin, and drank a mug of coffee, handed to him by the steward.

"I used to be the skipper of this vessel in my young days," said Coles, as he gazed about the cabin.

"Indeed! Then you are a sailor."

"O, yes. This was my state-room. I had it put up myself," he added, opening the door of the little apartment. "Just look in and see how convenient it is for a man of small desires."

Somers did look in; did more — he went in — was pushed in. The door was suddenly closed upon him and locked.

Apparently Mr. Coles's notable scheme had been entirely successful; but the thin-faced man was yet to be heard from.

CHAPTER VIII.

ON BOARD THE THEBAN.

"NOW make sail as fast as you can, Murdock," said Coles, in excited tones, when he had locked the door of the state-room.

"I don't know about this business, Captain Coles," replied Murdock, shaking his head, as he glanced towards the state-room.

"You don't know about it? Why, what do you mean by that?" demanded the polite friend of our middy, though he was not now quite so soft-tongued as he had been.

"That wasn't in the bargain," added the doubtful skipper of the schooner; for such was the position filled by Murdock.

"What wasn't in the bargain? Why don't you speak out, if you have anything to say?" added Coles, impatiently.

Somers's kind friend did not appear to be aware that he was engaged in a business in the slightest degree irregular. He looked virtuous and indignant at the scruples of his companion in treason, and bore himself as loftily as though he had been a loyal man on the deck of a loyal ship of war.

" Carrying that officer off in this kind of way is something rather different from running a cargo of merchandise into a blockaded port. I don't like the looks of the thing ; and I'm not paid for doing a job of that sort."

" Good! Then you shall be paid for it. You shall have a thousand dollars if we put him safe on board of the Snowden."

" That alters the case, Captain Coles."

" I thought it would," replied Coles, contemptuously.

" I reckon we have no time to spare. But the young cub will get out of that state-room."

" Drop the dead-light, and fasten it down. He will be safe enough then," added Coles, as he led the way to the deck, where Murdock proceeded to get the schooner under way, without the loss of another moment.

" Boatman," said Coles to the man who had pulled them off from the Brooklyn shore, " we have concluded to remain on board, and you may go back. Here is a dollar for you."

" Thank you, sir. What will I do with the young gentleman's bag?"

" Throw it on deck."

" I will, your honor," replied the boatman, as he tossed the bag on the deck.

"See here, my man : the young fellow got into a little scrape over in the city last night, and wants to keep out of sight for a few days. Here's another dollar for you, and don't mention to anybody that you have seen him."

"God bless your honor for a gintleman, as ye are; but I won't spake of it to any living sowl — not even to Biddy, and that's me wife, long life to her!"

The dead-light was fastened down, leaving the prisoner in total darkness; the mainsail was hoisted, the anchor hove up, and in less than half an hour the old craft was making her way down the harbor in the direction of Sandy Hook; and the man with the thin face had not been heard from yet.

While the Theban — for that was the classic name of the antiquated craft — is sailing down the bay, we will take a look at Somers, if the state-room is not too dark for such an operation. Mr. Coles was so polite and sincere that our hero did not suspect any immediate foul play. He knew, but, in his eagerness to obtain "valuable information" for the government officers, he had not kept it uppermost in his mind, that he was expected to be an involuntary passenger in the venerable schooner of which Coles had been skipper in his earlier days. He had a revolver in his pocket, ready for instant use; but with so amiable a person as his Newport friend, such an instrument had appeared to be entirely unnecessary, and it hardly occurred to him that he had it.

9

With the information Somers had of the intentions of the conspirators, we must say that he was careless to venture on board of the schooner; but we feel more inclined to excuse his want of caution when we remember that he had been impelled to do so by the desire to serve his government and defeat the purposes of traitors. When he looked into the state-room, he expected to find it stored full of percussion caps, or some other commodities contraband of war; which fact he intended to use as evidence against the traitors. He fully expected to obtain such proofs of the character of the vessel, and of her intended voyage, as would justify Captain Waldron in seizing her when he should impart the information. It would be a good thing for the new captain of the Rosalie to do a prompt act for the government service, and add to his credit at Washington. These considerations had caused Somers to forget his own relation to the conspirators.

He was angry with himself for his imprudence when the state-room door closed upon him, and he realized that Coles had actually made him his victim. He had been guilty of an indiscretion, which was more painful to him than the fact of his imprisonment. With the future he did not yet trouble himself; the present was too full of doubt and mortification to allow him to withdraw his thoughts from it.

"I can't stand this," said he, ready to cry with vexation, as he thought of his folly in getting into such a scrape.

"What are you going to do about it?" a voice seemed to reply from the thick gloom around him — a voice which appeared to embody, in mocking tones, the spirit of the conspirators who had been the cause of his misfortunes.

"I am going to fight my way out of this scrape as fast as I can," muttered Somers, in audible tones, as though he were speaking to the obstacles which surrounded him.

He took hold of the handle and shook the door, to test its strength. It was a thick, strong piece of joiner's work, and the trial did not afford a very encouraging prospect of making his way through it. He applied his shoulder, but with no better result. He then examined the stern-window. He could open the sash, but the dead-light was carefully secured on the outside for the present emergency. The partition was so thick and solid that Somers concluded the captain's state-room had been made for a specie room.

While everything looked thus hopeless, the unhappy prisoner bethought him of an expedient which afforded a slight prospect of success. He had his revolver, and plenty of metallic cartridges in his pocket. Placing the muzzle of the pistol near the bolt of the lock, he fired, and repeated the process several times, hoping to perforate the wood until it gave way. Perhaps this experiment might have been crowned with success, if the smoke of the burnt powder had not become so overpowering that he was compelled to suspend operations.

"Fire away!" shouted Coles from the cabin, with a hearty laugh, either real or forced, which grated harshly on the ear of the disconsolate prisoner.

"Open the door, or I shall suffocate," cried Somers.

"Go ahead and suffocate," replied the brute. "If you don't know any better than to fire a pistol in a close room like that, you ought to suffocate."

"Will you open the door?"

"I will, if you desire it very much," replied Coles. "But, Mr. Somers, you are a brave man, and I dare say you are a discreet one. My friend Captain Bankhead said you were as prudent as you were brave."

Coles chuckled as he uttered this remark, and Somers heard his step as he moved towards the door of the state-room. He was tempted to fire again, and wipe out his persecutor from the face of the earth, if he could hit him; but the chances of making a good shot through the door were so few, that he was discreet enough not to risk it.

"Now, Mr. Somers, I want to tell you, before I go any further, that I have a pistol in my hand. If you use yours, I shall use mine; in a word, if you don't behave yourself you are a dead man. What do you say?"

"Open the door; that's all I have to say," replied Somers, in savage tones.

"If that's all, I won't open it; and you can amuse yourself firing at a mark in the dark."

Somers was almost suffocated by the dense mass of powder smoke in the little apartment; and he was not in a condition to be very haughty.

"Open the door, if you please," said he, after he had chewed upon the matter for a while.

"Say that you will behave yourself like a man, and I will."

"I will behave myself like a man," replied Somers, who interpreted this promise as including the right to make a gallant and manly strike for his freedom, if the circumstances would permit such an attempt.

"You are a sensible fellow now," added Coles, as he turned the key, and opened the door a couple of inches.

The fresh air which came in through the aperture gave the prisoner a new life, and he inhaled the precious blast with grateful eagerness.

"Now, youngster, pass your pistol out, and I will open it wider," said Coles.

"I can't spare my pistol," answered Somers.

"All right," said Coles, as he closed the door, and locked it. "What do you say now?"

Somers did not know what to say. The room was still too full of smoke to enable him to breathe with

9 *

comfort. While he was confined, the pistol was a useless piece of furniture, and the chances outside were better without the pistol than they were inside with it.

"I will give up the pistol," said he.

"Sensible again," replied Coles, as he opened the door, and took the pistol. "There, Mr. Somers, you have now fully vindicated your reputation for bravery and prudence. You have fired half a dozen shots into that wooden door, which proves that you are a brave fellow; and you have given up your pistol, which proves that you are a prudent one. I honor you, and deem it a privilege to become acquainted with such a distinguished young gentleman."

"Your success has not impaired your politeness," answered Somers, rather tamely.

"Not at all. I was brought up as a gentleman, and I intend to be one till the last day of my life. I shall leave a letter of thanks for the sexton who buries me, to be delivered to him if he does his work well."

"You had better write that letter very soon then, for you will be introduced to a hangman before you are much older."

"My dear Somers, that is a very impolite suggestion. I was born a gentleman, as I just now remarked, and I intend to die like a gentleman."

"Were you a gentleman in your earlier days, when you commanded this old tub?" said Somers, who was amused, in spite of himself, at the conceits and oddities of his gentlemanly friend.

" My dear fellow, that was an amiable fiction of mine, intended to assist in quieting your nerves, before you took up your quarters in that state-room. You may come out now, if you desire to do so ; but I trust you will not attempt to leave this cabin, for that would reduce me to the disagreeable necessity of shooting you."

" And thus save your friend Phil Kennedy from any further uneasiness on my account."

" Ah ! " exclaimed Coles, starting back with astonishment at this obvious knowledge, on the part of his prisoner, of what no one was supposed to know. " You are wiser than the law allows young men of your age to be."

" I know why I am here," added Somers.

" Do you, indeed ? "

" Undoubtedly I do ; and wise as your age and experience have made you, I could tell you a dozen things that are worth knowing."

" Perhaps you will oblige me by doing so," sneered the hard-visaged man.

" Perhaps I will ; and then, again, perhaps I won't."

" Don't be unkind, my dear young friend. Confidence is a jewel between such friends as we are."

" You can sit there and crow over me, but my time will come by and by," said Somers, as he stepped out of the state-room, and sat down opposite his persecutor.

" Crow over you, my dear fellow? I have been treat-
ing you with the most distinguished consideration."

" You may think all your plans are crowned with success, but I assure you they will all fail," added Somers,
fearfully galled by the jeering tones of Coles. " You
have got almost to the end of your rope, in a double
sense."

" That is, my plans will fail, and I shall be hung for
my politeness to you."

" Exactly so. This old tub will never reach latitude
forty-one, longitude sixty-two."

Coles sprang to his feet, and his hard visage turned as
red as blood. His politeness suddenly deserted him, and
he clutched the pistol in his hand with convulsive energy.

" Neither will you ever pocket ten thousand dollars
for handing me over to Phil Kennedy," added Somers.

" Young man, it is evident that you know more of me
than I had supposed."

" And Phil Kennedy will never invite you to his wedding with Miss Kate Portington," continued Somers,
who could not resist the temptation to pour in one more
hot shot.

" I am afraid you know too much for your own safety,
young man," said Coles, with difficulty repressing his
emotions.

" Too much for *your* safety, you mean."

" For both, if that suits your humor better."

" Perhaps I do ; and I assure you, the best thing you can do will be to put me on shore at the earliest possible moment, and make your ten thousand dollars in a more respectable and gentlemanly way."

" I shall not do that ; you and I will hang together for the present."

" We shall be separated at the final hanging, which cannot much longer be delayed."

" Mr. Somers, I hold a pistol in my hand, and I will thank you not to indulge in any useless impudence."

Our middy was prudent enough to take this broad hint, and permitted Coles to do the talking for some time, without venturing to make a reply. There was not much, however, that the amiable gentleman could say, for Somers had taken the wind all out of his sails, by exhibiting his knowledge of the conspirators' mysteries. He was exceedingly troubled, and he could no longer conceal from his prisoner his anxiety and uneasiness. He made several efforts, more or less direct, to ascertain where Somers had obtained his information ; but the latter was too well satisfied with the change which had come over his persecutor to enlighten his bewildered mind.

. " Captain Coles, there is a steamer coming down the bay, which acts very strange. I reckon she is after us," said Murdock, at the companion-way.

" Nonsense ! " exclaimed Coles ; " it is some tow-boat."

" The men on board of her keep looking at us through their glasses."

" All right ! " said Somers, with emphasis, hoping and believing that the information he had given Mr. Revere was now to save him from a rebel prison.

The man with the thin face was beginning to make himself felt.

CHAPTER IX.

THE MAN WITH THE THIN FACE.

R. SOMERS, I will trouble you to remain in this cabin," said Coles, again assuming the polite manner which had distinguished him in more prosperous hours.

" I will stay here with the greatest pleasure. I shall make no attempt to escape, Mr. Coles, for I am too much interested in the results of this adventure to be voluntarily deprived of the pleasure of seeing the conclusion of the whole matter," replied Somers, with a bland smile, and a courteous bow.

" Don't flatter yourself just yet, my dear young friend," continued Coles, as he rose from his seat, and walked towards the companion-way. " You and I will not part company to-day."

Somers hoped they would, and fully expected that such would be the result of the excursion down the bay. He was satisfied that Mr. Revere had used the information he had given him, and it was hardly possible that the authorities would permit a vessel with important military supplies to leave the harbor.

Coles went on deck. Polite and easy as his bearing was, he was sorely tried by the difficulties of his situation. He was amazed and confounded at the information in possession of his prisoner, and he felt very much as though he stood on a volcano in process of irruption.

"There's the steamer," said Murdock, as Coles stepped on deck; "and, if I'm not greatly mistaken, she's after us."

"What makes you think so?" asked Coles, uneasily.

"In the first place, there are not less than twenty men on her deck, and it appears to me that about one half of them have spy-glasses in their hands, and are watching this vessel."

"I think you are right, Murdock," replied Coles, more nervously. "Where did you stow our cargo?"

"Under the groceries."

"Do you think they will find the kegs?"

"Nothing to prevent their finding them, if they look far enough."

"You have your clearance and other papers all right?"

"All right and straight, Captain Coles. I fixed everything just as you told me."

By this time the Theban was off "The Kills," which is the strait connecting New York and Newark Bays. The steamer that caused Coles and his companion in treason so much anxiety was half a mile distant. The wind, which was tolerably fresh, was from the southward, and the old schooner was close-hauled, lying as near the wind as she could, which, however, was not within eight points of her course. The steamer was headed due south, knowing that the Theban must presently tack, and stand out into the middle of the bay again.

" The steamer will overhaul us in fifteen minutes more," said Coles, as he glanced up the Kills.

" We can't expect to run away from a steamer in this old craft," replied Murdock.

" There are only two things that we can do."

" Not more than that," answered Murdock, with a grim smile.

" We can take our chance in being examined, or run up the Kills and take to the boat. Which shall we do? "

" There isn't much chance any way," said Murdock; " but I think we had better run up the Kills."

" Do so, then."

" What are you going to do with that young cub in the cabin? "

" I have a mind to throw him overboard. He knows too much for his own comfort and mine."

" He will blow on us the moment the officers come on board."

" We must get rid of him before any of them come," added Coles, as the schooner fell off, and stood up the strait. " We shall know, now, whether the steamer is looking for us or not."

"Ay, there goes her helm over to port, and she is headed this way," said Murdock.

"I am afraid it is all up with us," replied Coles, as he went down into the cabin.

"Well, Mr. Coles, how goes the battle?" demanded Somers, with abundant good nature. "You see I am taking it very coolly."

"Everything works right; but, my young friend, as I have now shown you my yacht, and exhibited my state-room to you, I think it is about time for you to join your ship," said Coles, with an effort to assume his former easy air.

"Thank you for your considerate regard for my welfare. Then you have concluded not to put me on board of the Snowden?"

"I am sorry that I shall be obliged to disappoint our friend Mr. Kennedy. I will trouble you now to go on deck, where I shall take the liberty to transfer you to a shore boat."

"Don't give yourself any further trouble on my account. I prefer to remain where I am."

"Do you? Then you shall be gratified. But I shall have to ask you to resume your place in the state-room."

"I shall be just as comfortable where I am," replied Somers, facetiously.

"You will be too comfortable," said Coles, producing

his pistol. " This is the only argument I can offer for your consideration at the present time."

" O, well, if you are in earnest, I will enter the state-room ; " and Somers, not doubting that he should be released in a few moments, obeyed the polite order.

The little room had been thoroughly ventilated, and was now quite comfortable. He sat down to abide the issue, fully satisfied that before noon he should grasp the hand of Lieutenant Waldron on board the Rosalie.

Coles went on deck again. He was nervous and uneasy, and occasionally glanced at the pursuing steamer as a condemned criminal looks at the gallows on which he is to be hung.

" Captain Coles, if you are going to stand an examination, I reckon we have made a blunder in coming into this channel," said Murdock.

" It's no use to run away in a place like this. Put your helm down, and come to anchor under the weather shore of the creek," replied Coles.

" Down with your helm ! " said Murdock to the man at the tiller. " Let go the anchor," added he, when the jib had been hauled down. " Here we are, Captain Coles."

" When they come on board, just say that we found the wind ahead, and concluded to anchor in this place till we could get a little slant."

" I understand," answered the intelligent skipper.

The Theban came up to her anchor, with her patched fore and main sails flapping in the wind. Murdock sat down on the rail, lighted his pipe, and looked as unconcerned as though he had been a loyal trader to a .yal port. Coles went aft, and busied himself in gazing up the creek, apparently unconscious that any great event was about to take place.

The steamer ran her bows alongside the schooner, while the eager crowd, including the man with the thin face, carefully scrutinized the old craft.

"Hallo, there!" shouted Murdock, suddenly springing up, as though he had just seen the steamer for the first time. "Hard a-port your helm, or you will run me down! What are you about? Do you mean to stave me in?"

The steamer's people made no reply to this warning, but as her bow came up with the Theban's side, one of the deck hands passed a small hawser through one of her channel plates, and the man with the thin face leaped on board of the schooner. He was followed by several other men, who appeared to be officers, though none of them were dressed in uniform.

"What are you about now?" demanded the innocent skipper of the Theban. "What are you all coming aboard of this craft for?"

"We have business here," replied the man with the thin face.

" O, have you ? "

" I have. Who is the captain of this vessel? "

" I am, for the want of a better," said Murdock, as he sat down again, and proceeded with the utmost deliberation to relight his pipe.

" But you are not the person I want," said the man with the thin face, who was a government detective officer.

He had been sent on from New York to " work up " the case of Coles and Kennedy, after Mr. Revere had telegraphed the information obtained by Somers.

" Then you don't want to see the captain of this vessel," replied Murdock, philosophically.

" Where is the other man? " demanded the officer.

" What other man? "

" The one that came on board just before you sailed — two of them, for that matter. Where is the elderly man? "

" Well, I reckon he isn't a great way off. He stood on the taffrail a few moments ago."

" Do you mean me? " said Coles, now coming up from the cabin, where he had gone, as the steamer was making fast to the Theban, to satisfy himself that his prisoner was not complicating his affairs.

" I mean you," answered the detective. " You are the man I want.''

" What do you want of me? " asked Coles, with as much simplicity as so artful a man could assume.

10.*

" There is a room in Fort Lafayette ready for your use," replied the facetious man with the thin face.

" What do you mean?"

" It's a plain case.   But I think we will overhaul your cargo a little before we go any farther."

" I reckon you will find it all right," said Murdock.

" Perhaps we shall.   We can tell better after we have examined it."

A dozen men were set at work in the hold.   Within an hour, they had brought to light a number of kegs, labelled " cut nails," which were found, upon further examination, to contain articles contraband of war, and to prove that the label was a lie.

" Exactly so !" exclaimed the detective, when the kegs were open.   " The facts correspond with the information."

" Just what the rebels want most," said a loyal member of the boarding party.

" Mr. Coles, you are my prisoner," continued the detective.   " Where is the other man?"

" What other man?" asked Coles, with genuine surprise.

" The young fellow in false colors — wearing the uniform of a midshipman."

" He's down below," answered Coles, actually chuckling, in spite of his own misfortunes, at the blunder of the officer.

" I want him too."

" What do you want of him ? "

" I don't like to separate two such loving friends as you are, and I think they can find a room in Fort Lafayette big enough to hold both of you."

" He is down in the cabin. Come with me, and I will show you where to find him," added Coles, maliciously.

"I can find him without any assistance from you," continued the detective, with highly commendable caution.

" Perhaps you can," said Coles, doubtfully.

The detective went below, but the " young fellow wearing the uniform of a midshipman," was not visible to the naked eye.

" Where is he ? " called the officer, who did not imme- diately discover the state-room.

Coles, followed by a couple of the detective's party, went below, and turning the key of the state-room, which he did in such a manner that the movement was not seen by his captors, he threw open the door.

" You are my prisoner ! " said the man with the thin face, slapping Somers on the shoulder, as he stepped out of his narrow quarters.

" Your what ? " demanded the young officer, astonished beyond measure at this unexpected demonstration.

" My prisoner, my gallant little fellow. You under- stand English — don't you ? "

" I don't understand you, sir."

" I can't stop to explain just uow ; but you will probably understand it by the time you find yourself comfortably quartered in Fort Lafayette," replied the enterprising detective, as he handed both of his prisoners over to his associates.

"In Fort Lafayette!" exclaimed Somers, filled with horror at the bare mention of the place in connection with his own name.

The officer in charge of the party hastened on deck, without paying any further attention to the complaint of the unfortunate young gentleman. The anchor of the Theban was hove up, and she proceeded up the bay in tow of the steamer.

"Well, my dear young friend, we are not to be rudely separated, after all," said Coles, in mocking tones, as he seated himself between the two officials who were charged with his safe keeping.

"I presume I am indebted to you for this insult," replied Somers, bitterly; for being put under arrest for treasonable practices was the severest trial which he had yet been called to endure.

He was not as patient as he might have been under this new misfortune, and he at once concluded that he was indebted to Coles for it. He believed that the malicious traitor had accused him to the officer of being his accomplice.

"Keep cool, my dear fellow," continued Coles. "Our mutual friend, Captain Bankhead, assured me you were the coolest young man he had ever known; but I must confess that present appearances do not confirm his good opinion of you."

Somers was disgusted with Coles, and disgusted with the results of the adventure; and he made no reply to the taunts of his companion in misery. He seated himself in a corner of the cabin, and maintained a savage silence till the steamer and her prize reached East River, where the latter was anchored under the guns of the Rosalie, which had just hauled out into the stream.

"Now, gentlemen, if you will step on board of the steamer, we will give you comfortable quarters behind a thick stone wall," said the polite detective.

"Thank you," replied Coles, with forced indifference.

"I should like a few moments' private conversation with you before you go any farther," said Somers, rising heavily from his seat.

"I can't spare the time."

"Then you will make a great mistake if you arrest me, for I assure you I am guilty of no crime, and am as loyal to the government as you are."

"I can't stop to discuss these questions now. It isn't my business to try the case. Hurry up, if you please."

"You will injure your credit if you go on with this matter."

"If you save your own credit, young man, I will take care of myself," replied the official, laughing.

" I gave the first information which led to the seizure of this vessel," whispered Somers.

" Come, come, my lively little bird, your tongue is a useful member to you, but it won't do you any good in the present instance."

" Very well ; if you won't hear me, will you, as a special favor, send a man to inform Captain Waldron, of the Rosalie, that you have arrested Midshipman Somers, of his vessel, on a charge of treasonable practices."

" I don't make any charges, young man — I leave that for a court-martial to do.   I found you in company with men engaged in smuggling percussion caps out of New York."

" I can explain why I happened to be on board of this vessel."

" You came from Newport with this man, Coles ; you were on intimate terms with him ; and you slept in his state-room.   Do you know Captain Waldron, of the Rosalie?" continued the officer, who seemed to be considering whether there might not, after all, be some mistake.

" I know him well, and am ordered to duty on board his vessel."

" I will send for him."

" Thank you, sir," replied Somers, now assured that he should soon be discharged from arrest.

CHAPTER X.

THE UNITED STATES SCHOONER ROSALIE.

ON'T you be kind enough to inform Captain Waldron that I am here also?" interposed Coles, as the boat with the messenger was about to shove off.

"Is he a friend of yours, too?" demanded the officer, as a momentary doubt overshadowed his thin face.

But the mocking smile on the countenance of Coles assured one so well versed in the expression of the human face that the remark was a facetious one; and he paid no further attention to the real traitor. While the messenger was absent, Somers and the officer compared notes in regard to the trip from Newport; and the detective was pretty well satisfied that the young man spoke the truth.

In less than half an hour the well-timed stroke of a man-of-war boat was heard near the Theban. Up went the oars, and Captain Waldron leaped on the deck of the old schooner.

"Good morning, Mr. Somers," shouted the captain, as he grasped the hand of his young friend.

"Good morning; I never was so glad to see a friend in my life as I am at this moment."

"What is the matter, Somers?" laughed Captain Waldron, who seemed to regard the whole matter as an excellent joke.

"Nothing in particular, only I am arrested for running contraband goods out the port."

"Is that all?"

"I have been watching this Coles for two days, and followed him from Newport. Mr. Somers has been his constant companion most of the time, and occupied the same state-room with him on the passage. I found him in bad company, and I concluded he was one of the traitors," said the man with the thin face, in apologetic tones.

"Well, I know nothing whatever about this matter," replied Captain Waldron; "but I will vouch for the loyalty of Mr. Somers against any charges that can be presented."

"You may be mistaken, as well as I," suggested the detective. "He was on board the schooner going down the harbor, and occupying the only state-room in the vessel."

"Yes, and I was locked in," added Somers; "I was a prisoner there."

" That may be ; but he seems to be on excellent terms with this man whom I was set to watch."

" I will take Mr. Somers on board of my vessel, and will be responsible for his safe keeping," said Captain Waldron.

The officer, who had no orders in regard to Somers, was satisfied with this proposition, and promised to inform himself forthwith in relation to the young man's complicity with the transaction he had been " working up."

" Captain Waldron, perhaps you will be kind enough to do me the same favor? " added Coles, who was determined to maintain his self-possession to the end.

" I haven't the honor of your acquaintance," replied the commander of the Rosalie, rather coldly.

" My particular friend, Mr. Somers, will vouch for me."

" Do you know this man, Somers? " asked the captain, as they went on deck.

" Never saw him in my life till three days ago. If you please, sir, I will tell you all about this affair when we get on board."

A few lusty strokes of the bargemen placed the boat alongside the Rosalie, whose fair lines and beautiful proportions Mr. Midshipman Somers was now, for the first time, in condition to appreciate. The side was manned, and Captain Waldron was received with the customary formalities as he went on deck. He repaired immedi-

11

ately to his cabin, to which his young companion was invited.

Though Somers had been very cautious in speaking about the information he had obtained at Newport, in the presence of his friends, or where it could possibly do any harm, he felt at liberty to tell Mr. Waldron the whole matter, not even excepting the part which was purely personal. It was entirely satisfactory to his partial auditor, and fully explained the mystery of his being on board the Theban, though Mr. Waldron could not help condemning the young man's want of prudence.

The man with the thin face went over to the city; the telegraph instruments clicked a few times, and Mr. Midshipman Somers was wholly exonerated from any connection with traitors and blockade-runners; indeed, the telegraph was so obliging as to inform the intelligent detective that the suspected person had actually communicated the information which led to the arrest of Coles.

The thin-faced man went on board of the Rosalie with the answers he had obtained, and made Somers the happiest man in the vessel by acknowledging the truth of every statement he had made. He apologized in the handsomest manner for his mistake; but Somers, with becoming moderation, assured him he had only done his duty.

"Now, Mr. Somers, you have removed the last shadow of a stain upon your good name, and you may go to your duty. I will introduce you to the executive officer, and I doubt not we shall all be friends. By the way, Somers, I have an old acquaintance of yours on board."

" Indeed! Who is he?"

" One Tom Longstone."

" Is it possible! The old man brought me up, and made a sailor of me. He is a splendid man."

" He is the boatswain of the Rosalie, just now — that is, he is a boatswain's mate, acting as boatswain."

" I am very glad to hear of it, for he is one of the best men in the service. I should like to see him a full boatswain."

" You may before long, when we get into a bigger ship than this."

Somers was then introduced to Mr. Layard, the executive officer, by whom he was duly presented to Mr. Jackson, the second lieutenant, Mr. Greene, the third lieutenant, and Mr. Brown, the sailing-master. The actual rank of the officers of the Rosalie did not correspond with that which they held on board of the vessel. Mr. Waldron was a lieutenant; but being in command of the schooner, he was called captain by courtesy. The three lieutenants were ensigns, and held the office of first, second, and third lieutenants, respectively, according to the dates of their commissions — the earliest commissioned taking the highest rank. The sailing-master was also an ensign, and the junior officer in the ward-room.

Our midshipman had not reached the dignity of being a ward-room officer, and he treated the lieutenants with the most respectful consideration. His peers aud equals were Mr. Midshipman Tubbs, whose warrant was two years older than his own, and two masters' mates, who had just received their appointments. Tubbs was the son of a naval officer, who had been relieved for obvious reasons. The mates had formerly been officers of merchant vessels, and had acting warrants, which would be annulled when the demand for their services ceased to exist.

The two midshipmen and the two masters' mates occupied the steerage, a snug little apartment, with only room to contain four berths, aud a small table, at which they were to take their meals. Somers examined this place with the deepest interest, for it was to be his home for some months at least. It was a very small room for four persons; but our middy never grumbled at manifest destiny, and the character of his companions was a matter of more consequence. But the place was well fitted up, and looked comfortable in spite of its narrow proportions.

Having been duly introduced to his messmates in the steerage, Somers went on deck to take a view of the vessel. She was a splendid craft in every sense of the word, and satisfied every requirement of a critical seaman. She had been built for a yacht by a wealthy

THE ADVENTURES OF A NAVAL OFFICER. 125

gentleman, who intended to take a cruise up the Mediterranean in her; but the war had interrupted his calculations, and he had sold her to the government for war purposes. She had been completely refitted for her present use, and Lieutenant Waldron had obtained the command of her, in preference to a small steamer, which had been available at the same time.

Her crew, consisting of fifty-two hands, had been on board of her several days; and when Somers reported for duty, everything on board was in working order. The officers and men had been assigned to their stations, and the Rosalie was ready to go to sea at a moment's notice. She was only waiting for her orders, which were hourly expected to arrive.

When Somers reached the deck, he looked about him for the familiar form and face of Tom Longstone; and it was with no slight emotion that he identified the old man, as he rolled aft to greet him.

"My blessed biscuit-nibbler!" exclaimed Tom, as he rushed forward to grasp his hand, in violation of all the traditions of navy discipline.

"I am glad to see you, Tom!" exclaimed Somers, as he grasped the hand of the veteran. "It does me good to meet you again, and be in the same ship with you."

"Thank you, Mr. Somers," returned the acting boatswain, recovering himself far enough to touch his hat, as he remembered what discipline required of him. "You

11 *

are as spruce as the cap'n's monkey on the Fourth of July ; and you look well in your new togs."

"I have worn these a long time, Tom; and they are an old story with me."

"I suppose so ; but I calculate you are the same chap that you used to be aboard the Harrisburg, and in the little Middy," said Tom, stepping back a pace, as the fact that Somers was now an officer became more real to him.

" The same person, Tom."

"I'm sorry we don't mess together in this craft; but you'll be an admiral one of these days," added Tom, rather sadly.

" We shall be good friends, as we always were, Tom. I am in the second lieutenant's watch, and my station is forward, where I shall have a chance to see you."

"Thank ye, Jack — beg pardon, Mr. Somers," said the veteran, touching his hat, as he corrected the mistake.

" Never mind, Tom ; when you are boatswain, and I call you Tom, instead of Mr. Longstone, you will forgive me for it."

" I will, my dear."

It took an hour to discuss the events of the past year, and to recall those of the memorable cruise of the Middy up the river. The little steamer, in which they had both seen some stirring work up the Mississippi, and on the coast of Florida, was affectionately remembered; but Somers thought she did not compare with the Rosalie.

"Isn't she a beauty!" exclaimed Tom, glancing around at her fair proportions."

"That she is."

"Look at that bow! Did you ever see anything go ahead of that? Look at her foremast! Did you ever see a prettier spar, or a more ship-shape piece of rigging?"

"Never; I am as proud of her as you are. I only want to get at something that wears the rebel flag, and then we shall soon find out what she is good for."

Tom then called the young officer's attention to her armament, which consisted of a fifty-pounder rifled gun amidships, with four brass howitzers, twenty-four-pounders, for broadside guns. There was a twelve-pound howitzer on the forecastle, with two swivels on the quarters.

"I suppose you have no idea where we are going, Mr. Somers?"

"Not the least; but I presume we are going on the blockade," replied Somers.

"I reckon we can hold way with some of their blockade-running steamers, if we have a decent wind. They say this craft has made her fourteen knots."

While they were talking about it, the orders came down for the schooner to put to sea at once. As usual, these orders were sealed up, to be opened when the vessel was outside of Sandy Hook.

"All hands, up anchor, ahoy!" shouted Tom, when he had received his orders from the officer.

The crew of the vessel, sharing the impatience of the officers to be on the blue sea, sprang to their stations with alacrity, and obeying the orders as they were issued, they were soon walking round the capstan. When the cable was brought to a "short stay," the capstan was pawled, and the vessel was ready for the second operation.

"Stations for loosing sail!" said Mr. Layard; and his order was repeated by the several officers on duty. "Lay aloft, sail loosers!"

The portion of the crew included in the last command was small; for, as the Rosalie carried only a foretop-sail, and foretop-gallant-sail, it did not require a heavy force to handle them. They were loosed and set, according to the strict rule of the service. The capstan was manned again, and when the boatswain reported the "anchor a-weigh," the jib and flying-jib were set, and the Rosalie went off, close-hauled, down the bay, with her port tacks aboard.

The wind was fresh, and her speed was apparent to all on board. She went by several little steamers, that happened to be going in the same direction, and her sharp bow cut the water as clean as a knife. Somers wanted to shout with admiration at her performance, and thought there was nothing in the world equal to her — unless it was Miss Kate Portington, who, in the whirl of exciting events since he left Newport, had by no means been forgotten.

At four o'clock in the afternoon, the Rosalie had worked her way down to Sandy Hook, and the sealed orders were opened. Shortly after this important event, Somers was sent for by the captain, and hastened to his cabin.

"Mr. Somers," said Captain Waldron, with a smile of satisfaction on his face, "I find my orders relate to the steamer you told me of this morning — the Snowden. It appears that there is no steam vessel available for the service, and we are sent out to intercept her. Notice of her coming has also been sent down to the blockaders off Wilmington. I am further instructed, that Mr. Somers can give me any further information I may require."

"Then I may chance to meet Mr. Phil Kennedy again," replied Somers.

"Perhaps you may; but the chances are rather against capturing a steamer with a sailing vessel."

"The Snowden can make but twelve knots under favorable circumstances. That was all that Coles claimed for her, and it is doubtful whether she will do even that."

"We are at the mercy of the wind. Without a breeze she could walk right away from us. My orders are, to repair to latitude forty-one, longitude sixty-two."

" Those are the right figures, sir ; and Coles expected to see the steamer about Saturday morning.   The
schooner was to burn a blue-light, if she happened to
make out a steamer in the night."

" Good ! Then I hope we shall sight her in the night,
for we can burn blue-lights as well as the Theban,"
added the captain.

" If you run a little farther to the northward, sir, you
might improve your chance of coming up with her in the
night."

" Very true, but we might miss her by that process. I
think our chances are rather small, Mr. Somers."

The midshipman thought so too ; and when he was
dismissed, he returned to the steerage, it being his watch
below, to meditate upon the matter ; but we are sorry to
say that he forgot all about the Snowden in three minutes,
and was wondering what Kate Portington was thinking
about at just that time.

CHAPTER XI.

MR. MIDSHIPMAN TUBBS.

"SO you are the captain's favorite — are you?" demanded Mr. Tubbs, when Somers returned to the steerage.

"Not that I am aware of," replied Somers, with proper dignity.

"You needn't put on airs, Somers," added the young gentleman.

"I was not conscious of putting on airs, Mr. Tubbs."

Somers was not so much astonished at this coarse salutation as the reader will be, for Mr. Tubbs, from the first moment of their acquaintance, had made himself as disagreeable as possible. He was very evidently bent on getting up a quarrel, reckless both of cause and consequence. He had been detailed from the Academy only a few days before Somers, but as they had been in different classes, they hardly knew each other by sight — at least, such was the fact so far as Somers was concerned. He had seen him with Kennedy once, but he had no reason to suppose they were friends. He could not, therefore, ascribe his apparent malignity to any sympathy with the man who had chosen to consider him an enemy.

"If there is any man about the ship that I despise, it is a fellow who claims to be the captain's favorite," continued Mr. Tubbs.

"I have made no such claim."

"Actions speak louder than words, Mr. Somers. You expect, under favor of the captain, to shirk your share of duty, and bear off all the honors, when there are any to be borne off. I despise such a fellow!"

"Well, Mr. Tubbs, you needn't waste any more breath on that subject; for whether you despise me, or despise me not, will not keep me awake one moment at night, or cause me to miss any portion of my grub."

"You mean to say that my opinion is of no consequence," growled Mr. Tubbs, beginning to feel that he had made some progress in getting up a quarrel.

"On the question at issue, precisely so, Mr. Tubbs."

"Do you hear that, Thompson?" added Tubbs, appealing to one of the master's mates, who happened to be in the mess-room.

"I hear it," replied Thompson, with indifference.

"What should you say to that?"

"Nothing; mind my own business."

"So should I," said Somers.

"If you think, Somers, that being the captain's favorite makes you chief of the mess, you are confoundedly mistaken."

" I have never assumed any such position, Mr. Tubbs."

" Yes, you have ; you carry it in your looks and man-ner. One can see that you look down upon the rest of us, and expect to bear off all the honors," replied Tubbs, who was not to be checked by any minor obstacles.

" As to the honors, let every tub stand on its own bot-tom."

" Sir ! " roared Tubbs, jumping off the stool on which he sat.

Now, Somers, being a most exemplary young man, had no more idea of making a pun than he had of mak-ing a quarrel ; and he did not realize that he had done so till the flushed face of his brother middy assured him of the fact.

" Good ! " said Thompson, with a low, inward chuckle, which assured his companions that he was listening, in spite of his determination to remain neutral.

" Do you mean to insult me, Mr. Somers ? " growled Tubbs.

" I had no such intention."

" Then you shall apologize."

" With pleasure — for what ? "

" For the remark you made."

" Then every tub should *not* stand on its own bottom. Is that satisfactory ? "

" No, sir ! It is not."

12

" Well, I have put it both ways, and you are not content with either."

" Will you apologize, or not? " demanded Mr. Tubbs,
striking the table violently with his fist.

" I am not conscious of having done anything for
which I should apologize."

" You intended to insult me."

" I have already assured you that I did not intend to
insult you."

" You made an unwarrantable use of my name."

" I simply quoted a common maxim, and I did it
without any reference whatever to your name.   That is
all I have to say about this matter, Mr. Tubbs," replied
Somers, as he took a book from his berth, and seated
himself near the door.

" That will not do, Mr. Somers !   You can't insult a
gentleman, and then refuse to give him satisfaction."

Somers found his place in the book.

" Do you hear me, sir? "

Somers began to read.

"·Mr. Somers, I demand satisfaction."

Somers finished a short paragraph.

" You have grossly insulted me !   You have made fun
of the honored name I bear, and I will not submit to it !"
roared Mr. Tubbs.

Somers began another paragraph.

" You are a mean, cowardly flunkey !   You can

toady to the captain, and put on airs among the men, but you can't insult a gentleman! Do you hear me, sir?"

Somers finished the paragraph.

"Will you answer me, Somers, or shall I kick you?"

Somers thought he had better not ; but he finished the second paragraph without making any reply.

"We have come to a pretty pass in the service when common sailors are made midshipmen, and put in with gentlemen."

"Shut up, Tubbs ! Stop your noise !" said Thompson, who rarely uttered two sentences without stopping to rest.

"Do you apply that language to me, Mr. Thompson?" demanded the irate middy.

"Shut up !" was all the taciturn master's mate would venture to reply, or all he had breath to utter.

"The service is going to ruin when such brutes are tolerated on board a man-of-war."

"Stop your noise, Tubbs," replied Thompson, in low and feeble tones, as though he had already exhausted himself by the long speeches he had made.

Somers was so much amused by the cool indifference of the master's mate to the abuse of the inflammatory middy, that he could not repress a laugh ; and he did laugh, without considering what the effect might be upon the stormy little monster.

"Mr. Somers !" said Tubbs, boiling with fury, as he

threw himself on a stool opposite the object of his anger.

"Mr. Tubbs," replied Somers, with great good nature.

"You cannot insult a gentleman!"

"I never tried."

"You insulted me! I am no gentleman — is that what you say?"

"No, you said it," laughed Somers.

"Mr. Somers, I know you! I know who you are and what you are! You have grossly insulted me; and I will pay you off for it, if it costs me my life;" and Mr. Tubbs, still foaming with wrath, rushed out of the mess-room, and went on deck.

"Mad," said Thompson, without looking up from the book he was reading.

"He acts like a crazy man," replied Somers.

"Look out for him," said Thompson, with a tremendous effort, for more than three words were a trial to him; and he never exceeded that number except on extraordinary occasions.

"I am not afraid of him by any means. I can't imagine what ails him. I haven't done anything to offend him that I know of."

"Tubs!" added the mate.

"That was an accident. I did not intend to insult, or to cast any reflections upon the honored name he bears, and I told him so."

"Means mischief."

" Well, it is all a mystery to me; he commenced almost as soon as I came on board."

" Hates you."

" I don't know of any reason why he should. I certainly never did him any injury."

" Pass the word for Mr. Somers," said the master; and the middy obeyed the call, leaving Mr. Thompson alone with his books, and to the silence in which he seemed to revel.

Eight bells sounded through the vessel, which was rolling along slowly before a very light breeze. The boatswain's whistle piped up the first watch; and presently everything was as quiet on board as in a well-ordered church.

" Pass the word for Mr. Somers," said the officer of the deck. And the order went from one mouth to another till it reached the midshipman's berth, where Mr. Tubbs and Mr. Walker were seated at the table reading by the dull light of a ship's lamp.

" Mr. Somers is not here," replied Mr. Tubbs, as amiably as though he had been the tenderest lamb in the fold.

Mr. Thompson, who was on duty, was sent to find Mr. Somers. He went to every place where a middy might be supposed to exist, but he was not to be found, and he so reported. It so happened that it was the captain who wanted Somers. As a zealous and devoted officer, he had hardly ceased for a single moment, since he opened his orders, to think of the difficult mission which had been committed •to him. Some point in regard to the Snowden, which Mr. Somers might possibly settle, had come to his mind, and he had sent for him in order to have another conference.

Captain Waldron was duly and properly surprised when it was reported that the young gentleman could not be found. The Rosalie was not large enough to afford many hiding-places. There was plenty of room outside of her, in the broad ocean, but very little within her wooden walls ; and Mr. Somers could not be far off. The captain ordered a more careful search to be made, which was done with no better result. He then went on deck, somewhat alarmed at the non-appearance of his young friend.

Strict inquiries were instituted. Mr. Layard had not seen him ; neither had Mr. Jackson, nor Mr. Greene. He had been with the captain after he had been relieved at eight bells in the afternoon watch. Mr. Thompson said he was in the mess-room at one bell in the first dog-watch.

The captain began to be very nervous, and feared that some accident had happened to the absentee ; but it was hardly possible that he could have fallen overboard· in broad daylight without being seen. None of the officers had assigned him to any special duty, and none of them had seen him for two hours and a half.

" Where is Mr. Brown?" demanded the captain.

" Below, sir."

" Send for him."   .

Mr. Brown, the sailing-master, presented himself. He had sent Mr. Somers down to open the after-hold, but the keys had been returned to him within ten minutes after the order was given. This was a little later news than any which had yet been furnished in regard to the absentee; but it did not solve the mystery. Another and still more careful search was made.

" Mr. Tubbs," said Thompson, as they walked forward together. .

" Well, what do you want?" replied the midshipman, with more suavity than he was in the habit of using.

" You know," added Thompson, significantly.

" Know what?" asked the innocent middy.

" Where Somers is."   .

" I haven't the least idea where he is. Do you suppose I should be looking for him, if I knew where he was?"

" Yes."

" Upon my word and honor as a gentleman, I haven't seen him since we parted in the mess-room," protested Tubbs.

" Stuff!"   .

" Don't you believe me, when I give you my word and honor?" added the middy, indignantly.

"No!"

The "vim" of Thompson's sentences compensated for what they lacked in length; and Tubbs had no difficulty, for the want of words, in appreciating his meaning.

"It's of no use to talk to one who don't believe what you say."

"Row in the mess."

"That wasn't my fault."

"Lie!"

"Do you mean to tell me I lie?"

"Yes."

Somehow Tubbs could not get up steam as readily as he had done in the afternoon; and he did not resent even the "lie given him," as might have been expected from one of his high notions and fiery temperament. In fact, he was comparatively tame; perhaps because he was aware that the taciturn master's mate regarded him with supreme contempt.

"He insulted me then, and I am not the man to submit patiently to an insult."

"Tell the captain."

"Tell him what?" said Tubbs, rather appalled at the idea of having the captain know what had happened in the mess-room.

"Row."

"Well, if you choose to tell him about that, you can, of course; but I don't know where Somers is any more than you do. The captain would blame me, punish me, when I am not to blame."

" Serve you right."

" If Somers has fallen overboard and got drowned, it is not my fault."

" Villain ! " gasped Thompson, as he seized Tubbs by the collar.

The master's mate had probably read the story of the dog and the fox, and come to the conclusion, rather hastily, that the young wretch had pushed the missing officer overboard.

" I don't say he has fallen overboard," protested Tubbs ; " and I don't believe he has. Let go of me — will you? Don't say anything to the captain, and I will make it all right with you."

" Where's Somers ? "

" I don't know — upon my life, I haven't the least idea. After the little row we had, it would make things look bad against me if you said anything about it."

A call from the officer of the deck caused Thompson to release his hold upon Tubbs, who was careful not to go too near him again. The mate was questioned about the absentee, and he cautiously acknowledged that there had been some dispute between Tubbs and Somers in the mess-room.

Tubbs was then called up by the captain, who was too much interested in the search to permit the first lieutenant to carry on the investigation. The malignant little wretch presented himself, but he stuck to his former text that he knew nothing about Mr. Somers, and had not seen him since he left the steerage at one bell in the dog-watch.

" You had a dispute with him?" said the captain.

" A little friendly sparring," replied Tubbs.

" What was it about?"

" About putting on airs, I believe; or something of that kind. Mr. Thompson was present, sir."

Mr. Thompson was appealed to, but he had all that sensitiveness about exposing his messmates to punishment, even if guilty, which prevails among sailors and school-boys. He did not deny Mr. Tubbs's statement, but he was fully resolved, on his own account, to bring the quarrelsome middy to justice, if Somers did not soon appear.

" Were there any hard words passed between you?" demanded the captain.

" No hard words; but there was some rather strong language used by both of us."

If Mr. Tubbs had any further information, he would not impart it. The master was examined once more. He was positive that the keys of the after-hold had been returned to him by Mr. Somers within ten minutes after he took them. It was useless, therefore, to examine the hold, and the search was sorrowfully abandoned; but there were some sleepless eyes in the Rosalie that night.

CHAPTER XII.

SOMERS IN DARKNESS.

THE keys of the after-hold are the especial charge of the master. It is never opened except in presence of a suitable officer, who is responsible for any neglect or carelessness of which the party taking out stores may be guilty. Somers had been sent down to attend to this duty. He had delivered the stores, or rather seen them delivered; and, in order to be sure that everything was right, he had stepped within the door to make a careful survey of the place. He had scarcely done so when the door was suddenly closed upon him. He was in total darkness, for he had left the lantern outside, that he might the better detect any appearance of fire within the store-room.

Somers groped his way back to the door, but found that it was locked. Of course he was greatly annoyed and astonished at the blunder some one had made. But it was a mistake which must shortly be corrected. He concluded that Mr. Brown, the sailing-master, had come below himself, and finding the store-room open, had closed it, and gone on deck to find the officer who had thus neglected his duty. He would soon return, and an explanation would make the matter all right.

Mr. Brown did not return; no one came to release him from his dark prison-house. The mistake began to appear unaccountable to him. He made some experiments with his voice, which, however, seemed to be failures, as they did not bring the needed relief from above. It was no use to fret about his situation, which he regarded as by no means desperate. At the worst he could only spend the night there, and some one would release him in the morning, if a call happened to be made for stores. It was a dark, disagreeable place in which to spend the night; but as that was the best which could be done, he decided to content himself with the situation.

The hours wore away very slowly; but Somers imagined himself in Newport, holding a skein of worsted for Kate Portington, and his fancy easily changed the gloomy apartment into the pleasant parlor of Commodore Portington. From there he went to Pinchbrook, and sat for an hour in the kitchen, talking with his father and mother about the Rosalie, and wondering how he could contrive to tell them about the fair young lady who always called him a prodigy. But, after all, the dark hold was neither the parlor at Newport nor the kitchen at Pinchbrook; and, in spite of his vivid fancy, he was occasionally brought to a realizing sense that he was surrounded by boxes and bags, casks, kegs, and cans.

At an early hour he made his bed on the floor, and in due time went to sleep. His sublime philosophy enabled him to accomplish this feat without any very severe exertions. The bed was very hard, and latterly he had not been accustomed to roughing it on a plank; so he waked up several times during the night, but, after a careful consideration of his position each time, he went to sleep again. On the whole, he passed a tolerably comfortable night, though he would have preferred to be in his berth in the steerage, or with his watch on deck. He did not regard himself as a martyr, and did not make any set statement of his sufferings, wherewith to regale his messmates after his escape.

Morning came, though Somers, shrouded in the deep gloom of the hold, was not conscious of the fact. He had slept all he could, and, being a resolute sleeper, he concluded from this fact that it must be daylight. But hour after hour passed away, and no one came for stores; and the darkness frowned upon him as savagely as ever. He could not hear the bells on deck, though the occasional footstep of an officer in the ward-room was audible.

In the mean time, Captain Waldron was greatly distressed about the absence of his young officer. On one occasion Somers had saved his life, and he was as grateful as one man could be to another for this service. In

13

addition to this fact, the absentee was a splendid fellow in his estimation ; and, for this reason alone, he could not afford to lose him.   He had not slept half as well in his comfortable cabin as Somers had on the soft side of the pine plank which formed his bed.

A careful consideration of all the circumstances, and a careful weighing of all the evidence in his possession, well nigh convinced him that Somers had not fallen overboard.   He was either in the vessel, or he had been swallowed up by the ocean.   As no one had seen him fall overboard, as no one had seen him in a position where he could fall overboard, it seemed more probable that he was still in the vessel.

At eight bells, when the forenoon watch came on deck, and the essential parts of the ship's work had been performed, the captain ordered a strict search to be made in every part of the vessel, not excepting the bread-room and magazine.   The master himself was ordered to superintend the search in the parts of the hold under his own care, and the first place he went to was the store-room.

" Good morning, Mr. Brown," said Somers, touching his cap, as by the light of his lantern he recognized the sailing-master.

" Good heaven, Somers ! you here ? " exclaimed Mr. Brown, as much astonished as though a ghost had risen from the depths of the ocean to confront him.

" I am here, sir, just where you left me last night,"
replied Somers, with undisturbed good nature.

" Where I left you?" demauded Mr. Brown; " I
didn't leave you here; I hadn't the slightest idea where
you were."

" I supposed not, and I concluded that you had fastened the door on me by mistake."

" It would have been a mistake if I had done so, but
I did not close the door at all. I don't understand this
matter."

" Nor I either, sir. It was rather too dark in there
to see into anything."

" But you brought the keys to me last night, and reported the after-hold closed," continued Mr. Brown.

" I beg your pardon, sir, but I did not."

" Then it was your ghost," replied the bewildered
master.

" That may have been, sir; but I am not responsible
for the movements of my ghost."

" But I am sure it was you who placed the keys on
my desk, and reported the after-hold all secure."

" You will excuse me, sir, if I deny it again. It
would not have been convenient for me to lock myself
into the store-room, and carry the keys to you."

" I should say it would not. It is all a mystery to
me, for I would have taken my oath you brought me the
keys. But I am glad to find you again. Now come on

deck, and show yourself to the captain, who has almost had a fever on your account."

It was instantly reported through the vessel that Mr. Somers had been found, and under the direction of acting Boatswain Longstone, three lusty cheers were given by the men, of which manifest breach of discipline no notice was taken by the officer of the deck, for Captain Waldron was pacing the weather side of the quarter-deck with him.

" I have the honor to report myself, sir," said Somers, touching his hat to the officer of the deck.

The captain grasped his hand with enthusiasm, and his example was followed by the executive officer. Somers's face was radiant with smiles, and it was plain that he was not in a suffering condition, and had undergone no severe hardships during his absence.

" Have you been ashore, Mr. Somers?" asked the captain, as he wrung his hand.

" No, sir, I have not."

" Where have you been?"

" Down in the store-room, sir. I got locked in by some mistake."

" By some mistake? How did it happen?"

" I have not the least idea, sir. I only know that I was sent down with the keys by Mr. Brown. When the steward had taken his stores, I went in again, to be sure there was no fire there. I left the lantern in the passageway, and was making a careful examination, when the door was closed and locked. That is all I know about it, sir. I supposed it was an accident, and that Mr. Brown had locked the door himself."

"I did not, sir," added Mr. Brown.

"You said that Mr. Somers brought you the keys," said the captain.

"I said so, sir, and I would have sworn to the fact ten minutes ago, though, of course, that could not have been the case."

"Well, who did bring you the keys?" demanded the captain, impatiently; for every thing did not look regular and ship-shape to him.

"I do not know, sir. I was making an entry in one of my books at the time. The keys were laid on my desk, and the after-hold reported secure for the night. I believed at the time, and did believe till the evidence of my own senses assured me I was mistaken, that Mr. Somers was the person who had reported," continued the master, very much annoyed and confused by the situation in which he found himself placed.

Captain Waldron was as much mystified by the explanation as he had been by the fact of the midshipman's disappearance. If Mr. Somers had not returned the keys to the master, who had? On this point Mr. Tubbs and the two master's mates had been questioned; but they could not solve the problem. Neither of them had returned the keys to Mr. Greene. As no further information could be obtained, the officers returned to their usual duty, and the captain, in despair, gave up the attempt to unveil the mystery. Mr. Somers went to the mess-room to obtain his breakfast. Mr. Tubbs and Mr. Thompson had preceded him.

" Well, Mr. Somers, may I be allowed to inquire how you liked your quarters last night?" asked Mr. Tubbs, when Mingo, the mess steward, had gone for the absentee's breakfast.

" As well as could be expected, Mr. Tubbs," replied Somers, with the most provoking good nature; for our hero was expected, under the circumstances, to be very much dissatisfied, and very indignant.

" I am glad you liked them ; but I suppose you got used to such accommodations when you were before the mast."

"O, yes," replied Somers, refusing to take offence at the intended insult. "I have slept in worse places than that."

" By the way, Mr. Somers, it is a little strange how you contrived to lock the door of the store-room, and give the key to Mr. Brown, while you were shut up in the room," added Tubbs, facetiously.

" Mr. Brown explains that."

" Does he? "

" Yes. He suggests that it was my ghost who gave him the keys. I think it was a ghost, but one of another color ; a fellow about your height, Tubbs."

"Do you mean to say that I locked you up in the store-room?" demanded Tubbs, his face turning red.

"If it wasn't you, it wasn't anybody else," answered Somers, with a pleasant laugh.

"Mr. Somers, you make a grave charge against me. You took occasion last evening to make a quarrel with me — "

"I took occasion to make a quarrel with you!" exclaimed Somers. "Why, man, you pitched into me as though you had a seven years' grudge to wipe out."

"I made some playful remarks, and you took advantage of them to insult me. During your absence I was compelled to suffer on account of the words we had. In short, I was suspected of having helped you overboard, or spirited you away in some other mysterious manner. If you hadn't returned as you did, I have no doubt I should have been accused of your murder."

"That's so," muttered Thompson.

"If there is any man I despise, it is one that wants to get up a quarrel in the mess-room," added Mr. Tubbs, with the utmost self-complacency.

"I am exactly of your mind, Mr. Tubbs," said Somers.

"Do you mean to accuse me of getting up a quarrel in the mess?"

"As I am not disposed to get up another quarrel, we will drop that, if you please, Mr. Tubbs," replied Somers, as Mingo brought in his breakfast.

"After you have insulted a gentleman, you want to let

it drop. I know all about you, Mr. Somers. You have insulted me, and you will find it no easy matter to let it drop, as you call it."

"Mr. Tubbs, you will oblige me by holding your tongue long enough for me to eat my breakfast," continued Somers, playfully.

But the irate middy was in no mood for a playful remark, and he worked himself up into a passion, though Somers took no further notice of him.

"Shut up!" said Thompson, who was trying to improve his mind in the mysteries of great circle sailing, and was much disturbed by the vaporings of the angry youngster.

"Mr. Somers, the day of reckoning will come, and come soon. I want you to understand that I cannot be insulted with impunity, and you have done it twice. Will you apologize or fight?"

"Neither," replied Somers, as he stuffed half a biscuit into his mouth. "But if you will let me eat my breakfast in peace, I will talk over the matter with you when you are entirely cool; then, if I have done anything wrong, I shall be happy to make it all right with you."

"No words over an insult," foamed Tubbs. "I will give you till eight bells to apologize; if you don't do it, you may look out for breakers."

"Bah!" growled Thompson, in a significant tone; but for some reason or other, Mr. Tubbs refused to consider himself insulted by anything which the burly master's mate could say.

Mr. Tubbs went on deck, and Somers finished his breakfast — which was an unusually long operation in the present instance — without further annoyance.

"Mr. Thompson, who do you suppose locked me in the store-room?" he asked, when he had finished.

"Tubbs."

"What makes you think so?"

"The row."

"I am satisfied myself, but there is no evidence."

"No."

"In my opinion Tubbs followed me into the hold to get up a fight with me; and when he saw me in the store-room, he took his revenge by locking me in."

"Told you," added the mate, raising his eyes from his book for the first time.

"Told me what?"

"To look out."

"So you did; but I didn't think of his playing a little dirty trick on me."

"Malicious wretch."

"I will keep my eye on him after this."

"Do."

To Somers and Thompson the mystery was satisfactorily explained; but as there was not a particle of proof of Tubbs's agency in the matter, they agreed that it was useless to say anything.

CHAPTER XIII.

MR. TUBBS BECOMES BLOODY-MINDED.

M R. TUBBS was not satisfied — he was very far from being satisfied. He felt that the "honored name he bore" was suffering for an expiatory sacrifice, for it had been ignominiously punned upon — used as a synonyme of a vulgar household utensil, closely allied to dirty shirts and befouled dickies. He was evidently spoiling for a quarrel with Mr. Somers. He made no issues with the master's mates; and it looked very much as though he had a special object in picking a fight with his brother middy.

He was silly enough to do any ridiculous thing; and before noon he rushed down into the mess-room with a desperate resolve burning in his heated brain. Taking his bag from beneath his berth, he drew from it a dirty portfolio, into which his papers had been thrust without order or method. He searched diligently for a clean sheet of note paper, but he did not find it. Taking the nearest approach to it he could find, he sat down at the table, and wrote this luminous epistle : —

Mr. John Somers. Sir : You have insulted me, and you have refused to apologize. There is but one alternative among gentlemen, and I take this method of formally demanding the satisfaction which nothing but blood can wash from the stain upon mine honor.

By communicating your answer in writing, you will greatly oblige

Yours, respectfully,

Timothy Tubbs.

With convulsive energy Mr. Tubbs folded this savage document and thrust it within an envelope.

" Mr. Somers," said he, as he laid the note upon the table at which the object of his wrath was still seated.

" What's this? — a challenge?" laughed Somers.

" Read for yourself," replied Mr. Tubbs, as he sailed out of the mess-room, unwilling, perhaps, to trust himself any longer in the presence of his enemy.

Somers read it, and laughed again. He handed it to Thompson, who read it, and laughed also.

" Savage," said Thompson, as he returned the note.

" I suppose I must accept it, or be branded as a coward," added Somers, as he turned the dangerous paper over in his hands, as persons often do, when they have read a letter, to ascertain if there is any more of it.

" Bosh !" ejaculated Thompson.

In the present instance there was something more in the letter to reward the receiver for his search — something which seemed to be of greater importance than the silly challenge it was intended to convey. On the third page there was another note, which Mr. Tubbs had turned in without noticing it. As it was part and parcel of the terrible document which Somers had received, he ventured to read it, as follows : —

Wednesday.

MY DEAR TUBBS: I am sorry I was not able to see you last night, as arranged. The unexpected arrival of a business associate prevented me from keeping the appointment, which you will please excuse. My offer is still open, and will remain so. I don't know of any easier way by which you can make five thousand dollars, and thus relieve your father's present necessities.

Yours, ever,

P. KENNEDY.

"Five thousand dollars!" exclaimed Somers, when he had read the note. "That's a great deal of money, and I hope it was not offered for doing any mean or wicked act."

Thompson did not understand this remark, and it was too great an effort to ask an explanation; therefore he said nothing. Somers was serious now, for this note from Kennedy was suggestive. Tubbs had been offered a large sum of money for doing some unwritten act. Coles had been offered double the sum to deliver him as a prisoner on board of the Snowden. Tubbs had manifested a decided hostility towards him since the first moment they met.

There was no date to the note, only the day of the week; and the only thing that it proved was the fact of a negotiation of some kind with Phil Kennedy. He suspected that the offer related to himself — that at the most convenient time he was, by some underhand means, to be given into the power of the rebels. He was not willing to believe anything worse than this of Mr. Tubbs, malicious as he had shown himself.

If Somers's supposition was correct, Mr. Phil Kennedy had been singularly unfortunate in the choice of the instrument of his evil purpose. Tubbs was little better than an idiot; and by his display of hostility towards his assumed victim, he had almost destroyed his chance of carrying out his plan, whatever it was.

Somers decided to take no notice of the challenge at present, but to keep both eyes wide open to defeat any evil intention his messmate might cherish. He did not see Tubbs again till dinner-time, when that gentleman seemed to be cooler and more reasonable than when they had last met.

" You received my note, Mr. Somers?" said he, after dinner, when they happened to be alone.

" I did."

" Have you a note in reply?"

" No, sir."

14

" What have you to say in regard to the contents of my note?"

" Nothing."

" What do you propose to do about it?"

" Nothing, unless I hand it to the first lieutenant," replied Somers.

" I might have expected that; but I will do you the justice to say, Mr. Somers, that I did not expect it. If there is any person I despise in the mess, it is a tattler. I have never believed you to be a gentleman of that description," replied Tubbs, who was evidently much in dread of such a disaster.

" What did you mean by the note, Mr. Tubbs?" demanded Somers, who could not lose sight of the ludicrous event which the contents of the epistle suggested.

" Don't you understand it?"

" It looked very much like a proposition to fight a duel; but as I don't believe you have courage enough to do anything of that kind, I confess I am very much in doubt in regard to its real signification."

Mr. Tubbs looked as dark and threatening as a thunder-cloud. Another insult had been added to the list of his grievances, real or imaginary.

" I meant to fight, Mr. Somers! Can you understand that?" said Tubbs, with emphasis.

" Where? — here in the mess-room?"

"The time and place are after-considerations, which can be adjusted when you accept the challenge."

"How would the fore-yard do for the conflict?" laughed Somers. "I will take the lee, while you perch yourself on the weather yard-arm. That would be a novel idea in duelling, and it would afford half an hour's amusement for the whole ship's company. What do you say?"

"You may treat this matter as lightly as you please. I am in earnest, and I will convince you that I have the courage to fight a duel."

"If that is your object, you may soon have an opportunity to show your pluck in a more sensible way — in close conflict with the enemies of your country."

"This is subterfuge, sir. In plain words, sir, will you apologize, or will you fight?" demanded Tubbs, working himself up into a frenzy beneath the galling sarcasm of his cooler companion.

"In plain words, Mr. Tubbs, I will not fight, nor apologize. I will talk the matter over in a friendly way with you, and if I have done anything wrong, I will make it all right. That's all I have to say about it."

"Then I brand you as a coward!" exclaimed Tubbs, bringing his fist down on the table.

"You can brand me as much as you please. Now, sir, you have carried this ridiculous farce far enough, and if you allude to it again, I will hand your note to the first lieutenant."

" I might have expected that," said Mr. Tubbs, in utter disgust. " But the day of retribution will come."

" Let it come ; when it does, I am ready for it. I will not fight a duel with any man, least of all with a little bully like you."

" 'Sdeath, sir ! " ejaculated Tubbs, springing to his feet.

" Keep cool, Tubbs. I have only one word more to say. I have listened to your nonsense till I am disgusted with it and with you. If you should venture to put a finger on me, in carrying out any of your notions of retribution, I will thrash you so that you will remember it to the end of your natural life."

" You are insolent, sir," said Tubbs, more tamely.

" I can afford to be, under all the provocation you have given me. In conclusion, Mr. Tubbs, if you propose to deliver me over to your friend Mr. Philip Kennedy, and put five thousand dollars into your pocket by the operation, you must do the job within a very few days."

With this remark Somers rose from the table, and abruptly left the mess-room. Mr. Tubbs wilted ; his face turned deadly pale, and his knees smote each other in the extremity of his terror. Somers must be in communication with the evil one — else where had he obtained a secret which was locked up in the breasts of himself and his co-conspirator? It was strange, it was unaccountable ; and he racked his slender brain to explain how Kennedy's offer had become known to the person who had the least right to know it.

Neither Mr. Tubbs's memory nor his speculations afforded him the slightest clew to the mystery. He was perplexed and troubled, and endured the most intense sufferings in view of an expected exposure of his purpose. He behaved himself with the utmost propriety during the succeeding three days; in fact, he was as subdued and tame as a whipped poodle.

"Mr. Somers," said Tubbs, on the third day after the conversation in regard to the duel, "may I beg the favor of a few moments' private conversation with you?"

"If you wish to talk about your challenge, I must decline," replied Somers, promptly.

"I do not; I concluded to accept your apology."

"What apology?" demanded Somers.

"You observed that if you had done me any wrong, you would make it all right. That is the spirit of a gentleman, and I am entirely satisfied. At the close of that interview you made a most extraordinary remark."

"I wasn't aware of it."

"Something about my friend, — and yours, I trust, — Mr. Philip Kennedy."

"Well, Mr. Tubbs."

"And about a sum of money — five thousand dollars, I think you said."

"Well, Mr. Tubbs."

"It was a very extraordinary remark."

"Possibly it was."

14 *

" Will you do me the favor to explain that remark?'
said Mr. Tubbs, with the most insinuating eloquence.

" It explained itself."

" But it was incomprehensible to me."

" O, well, let it drop, then ! If there is anything in it,
it will come out in due time. I wouldn't worry myself
about it."

" But if I remember rightly, it involved a very grave
charge against me."

" Perhaps it did."

" Will you be so kind as to give me the name of your
informant — in other words, the person who fastens such
a disreputable charge upon me?"

" I shouldn't dare to do it, my dear Tubbs," replied
Somers, with a tantalizing smile.

" Why not?"

" Because you would challenge the poor fellow, and
shoot him down in cold blood."

" I give you my word and honor that I will not molest
him."

" I don't know that it is exactly safe to trust such a
sanguinary person as you are in a delicate matter of this
description."

" Pray be serious, Mr. Somers. This is a matter of
great importance to me. Of course you did not believe
the nefarious charge. Some one has been taking liberties
with my good name. My reputation, which is far dearer

to me than life itself, is involved in this cruel imputation. You owe it to me, as a shipmate, to give me the name of the person from whom you obtained this false imputation."

"Really, you must excuse me, Mr. Tubbs."

"Just give me his name. An enemy hath done this thing, and I wish merely to defend my own character. Give me his name, only his name, and I will ask nothing more."

"Nothing more?"

"Not another particular."

"Then I will give you his name," replied Somers, biting his lips to repress a struggling smile.

"Thank you — nothing but his name. I shall understand it all then — only his name."

"Mr. Timothy Tubbs," replied Somers, rising and hastening out of the mess-room.

Mr. Tubbs was not satisfied.

CHAPTER XIV.

LATITUDE FORTY-ONE, LONGITUDE SIXTY-TWO.

THE Rosalie took her " departure " from Sandy Hook at four o'clock on Saturday afternoon. She had to make nearly six hundred miles before she could reach the latitude and longitude to which the commander's orders required him to proceed. But as she had about six days and a half to accomplish this distance, Captain Waldron had but little doubt of his ability to obey his instructions. Under favorable circumstances, he would have had two or three days to spare. It happened that she had several days of light or head winds ; and when the master had reported the position of the ship on the Friday following, at meridian, the captain had some serious doubts about the success of his expedition, especially as the sea at this time was hardly ruffled by a breeze, and the log showed that the schooner was making only three knots an hour.

Captain Waldron was very nervous and uneasy. He paced the deck impatiently, occasionally casting his eyes to windward, as if invoking the favor of a fresh breeze.

His instructions informed him that a steamer would be sent to assist in the capture of the Snowden, if one was available. He hoped to accomplish his work before any such aid arrived, and he was anxious to make out his expected prize before the daylight betrayed the true character of his vessel to the blockade-runner.

Hour after hour he paced the deck, and at eight bells in the afternoon he was absolutely in despair, for the wind had subsided almost to a calm.

" Did you hear anything about waiting for the schooner? " asked Captain Waldron, as he called Somers over to the weather side of the deck.

" No, sir ; but I should suppose that would be understood," replied Somers.

" It looks bad for us just now. If we don't have a wind, we cannot reach the spot in season."

" I think the Snowden will wait, for Kennedy expects Coles to go with him into Wilmington."

Somers went over to the lee side again, which is the part assigned to midshipmen, and master's mates, and commissioned officers not on duty, while the weather side is exclusively appropriated to the captain and the officer of the deck.

Shortly after, it was a dead calm, and the sails of the Rosalie hung useless from the spars, flapping idly, as the vessel rolled on the long swell of the ocean. The captain looked as blue as a whetstone ; and the more the vessel didn't go, the faster he walked up and down the quarter-deck. His example was contagious, and the "people" looked as if there had been a funeral on board.

Mr. Midshipman Somers tried to keep cool, but it was hard work. Only a few of the officers on board besides himself knew the destination of the vessel, and the depression of the rest, and of the crew, was wholly from sympathy, or from the natural effects of a calm at sea, which is the bluest thing in the vocabulary of a sailor. There was an evident want of faith on board, from the captain down to the side-boys, which nothing but a lively breeze could dissipate.

Fortunately for the captain's peace of mind, if not for the actual preservation of his sanity, — for he was now walking at a fearful pace, — at two bells, in the first dog-watch, a change came over the bosom of the throbbing ocean. A slight ripple was observed far to the southward, which travelled slowly up towards the Rosalie. The last wind had come from the north-east, and she had her port tacks aboard; but before "the breath of the gentle south," as Mr. Walker, the senior master's mate, who was a salt-water poet, called it, the sails were trimmed on the other tack.

The wind struck the waiting sails, and the captain very sensibly abated the speed of his monotonous peram-. bulation. It came fresher in a few minutes, and he "planked the deck" more like a sane man. At four bells he smiled as blandly as a man on his wedding day, when the officer of the deck reported that the ship was making ten knots. At eight bells it was blowing half a gale, and the captain, mindful of the safety of his spars, ordered the fore square-sail to be taken in. The Rosalie was now flying through the water, and Captain Waldron was providentially saved from reporting at a lunatic asylum when he went on shore. He was satisfied, and went below.

If the decks of the vessel, reflecting the sombre looks of the people, had worn a funereal aspect before, it now looked like feast time on board. The officers on duty walked with a buoyant step, and the old sheet-anchor men spun jolly yarns about festive scenes on ship and shore, instead of gloomy tales of blood and death, inspired by the depressing influence of the calm.

Even Mr. Midshipman Tubbs was happy; for, whatever else he knew, he was not aware that only a few leagues lay between him and his particular friend, Mr. Philip Kennedy. He had no suspicion that his confiding co-conspirator was in immediate danger of being "gobbled up." He was happy because others were; and, seeing everybody so good-natured, he ventured again to open the subject nearest to his heart to Somers.

"You promised not to ask me anything but the name of my informant," laughed Somers.

"Yes, but your answer was a jest, a mere evasion;

for how could I have informed you of that which never entered into my head."

" Nevertheless, Mr. Tubbs, I told you the truth, the whole truth, and nothing but the truth."

" Come, come, Somers, this is absurd ; you trifle with my feelings. I am only anxious to vindicate my fair fame."

" I must hold you to your promise, Mr. Tubbs ; but I will add, for your consolation, that you will probably have an opportunity to vindicate your fair fame in the course of the next twelve hours. I hope you will be able to do it successfully."

" Really, Mr. Somers — "

" You must excuse me if I decline to hold any further conversation with you."

" If there is anything I despise in the mess-room, Mr. Somers, it is mystery," replied Tubbs, impatiently.

" So do I ; therefore I advise you to make a clean breast of it."

" You speak in riddles," added Tubbs, more tamely. " You seem to imply that I have some designs against you."

" I don't imply it ; I say it. Now, I am as curious to know in what manner you proposed to hand me over as a prisoner to the rebels, as you are to know how I obtained my information."

" I hand you over to the rebels ? Why, that would

·be treason ; it would be giving aid and comfort to the enemy."

" It is liable to that construction."

" That is a grave charge," added Tubbs, shaking his head.

" If you wish to own up, I will give you all the information in my power. Will you do it? — yes or no?"

" Of course I will not, for no such thought ever entered my head."

"I have nothing more to say. I must turn in now, for it is my watch at twelve."

Somers did turn in, and Mr. Tubbs left the mess-room more bewildered and uneasy than before. The latter was what is technically called an " idler " on board ship. This term is applied to officers and others who are not in either of the watches, being what is called " day officers." The captain and executive officer, who occupy the most responsible positions on board, are, by this queer anomaly, the principal idlers. Mr. Tubbs was on duty on the berth-deck during the day ; hence he was an idler, which will account for his being in the mess-room with Somers during some of the long conversations we have had occasion to report. Mr. Tubbs could obtain no satisfaction below ; so he went on deck, to nurse the venom of his discontent, leaving Somers to sleep out his watch below.

The wind continued to blow very fresh all night, and

15

the captain was happily relieved from all doubts and fear on that account. Although we are not permitted to invade the sanctity of the captain's cabin, we will venture to say that he did not sleep much during that anxious night. At six bells he was up and dressed, engaged in overhauling certain reports which had been made to him in regard to the position of the vessel. When he had carefully examined the sailing-master's figures, he went on deck.

It was seven bells in the mid-watch, or half past three in the morning, when he took his place by the side of the officer of the deck.

" Sail ho ! " shouted the forecastle man, who had been stationed on the fore-yard as a special lookout.

" Sail ho ! " repeated Mr. Midshipman Somers.

" Where away ? " demanded the officer of the deck.

" On the lee bow, showing a green light and a white light."

" That's a steamer ! " exclaimed the captain, when the report reached him.

All steamers belonging to the United States, as well as English, French, Dutch, and Russian steam vessels, carry, in the night, a bright white light at the foremast head, a green light on the starboard side, and a red light on the port side. This is done in order to prevent collisions at sea ; but it also enables those in charge of other vessels to tell which way the steamer is going. Suppose the reader is standing on the forecastle of the Rosalie, and sees a red and a green light with a white one between them; then the steamer is approaching you.

The white light, which is placed higher on the vessel than the colored ones, should be seen, in a clear night, at the distance of five miles. It is the warning light. The red and green lights, being lower down, can be seen only two or three miles. If the lookout sees the white light, he watches till the others, or one of them, can be seen. If the Rosalie were headed to the east, and a red light only were reported, her commander would know that the steamer was coming up from the southward; for then she would show her port side. If the green light were seen, it would prove that she was coming from the north. If any of our young readers wish to remember this explanation, so that they may test it when they go to sea, they have only to call to mind the fact that port wine is red — port is the side, and red the color. If they cannot remember the color on the other side, they have only to think how *green* they are in a knowledge of nautical night signals.

The green light seen over the port bow assured Captain Waldron that the steamer was coming from the north, and that her course was at right angles with that of the Rosalie. He had no doubt that the, steamer was the Snowden, and his hopes ran high. The circumstances could hardly have been more favorable, for the wind was fresh enough to make the schooner almost, if not quite, a match for the Snowden in point of speed. But the captain did not care to reduce the question to a mere matter of speed; so he ordered the signal quarter-master to burn blue lights on the quarter of the Rosalie.

The steamer replied by burning another blue light; and her identity was fully established. Mr. Phil Kennedy had precisely carried out his part of the arrangement; but it soon appeared from the movements of the Snowden, that he had no intention of being boarded, at present, by his fellow-conspirator. Instead of bearing down for the schooner, he held his course to the southward, occasionally burning a blue light, to assure the schooner that she was aware of her presence.

Captain Waldron was perplexed at first, but he finally interpreted the movement to mean that he must wait for daylight before he boarded her. In confirmation of this supposition, it was found that the Snowden had reduced her speed one half at least. The Rosalie could not follow her, as the wind was exactly south; but she came about on the port tack, and sailed within six points of her course.

The Snowden exhibited no intention to run away, and therefore Captain Waldron did not deem it prudent to open fire upon her, and thus disclose what he really was. The fifty-pounder amidships was loaded, ready for use.

This ugly gun would betray the vessel as soon as there was light enough to make it out on board of the Snowden. To prevent so undesirable a recognition, one of the boats was hoisted on board, and turned, keel up, over the piece. The broadside guns were covered with sails, and as much of the man-of-war appearance of the schooner as time would permit was removed.

At daybreak the Rosalie was about three miles from the Snowden, and rather to the windward of her, when the latter indicated by signal that she was ready to have the schooner approach. The critical moment was at hand. The Rosalie went about on the other tack, and easing off her sheets, went off towards the Snowden with the wind abeam.

In a quarter of an hour the Rosalie hove to under the bows of the steamer. The men, except those necessary to work the vessel, were sent below, and there was as little display as possible of " blue coats and brass buttons" on the quarter-deck. One of the quarter-boats was lowered, and Mr. Jackson, the second lieutenant, was ordered to board her. Somers, at his own request, was allowed to go in her. The men were armed to the teeth, for it was not impossible that a conflict might occur; but their arms were carefully concealed at first, and another boat was in readiness to pull off to her assistance if necessary.

15 *

CHAPTER XV.

THE SNOWDEN AND HER COMMANDER.

CAPTAIN WALDRON had at first objected to the request of Somers to go in the boat, fearing that the sight of him might raise a suspicion in the mind of the commander of the Snowden. But our Yankee middy, who was a bit of a lawyer as well as a sailor, argued that his presence would be the very thing to allay any suspicion on the part of Kennedy, since it was hoped, if not expected, that he would be a passenger in Coles's schooner.

"What vessel is that?" demanded a voice on the quarter-deck of the Snowden, as the boat approached the steamer.

"That's Kennedy," said Somers to Mr. Jackson, who had been partially informed in relation to the event in which he was an actor.

"The Theban, of New York, with caps on board," replied the second lieutenant.

"All right!" shouted Mr. Phil Kennedy. "Where is Coles?"

" On board the schooner."

" Where did you get so many men?" asked Kennedy, when he saw au unusual number in the boat.

" They are good fellows that want a passage to the south, and are willing to ship in a good steamer at Wilmington."

" All right! — the more the better," responded Kennedy, to whom the replies were sufficiently intelligible.

By this time the boat came up under the lee of the Snowden, abaft the paddle-box. A rope was thrown to her, and she was hauled up at the accommodation ladder.

" 'Pon my word and honor as a gentleman and a sailor!" exclaimed Mr. Phil Kennedy, who had grasped the man-ropes, and was now looking down into the boat. " Whom have you there?"

" Mr. Midshipman Somers, the prodigy," replied Jackson, who had been instructed in his part; for it was very necessary that Mr. Kennedy should be kept quiet until force enough had been transferred to the deck of the steamer to prevent anything like reaction.

If the commander of the Snowden suspected any foul play, he had only to ring the bell to start the engine, and the boat might have been swamped in the heavy sea, or at least placed in a position where it would be impossible for the gallant blue-jackets to board her.

" Somers, upon my word!" added Kennedy; " Coles

is a jewel, and ought to be made an admiral.   Come on board.   Have you any caps in the boat?"

" Ay, ay, sir ; a few," replied Mr. Jackson, though he neglected to say there was a head under each one of them.

" Pass them up, as lively as possible."

" Let some of these men come on board first; they are in the way here."

" Pipe them up, then."

Mr. Jackson went up the accommodation ladder first, and was followed by Somers.   Kennedy looked sharp at the second lieutenant, as he stepped down from the rail. He evidently did not like the looks of the uniform he had on, though Mr. Jackson wore an old coat, from which the shoulder-straps and sleeve-band had been removed.

" Who are you, sir?" demanded Kennedy, rather roughly, as he stood off and eyed the lieutenant.

" My name is Jackson, sir, at your service ; and I hope to obtain a position on board of this vessel when she goes into commission, even if it is no better one than master's mate."

" You are the man we want, then ; Coles has been doing a lively business in New York," added Kennedy, as the old salts, who had been carefully instructed to hold their tongues, poured in upon the deck, fourteen in number.   " These are good fellows, and I see they bring their arms with them, which is better yet."

" Yes, sir ; when we heard what sort of a man we

were to have as commander, we thought it likely we should want to use these playthings before we got into port," replied Jackson.

"Very likely you will," returned Kennedy, pleased with the compliment contained in the remark. "If Coles will consent, we will capture the first Yankee ship we meet."

"I think he will agree to it, from what I heard him say."

"My dear Mr. Somers, I am delighted to see you!" exclaimed Mr. Phil Kennedy, who had hardly removed his eyes from our middy during the conversation with the second lieutenant. "Pray, how did you leave Miss Portington?"

"She was in excellent health and spirits the last time I saw her," replied Somers, in a tone suited to the trying occasion.

"I am glad to hear that she was well. Possibly she was rather sad when you informed her of your intention to leave Newport."

"She did not seem to be much affected."

"And how were the rest of the family in Newport?" continued Kennedy, rubbing his hands with delight.

"They were all well."

"Was Kate really willing to let you go from her side?"

"Not very willing; but I consoled her with the assurance that you would soon return, and she would be happy again."

" 'Pon my word as a gentleman and a sailor, that was very kind of you to remember the absent. I shall reciprocate that favor; for I shall probably see her before you do."

" Very likely."

" Really, Mr. Somers, this is a very unexpected pleasure. I hardly anticipated seeing you again so soon. Do I understand that you are tired of serving in the old navy, and intend to try your luck in the gallant little marine of the south?"

" No, sir! I don't intend to do anything of the sort, Mr. Kennedy. You know me well enough to be satisfied that I would never desert the flag of my country," said Somers, with proper spirit.

" Bravo, my little bantam!" replied Kennedy. " So much the worse for you. If you wish to serve the Confederate States of America in the capacity of midshipman, I think I have influence enough to procure you a warrant."

" You know me better than that, Mr. Kennedy. I would cut my right hand off before I would do anything of the kind."

" Then your right hand must be a very useless member to you, my dear Somers, or you would not be willing to get rid of it so easily."

" Excuse me, Mr. Kennedy, but the remembrance of our past intercourse brings to my mind a very pertinent question."

" Good on your dictionary, Somers ; I wish Kate could have heard that remark. But what's the pertinent question ? "

" Commodore Portington and all his family, as you are well aware, are intensely loyal. The question which occurred to me was, how you intend to make your peace with them after engaging in an enterprise of this description."

" My dear and astute friend, that question has already been up for consideration in my mind ; and I am very happy to answer you. In less than six months from the present time, that which is now called the United States of America will have ceased to exist ; or if it exists at all, it will only be as a rival, but not an equal, of the Confederate States of America. Doesn't that answer the question ? "

" Hardly, Mr. Kennedy."

" We who have fought for southern independence will not then be regarded as rebels and traitors. What is now called treason will shine out as the glorious deeds of brave and self-sacrificing men. What looks black now to the benighted eyes of those whom you call loyal — 'pon my honor, I hate the sound of the word — will glow like living fire. Those who are now fighting the

battles of the North will sneak off like whipped puppies,·
and return to the mud from which they came, there to
dig till your huge debt is paid.   Then, my dear Somers,
the officers of the southern army and navy will not have
to apologize for what they have done."

" They will not, if things turn out as you predict,"
replied Somers.

" They will turn out just as I predict.   Long before
you ever see your native town again, France will have
recognized the Confederate States ; England will follow
her example, and the great work of the nineteenth cen-
tury will be accomplished.   But, my dear Somers, I cannot stop to discuss this question now, and we shall have
plenty of time for it, as we cruise to the southward."

" Then I am to be a cabin passenger — am I ? " asked
Somers, in rather doleful tones.

" Certainly, for the friendship I bear you, I must
accord you that privilege ; but when we get into port, of
course I can do nothing more for you."

" What is to happen to me then ? "

" I am very sorry, my dear fellow, but the fortunes of
war have placed you in my power, and I can do nothing
less than hand you over to the authorities as a prisoner."

" Do you think my capture was entirely fair and hon-
orable ? " asked Somers, who was prolonging the interview to enable Mr. Jackson to make his dispositions of
the men about the deck and below.

" Perhaps not exactly in accordance with the strict letter of the rules of war ; but you see, my dear Somers, I had a particular liking for you, and wanted you very badly. I hope Kate will be able to get along without you."

"Probably she will not miss either one of us very much. In a word, I suppose I happen to be here to gratify your malice towards me."

" Don't use hard words, my dear Somers. You were certainly in my way, and it was necessary to remove you. Here you are, my fine fellow, and it will be many a day before you see Newport again."

" I am satisfied if you are, Mr. Kennedy."

"Well, I ought to be. I have won the game," added he, rubbing his hands again, in the exuberance of his delight. " That's a very fine pistol you wear in your belt, my dear Somers ; allow me to look at it."

" Excuse me, Mr. Kennedy, it is loaded, and you might get hurt with it," replied Somers, as Mr. Jackson approached the quarter-deck.

" I'll trouble you for that pistol, Somers," repeated Kennedy, rather sharply.

" I can't spare it."

" You are my prisoner, Somers."

" Not yet, Mr. Kennedy."

" I am sorry to interrupt you, gentlemen," interposed the second lieutenant of the Rosalie, " but I think it is about time to proceed to business."

16

" I think so, too. Have you brought your caps on board? " demanded Kennedy.

" Yes, sir ; all on board."

" Very well; but the first business is to disarm this young puppy."

" I think I wouldn't stop to do that just now, Captain Kennedy," replied Jackson, hardly able to keep from laughing. " He will do no harm."

" Where are your caps, Jackson? " demanded Kennedy, glancing around the deck for the valuable stores.

" They are on the heads of the men."

" I am in no humor for jesting," growled Mr. Kennedy.

" Neither am I ; and I think we will bring this farce to an end."

" Pray what do you mean by this farce? " demanded the commander of the Snowden.

" Well, sir, you have had all the fun to yourself thus far, and I think it is time for us to have our turn," replied the lieutenant.

" Confound your impudence, sir ! " exclaimed Kennedy. " I put you under arrest for insolence ! "

" Pardon me, Captain Kennedy, but that is just what I was about to do with you. Without further jesting, which I find is offensive to you, allow me to add, that you are my prisoner."

" Your prisoner? "

" My prisoner, sir, I repeat; and your vessel is the prize of the United States schooner Rosalie, Captain Waldron. I think I have been sufficiently explicit, Mr. Kennedy, to leave you no further doubt in regard to our relative positions. Mr. Somers, the prisoner is in your charge."

Mr. Phil Kennedy sank down on a seat by the side of the skylight. He turned deadly pale, and the terrible revulsion of circumstances shook every fibre in his frame.

" That's a fine pistol you have in your belt, Mr. Kennedy; allow me to look at it," said Somers, as he discovered the weapon beneath the frock-coat of his prisoner.

" Don't insult me, Somers," said he, savagely.

" I don't mean to insult you; but I will trouble you for your pistol."

" You can't have it," growled the wretched man.

" Take it from him," said Somers to the ship's corporal and a quarter-master, who had been detailed to guard the prisoner.

Kennedy sprang to his feet, and attempted to draw the pistol, evidently with the intention of taking a sweet revenge upon the man whom he hated. The ship's corporal was too quick for him, and before he could disengage the weapon from his belt, the burly chief of police of the Rosalie was hugging him, as a bear hugs his prey; while the quarter-master wrested from him the weapon which would have been dangerous in the hands of a desperate man. Having deprived the prisoner of his power to do injury, the men released him at a signal from Somers. In the mean time, Mr. Jackson had effectually secured possession of the vessel, and the trusty blue-jackets stood ready, with cutlass and pistol in hand, to enforce the orders of their officer. But no resistance was made.

"What does all this mean, Somers?" asked Kennedy, in a more subdued tone. "Where is Coles?"

"A prisoner in Fort Lafayette. We came out after this vessel, and we have her."

"You expected her, then."

"We did."

"Some one has betrayed me," groaned the traitor.

"No, sir; you betrayed yourself. When those living fires of which you spoke begin to glow, you will not be *there*," replied Somers.

CHAPTER XVI.

MR. TUBBS COMES TO GRIEF.

THE Snowden was a steamer of about eight hundred tons. Her capture was complete, and it only remained to make the proper dispositions for sending her into port, which, of course, could only be done by the captain.

"Mr. Somers, you will proceed to the Rosalie, with your prisoner, and report to the captain the capture of the steamer," said Mr. Jackson, when he had placed his little force in positions where they could repel any attempt to recapture the vessel.

Somers touched his cap, and requested his prisoner to go over the side into the boat. Kennedy was silent and sullen. He had been robbed of his last hope, and the glowing fabric he had painted of the great Southern Confederacy suddenly crumbled into ruins, for most men identify their own fate with that of their nation. He went below with the ship's corporal, and pointed out his personal effects, which were put into the boat. Without a remark, he went down the accommodation ladder, and seated himself in the stern-sheets.

16 *

"I have to report the capture of the Snowden, sir," said Somers, touching his cap, as he reached the deck of the Rosalie, and met the captain, who was eagerly waiting for intelligence from the prize. "Her commander accompanies me, sir," he added, when Mr. Phil Kennedy appeared, in charge of the acting master-at-arms.

"I am happy to receive your report, Mr. Somers," said the captain, glancing at the disconsolate prisoner.

"Mr. Jackson directed me to say that he was waiting further orders."

"They shall be sent to him presently."

Mr. Jackson was immediately detailed as prize-master, with Mr. Somers as first and Mr. Thompson as second officers.

"But before you go, Mr. Somers, there is a matter of some importance to be adjusted. Pass the word for Mr. Tubbs," said the captain. "Mr. Kennedy, may I trouble you to go below?"

"I am your prisoner, and you can do with me as you please," growled Kennedy, sulkily.

The captain went down into his cabin, followed by the prisoner, and by Somers, who was ordered to be present at the interview.

"Captain Waldron, if you propose to question me in regard to the steamer, I have only to say, that this business is wholly irregular," said Kennedy, as he threw himself into a chair; "and I intend to let the conse-quences rest with you."

" I am entirely willing to bear the responsibility."

" You have captured my vessel without even exam-ining her papers."

" I think I understand perfectly what I am about, Captain Kennedy."

" My ship is a British steamer, bound from one British 'port to another."

" Are you a British subject?" demanded the captain.

Kennedy wilted.

" I do not intend to answer any question in regard to my vessel," he replied, at last, in surly tones.

" It is not necessary for me to ask any questions on that subject."

At this moment, Mr. Tubbs entered the cabin, where he had been ordered to appear. He looked very much astonished at the invitation he had received, and it was clear that he did not know whether to expect a shock, or an appointment on board of the prize. Kennedy took no notice of him as he entered, and perhaps this fact had some influence in shaping the young gentleman's future course.

" Mr. Tubbs," said the captain, with a queer smile, which the senior midshipman of the Rosalie could not fathom, " we have a friend of yours here, and I thought it probable you might wish to see him."

" A friend of mine ! " exclaimed Tubbs. " Ah, Mr.
Somers? I learn that he is about to leave us for a time.
I am sorry to part with him."

" No doubt you are ; but I did not allude to him, but
to your friend Mr. Kennedy, commander of the steamer
just captured."

" I beg your pardon, sir, but I have not the honor of
the gentleman's acquaintance," replied Mr. Tubbs, with
a polite bow to the prisoner.

" Indeed? I thought you were old friends."

" No, sir ; it is quite possible that I have seen the
gentleman before."

" Your memory is astonishingly poor, Mr. Tubbs.
Perhaps Mr. Kennedy's is better."

" The gentleman is a stranger to me," said the prisoner, who was so strongly desirous of annoying the
captain, that he immediately fell in with the course laid
out by the midshipman, though it is possible he had
some stronger and more interested motive in view.

" This is very singular, Mr. Tubbs," added the captain, taking from his pocket a paper, which proved to be
the challenge sent to Somers. " Did you ever see this
letter before, Mr. Tubbs? " continued the inquisitor,
handing him the treacherous document, opened so as to
exhibit only Kennedy's letter to his fellow-conspirator.

" Really, I do not just now remember to have received
any such letter, though it is certainly addressed to me,"

stammered the senior middy, his face growing crimson, as he turned over the fatal missive.

"Did you ever have that letter in your possession, Mr. Tubbs?" demanded the captain, sternly, for he was disgusted with the duplicity of the wretch.

"If I ever did, I really cannot call to mind the fact. I was trying to think."

"Really, sir, your memory is the most unserviceable one a young man ever had. You are offered five thousand dollars for performing some act which does not appear in the letter, and you have the audacity to tell me you don't remember about it."

"Excuse me, Captain Waldron; but I was trying to think," stuttered Tubbs.

"You are conjuring up a new lie, sir. The letter is signed by Mr. Kennedy, and he made you this offer."

"I cannot now recall the circumstances connected with this letter, sir."

"It would be very-inconvenient, no doubt, to do so," added the captain, severely. "May I ask if you can recall the circumstances connected with this letter?" continued the commander of the Rosalie, as he took the paper, and, turning it over, exhibited the challenge.

Mr. Tubbs was overcome — had not another shot in the locker; and there was no decent course left to him but to surrender at discretion. Unfortunately for the young gentleman thus convicted, he chose still to shuffle and deceive.

" I took Mr. Somers for a gentleman," said he, when he had slightly recovered from the shock. " He insulted me, and I demanded satisfaction."

" Pshaw ! " exclaimed the captain ; and even Mr. Phil Kennedy, laboring under the heavy burden of his own griefs, could not restrain a smile as he glanced at Tubbs, and fancied him engaged in a duel.

" It seems he has betrayed me to the captain — a piece of treachery to which no gentleman would descend," added Tubbs.

" The challenge is too ridiculous for a moment's consideration, though it is sufficient to procure your dishonorable discharge from the navy. It would never have been brought to me but for the more important matter on another part of the sheet."

" I deny all knowledge of that matter," said Tubbs, with sudden energy, as if he had resolved upon a plan to fight the desperate battle.

" The original letter was in your possession."

" And it was stupid of you to write a challenge on an old note," interrupted Kennedy.

" I didn't see it," answered Tubbs, rallying to defend himself from this new charge.

The captain laughed at this unguarded admission, and Tubbs sank back into a corner, utterly overwhelmed with confusion, when he realized what a blunder he had made.

" Hold your tongue now, Tubbs, and face the music

like a man," added Kennedy, who evidently had a very mean opinion of the ability of his companion in misery.

" Mr. Tubbs, it appears, that you are in correspondence with Mr. Kennedy ; that you are engaged together in a conspiracy ; and it is strongly to be suspected that you have received, and perhaps accepted, an offer to give aid and comfort to the enemy. You are, therefore, placed under arrest."

" O, Captain Waldron !" exclaimed Tubbs, bursting into tears, " do not ruin me ! "

" You have ruined yourself."

" But I am not guilty of these charges. I appeal to Captain Kennedy," pleaded the unfortunate middy.

" Don't appeal to me, you whining puppy," said the late captain of the Snowden, incensed at his want of manhood.

" My poor father !" sobbed Tubbs.

" You should have thought of him before," replied the captain.

" I meant no harm, Captain Waldron."

" Haven't you plotted with this man to fit out a gunboat to prey upon the commerce of your country ? "

" Indeed I have not ! I had no suspicion of the intentions of Mr. Kennedy when he wrote me that note. I can prove it, sir."

" You will have to prove it in some other place, Mr. Tubbs."

" If I had had any intention, as you say, of fitting out a gunboat, do you suppose I would have confided my plans to such an idiot as this boy?" interposed Kennedy.

" For what were you offered five thousand dollars, Mr. Tubbs?" asked the captain.

" If you will permit me, I will explain."

" Go on ; but be brief."

" Mr. Kennedy, as you are all aware, was the accepted suitor of Miss Kate Portington," Tubbs began.

No one present was aware of it; but as that was the speaker's view of the matter, it was not thought necessary to controvert the statement.

" An accident placed Mr. Somers in a very favorable situation before the lady. In fact, he saved her life, for which she was very grateful, as she ought to have been. Mr. Somers made a very unfair use of the advantage thus obtained. There was an entire want of magnanimity on his part."

" Confine yourself to a statement of facts, Mr. Tubbs," said the captain, indignantly.

" I will, sir. Mr. Somers used the advantage he had thus obtained in supplanting Mr. Kennedy. In other words, he attempted ' to cut him out.' "

" That is all an idle tale," sneered Kennedy. " Do you think I could ask any favors of such a person as Mr. Somers?"

" I only state what Mr. Kennedy told me," replied

Tubbs, resolutely. "Captain Waldron, I mean to tell nothing but the truth now."

"That's the greatest lie you have told yet," snarled the "accepted suitor."

"When Mr. Kennedy told me this tale of his wrongs, I very naturally felt indignant, as any high-minded person would have felt."

The captain opened his eyes very wide, and Kennedy uttered a brief exclamation indicative of his contempt.

"I thought Mr. Somers had played a very mean part in a delicate matter, and I did not hesitate so to express myself. My father, having a large family to maintain, with his pay greatly reduced, was in very straitened circumstances; and Mr. Kennedy proposed to point out a way by which I could make five thousand dollars. For my father's sake I listened to the offer."

"Well, sir, what were you to do for the five thousand dollars?" asked the captain, as the speaker paused in his narrative, when he came to the disgraceful part thereof.

"I was to get Mr. Somers into difficulty, and injure his credit with the officers."

"Was that all?"

"I was to dispose of him as I could."

"Dispose of him? Do you mean that you were to take his life?"

"Mr. Kennedy may have entertained that view, but I never did."

" Mr. Kennedy never entertained any such view," interposed that gentleman ; " speak for yourself, if you must speak at all."

" Indeed, sir, I never accepted the offer," added Mr. Tubbs, brightening up, as though he had found a means of clearing himself from all blame.

" But you commenced operations when you locked Mr. Somers up in the store-room."

" No, sir ; I am willing to acknowledge that I despised him for his meanness in the matter I have mentioned, and was willing to play him a trick when I got a chance. I never intended to injure him — only to annoy him."

" How came Mr. Kennedy to make you this offer?"

" I heard that Somers and myself were to be appointed to this vessel a week before I was sent on board ; and I told Mr. Kennedy so."

" Mr. Kennedy bargained with another man to hand Mr. Somers over as a prisoner on board the Snowden," added the captain.

" I did not know that, sir," replied Tubbs.

" As nearly as I can judge, you were to do the dirty job if the other man failed."

" I was not to do that — at least I never intended to injure Mr. Somers."

" You have done enough to disgrace any officer. You are under arrest."

" I beg you — "

" I have nothing more to say. Report tó the master-at-arms, under arrest."

" I wish to say, sir, so far as Miss Portington is concerned, I never had the remotest idea of supplanting Mr. Kennedy," interposed Somers, blushing like a child. " I never paid her any attentions such as Mr. Tubbs mentions. I never made love to her, in a word."

Mr. Somers thought he had not ; he had no " serious intentions " — indeed, no intentions at all ; but it is quite likely he did not understand the matter.

The captain went on deck, followed by Somers, while Kennedy and Tubbs were banded over to the master-at-arms.

CHAPTER XVII.

THE ROSALIE IN DOBOY SOUND.

WHILE Captain Waldron was in the cabin, "working up" the case of Mr. Midshipman Tubbs, the first lieutenant was making the details for the crew of the Snowden. Somers and Thompson brought up their bags, and the boat put off. The engineers and fireman of the steamer were willing to retain their positions on certain conditions; but it was deemed necessary to have a large force of Yankee sailors on board, in case of any attempt to recapture her. The Rosalie was to keep near her, and to be towed by her in light or head winds.

Mr. Midshipman Somers was now first officer of the steamer, and the place had been assigned to him at the special request of Mr. Jackson. He was young, but he was considered fully competent to perform the duties of the position. The boat returned to the Rosalie, which immediately filled away on her course.

The wheels of the Snowden were started, and with a quarter-master to con the wheels, she followed in the

wake of her little captor. During that day the Rosalie was able to hold way with the steamer; but at sunset
the wind subsided, and a hawser was passed from her to
the Snowden.

. The purposes of our story do not require us to follow
the return voyage in detail, and we pass over the tame
incidents of an unbroken passage, till the Snowden took
on board a pilot, about a hundred miles east of Sandy
Hook. Though our voyagers had been absent from
home but a brief period, they were anxious to learn the
war news, and the bundle of papers which the pilot
brought on board were examined with great eagerness.
They were three days old, but they were nearly a week
later than any the officers had seen.

There was no very exciting news; but Somers, who had
a very decided relish for newspapers, devoted himself to
a careful perusal of them, as soon as he was relieved
from duty on deck. Of course he read the war news
first; and while looking over the paper for other matters
of interest, his attention was attracted by a familiar
name — no other than that of "Portington." His gaze
was instantly riveted to the paragraph, for everything
connected with that name had a kind of charm about it.

The paragraph in which he had found it, announced
the dangerous illness of General Portington, who had
been attacked by paralysis. The papers were sent on
board the Rosalie, with this sentence marked, that it

17*

might not escape the attention of the captain. The announcement would give Mr. Phil Kennedy a thrill of anxiety, but it would not be on account of the impending death of one who had been his guardian and protector, but for the final disposition of his large property.

Perhaps the general was already dead ; and it was not impossible that the prisoner on board the Rosalie was the heir of a quarter of a million. Money covers a multitude of sins ; and if the general had carried out what was understood to be his intention, and made Phil joint heir with Kate of his estates, it would not be a difficult matter for him to break through the meshes of the law. From this point of view the matter was one of no inconsiderable interest to Somers.

On Tuesday morning the Snowden steamed up the harbor of New York, followed by the Rosalie, which had cast off the hawser, and run up, in gallant style, before a fresh breeze. Both vessels came to anchor off the navy yard, and the first edition of the evening papers contained full accounts of the chase and the capture. Somers bought two of the papers, and mailed one to Pinchbrook, and the other to Newport.

His first care, after he had discharged the duties incident to the arrival of the vessel, was to examine the papers of each day, since the date of the one brought off by the pilot, to ascertain the result of General Portington's illness. He could obtain no further information from the papers, nor from any of the officers with whom he was brought into official connection.

Mr. Phil Kennedy was sent to Fort Lafayette as soon as the Rosalie's anchor struck the mud. Mr. Tubbs's case was reported to the authorities, and he remained under arrest, awaiting orders. On the following day, orders came by mail from Washington for the Rosalie to put to sea again as soon as practicable. While the few stores she needed were coming on board, the depositions of the officers were taken, to be used in the prize court in the case of the Snowden.

Our younger readers may not understand that, when a ship is taken in war, the captors cannot sell nor use her at their own pleasure. The customs or practices of maritime nations, embodied in what is called " international law," regulate all these affairs. A vessel may be captured as the property of an enemy in war, or of a neutral while engaged in entering a port legally blockaded, or when it appears to the satisfaction of the officer making the capture, that she is conveying goods contraband of war to the enemy ; but she is not yet the property of the nation under whose authority the capture was made.

If this were the law, or the fact, vessels might be unjustly taken from their owners. After the vessel or the goods are captured, they still belong, in theory, to the original owner, and the officer who captures them is responsible for his act. The captured ship is sent into

a port of the captor, or of a neutral, and the case
brought before a court created for the purpose, which
must sit in the country of the captor or his ally. The
evidence on both sides is then heard, and the court de-
cides whether or not the vessel was legally taken. All
the testimony respecting the vessel's nationality, the object of her voyage, indeed all the information that can
be obtained, is presented to the court.

On this evidence the decision of the court is made.
If the testimony is not sufficient to prove that she is a
lawful prize, she is acquitted, and the government must
pay any damage which may be caused by her capture.
If the evidence is sufficient, the vessel is condemned, and
handed over to the marshal of the district to be sold. If
the government wants the vessel, it must buy her at auc-
tion, the same as a private individual, for the sale is
necessary in order to establish the value.

The distribution of the proceeds of this sale is also
regulated by law. When the vessel is taken by a man-
of-war, if the captured ship be armed and of greater force,
all the money she brings goes to the captors ; if she is of
equal or of less force, one half goes to the government,
and the other half to the officers and crew making the
capture. If we divide the whole sum into twentieths,
the captain has three parts, or, if his vessel belongs to a
squadron, he has only two, the admiral taking the other
part. Two parts are divided among all the lieutenants,

the captain of marines, and the sailing-master; two parts among the chaplain, surgeon, paymaster, master's mates, and similar officers; three parts and a half among the midshipmen, armorer, boatswain's mates, cockswain, and other officers of approximate rank; two and a half parts among certain petty officers; and seven parts to all the seamen, marines, and all other persons not included in other grades. If there are, for example, three lieutenants and a sailing-master, each of them receives one fourth of two twentieths of all the money — that is, one fortieth. If there are fifty sailors of all degrees, each one receives one fiftieth of seven twentieths, or seven dollars of every thousand divided.

The Snowden and her cargo brought sixty thousand dollars above the expenses, one half of which was divided among the officers and crew of the Rosalie. There were twelve persons of the class to which Somers belonged; therefore he received one twelfth of three and a half twentieths of thirty thousand dollars, which is four hundred and thirty-seven dollars and a half—no small sum for a young man of eighteen to make in less than a fortnight.

Somers and his fellow-officers of the Rosalie made depositions before a magistrate in regard to their knowledge of the Snowden, to be used in the prize court if they should be absent on duty when the case was adjusted. The officers and sailors of the captured steamer would also be required to give their evidence.

All these matters were disposed of, and Somers thought the importance of the events in which he had been an actor was sufficient to warrant him in writing a letter to Kate, as he had promised. He did not write the playful letter he intended, fearing that such an epistle might be distasteful to her while the family were waiting to hear of the death of her grandfather, if the news had not already reached them.   He scarcely alluded to Phil Kennedy, for her relations with him were too intimate to permit a full statement of his infamy.

At meridian, on the following day, the Rosalie went to sea again, and, as usual, not a soul on board knew where she was bound.   But everybody was contented and happy, for the success already obtained was an earnest of the future. The vessel and her commander had received a great deal of credit for the capture of the Snowden, and the prospect of a handsome sum of prize money was calculated to make all hands good-natured.

The officers and crew were the same as before, with the exception of Mr. Tubbs, who had been relieved from duty, and ordered to hold himself in readiness for trial by court-martial; and we may as well anticipate the event, and say that he was dishonorably dismissed from the navy, the charge of aiding and comforting the enemy not being fully established.

Everything proceeded with the utmost regularity on board, after the Rosalie passed Sandy Hook, where the sealed orders were opened and read. The schooner was to go upon the blockade on the coast of Georgia, where sundry schooners laden with cotton had eluded the vigilance of the steamers, so few in number that it was impossible to cover the numerous watercourses which ran inland from the ocean. The particular point to which the Rosalie was ordered was the mouth of Doboy Sound ; and she reached her station after a rather rough passage of twelve days.

" Here we are," said Captain Waldron, when the vessel came to anchor to the southward of Chimney Spit.

This remark was addressed to Somers, who was on duty near the speaker.

" Yes, sir ; but I hope we shall have something better to do than lie at anchor."

" Patience, Mr. Somers. I have no doubt we shall find occupation before many days have passed away. This Doboy Sound is one of the back doors of the Altamaha River. So many of the vessels of the navy have been engaged in the attack upon Sumter, that the rebels have been encouraged to send out vessels, and they have done so with some success. This region has been pretty thoroughly explored and burned over by the negro troops. Darien was destroyed not long since, and vast quantities of property captured and burned. The place had a large trade in lumber."

" I suppose they don't run the blockade with lumber,

sir," added Somers, who did not think such a cargo would pay for the risk.

" No; but a great deal of cotton comes down the Altamaha River, which the rebels are anxious to get out, in order to pay the cotton loan."

" I hope we shall have a chance to do our share in putting down the value of the cotton loan."

" Probably we shall; for it is reported that blockade-running is quite brisk in this vicinity at the present time. Though it is rather a narrow field, we have this sound entirely to ourselves."

But the Rosalie mocked the expectations of the commander and his officers for a fortnight; for there was no appearance of a vessel going in or out of the inlet during that time. The weather had been remarkably fine, with bright moonlight evenings, which was not favorable for blockade-running, and all hands whistled for a change of weather. A rainy, misty, foggy day soon rewarded the seamen's prayer, and extra precautions were taken to entrap any vessel which might attempt to run out. The darkness set in with a fog so dense that the lookouts could not see a ship's length in any direction. Mr. Greene, the third lieutenant, was sent off in the second cutter to do picket duty inside of the sound.

At eight bells in the first watch, when it was dead low tide, and the wind was blowing in fresh from the eastward, this boat was recalled; for it was not considered possible that any vessel would attempt to run out at that stage of the tide, and with a head wind. At two bells in the mid watch, the lookout on the forecastle reported a noise like the puffing of a steamer up the sound. In an instant everything was alive on board the Rosalie. The order to call the men to quarters was given ; but everything was conducted in silence, that the position of the schooner might not be revealed to the approaching vessel.

18

CHAPTER XVIII.

IN THE FOG AND DARKNESS.

CLEAR away the first cutter, Mr. Jackson," said the captain, who, when the order had been repeated, gave the second lieutenant his directions, which were to proceed towards the approaching steamer, and carry her by boarding, if practicable; if not, to throw up rockets, slanted towards the position of the blockade-runner.

At this moment Somers contrived to place himself in such a situation that the captain might see him. He had heard the order given to carry the steamer by boarding, and he had a Yankee sailor's taste for this exciting employment. Captain Waldron, however, did not see him, for the fog and the darkness were very dense; but, as our middy almost invariably formed one of Mr. Jackson's crew, when he was sent away in the boat, he ventured to go a step farther than "hanging around."

" Shall I go in the first cutter, as usual, sir? " asked he, stepping forward and touching his cap.

" Certainly, Mr. Somers, certainly," replied Captain Waldron, smiling at the eagerness of the young officer.

The Yankee middy rushed to the deck, and obtained a cutlass, which, in addition to his usual arms, rendered him quite a formidable person.

" You will hardly need that, Mr. Somers," said the captain, as the young gentleman sprang to the accommodation ladder. " Boarding a blockade-runner is quite a peaceful occupation."

" It is best to be ready for anything that may turn up, and I should feel bad if there were to be a fight, while I was not in condition to have a hand in it."

" Up oars ! " shouted the cockswain of the cutter.

" Silence there ! " said the captain. " You will wake up every man within ten miles of us."

" Shove off ! " added the cockswain, in more cautious tones.

" Hold on a moment, if you please," called Somers, finding the boat was going away without him.

" Haul in again, bowman," said Mr. Jackson, who was always glad enough to have Somers in the boat with him ; not only because he was a faithful and reliable officer, but because he was a pleasant companion.

Somers leaped into the fore-sheets of the cutter, and made his way aft, where he reported himself in due form to his superior.

"Glad to have you with me, Mr. Somers," said Mr. Jackson. "We may have a little fun to-night."

"Shove off!" repeated the cockswain; and the boat left the schooner's side, and plunged into the fog and darkness. "Let fall!" he added; and the oars, poised in a perpendicular position, all dropped into the water.

"Less noise, men!" interposed Mr. Jackson, sharply, for the men, excited by the prospect of a stirring event, and perhaps by the hope of a handsome sum of prize-money, were in a fair way to defeat the object of the expedition by their own enthusiasm.

"Give way together," continued the cockswain, giving the last order.

A boat compass, enclosed in a brass case, with lamps inside, so that the points could be seen without shedding any light outside, had been placed where the cockswain could see it, and he was ordered to keep her head to the north-west, which would carry the boat directly up the sound. The men had been directed to pull in silence, and the oars had been carefully muffled; that is, a piece of sail-cloth had been wound around the loom where it played in the rowlock, thus preventing its motion from making a noise.

"One thing is plain, Mr. Somers," said the second lieutenant, in a low tone — "the steamer we have heard is not a blockade-runner."

"She is a high-pressure boat, sir, or she wouldn't make that noise."

"She is evidently a river steamer, and I suppose she is towing something out."

"I thought of that before I came into the boat," replied Somers.

"You have seen some service on the southern rivers."

"A little, sir, on the Gulf."

"Perhaps the steamer is armed."

"It may be that she is. If so, we may have a brush before we return."

"We are all ready for it," replied Somers, picking up his cutlass from the bottom of the boat, and placing it by his side.

"We always are," added Mr. Jackson. "It is low tide, and the wind is fresh from the sea. We must stop this craft before she passes the Rosalie, for she cannot follow her."

"That is the disadvantage of a sailing vessel."

"Yes; and I suppose the rebels who planned this movement intend to profit by our weakness. Where is the steamer now? Dixon, lay on your oars," added Mr. Jackson to the cockswain.

"Stand by to lay on your oars!" said Dixon. "Oars!"

At this order, the oarsmen levelled their oars, with the blades feathered, and in a perfect line, though it was too dark for any one to see and admire the precision with which the commands were executed.

"Can you hear the steamer, Somers?" asked Mr. Jackson.

18 *

"No, sir; they must have stopped her."

"Steerage-way gone, sir," said Dixon, after they had waited a moment for any sounds from the approaching vessel.

"Give way, then!"

"Give way!" repeated the cockswain; and again the men pulled their steady, silent stroke.

Mr. Jackson was perplexed at the discontinuance of the sounds on which he had relied to guide him to the expected prize. After the boat had proceeded a short distance farther, he again ordered the men to lay on their oars; and the officers listened for any indications of the steamer, but there was nothing to be heard but the dashing of the waves. The men pulled again; and this time they went about a mile up the sound before another stop was made. It was certain that the steamer was not near the boat; for even if she was not in motion, the noise of the escaping steam must have betrayed her presence.

"Is it possible that we have passed her?" asked Mr Jackson, appalled at the very thought of such an event.

"Hardly possible, sir," replied Somers.

"I don't understand it. We are at least two miles from the ship, and the steamer could not have been that distance from us when we heard her."

"She may have come out of one of these creeks, and gone up the sound," suggested Somers. "It looks as though there was no blockade-runner in the scrape, after all."

"I am very confident she could not have passed us. I know we should have heard her, for this sound is not much over a mile in width. I doubt whether anything will happen to-night to reward our patience. However, we will go up a little farther, and see if we can get any information, if we don't obtain anything else."

The men beut to their oars once more; and, after going another mile, the boat was again stopped: still there were no sounds to disclose the preseut position of the steamer. Mr. Jackson's hopes had been abating, until he gave up the chase in despair. He had given the order to return to the Rosalie, when a voice was heard from the depths of the fog and gloom. It came from over the starboard bow, and immediately excited a profound sensation on board of the first cutter.

"Who dar? Who dar?" demanded some invisible person from the mass of fog; but his quality and social station were sufficiently indicated by his dialect.

"It's a darky," said Mr. Jackson.

"And for that reason, sir, the most valuable person we could meet at the present time," replied Somers. "The negroes are all loyal; and if this man has any information of the steamer, he will give it to us.

"Who dar?" shouted the negro again.

"Boat ahoy!" replied the second lieutenant.

"Is you de Yankees, massa?". asked the cautious darky, who was still unseen by the cutter's crew.

"Yes; where are you? — on shore?"

"No, massa; dis nigger's in de dug-out."

"What are you doing at this time of night?"

"Trying to find de Yankees, massa," replied the occupant of the dug-out, as the craft emerged from the mass of fog, and ranged up astern of the cutter. "Dis nigger been tryin to get off dis tree weeks: now, here he is, glory be to Massa Ole Abe!"

"Where have you been these three weeks?" asked Mr. Jackson.

"Been loadin de schooners wid de cotton."

"O, indeed! Have you?"

"Yes, massa."

"There is one up here now — is there?"

"Yes, massa — fourteen ob 'em."

"Fourteen!" exclaimed the lieutenant, incredulously.

"Well, sar, dis chile can't edzactly say dare's jes fourteen ob 'em; but dar's a big pile ob 'em, as sure as you lib, massa."

"Where's the steamer?"

"I kin told you all about de steamer, massa."

"Can you? Then you are just the man we want."

"Dis chile kin tell you all about her, sar; but dis chile want to go to de Norf."

"Very well; you shall go to the North, if you know how to tell the truth."

" De truf! Golly! Dis chile neber tells nossin but de truf, as shore as you was born ! "

" Where is the steamer? " asked Mr. Jackson, now fully satisfied that he had captured a prize who would add a large sum to the credit of the officers and crew of the Rosalie.

" She done gone ober dar, massa," replied the contraband, pointing out into the gloom.

" What's she doing here? "

" She was gwine to take one ob de schooners down ober de bar."

" Where is the schooner? " demanded the lieutenant, impatiently.

"Dey bof gone ober dar ! " replied the negro, again pointing into the banks of fog.

" Why don't she go down the sound, if she is going?"

" Dar's de trouble, massa," said the black man, significantly.

" What is the trouble? "

The intelligent contraband then proceeded to explain the whole matter. He informed the lieutenant that the steamer, with a schooner in tow, got within a short distance of the Chimney Spit, off which the Rosalie lay, when a boat, which had been sent ahead to feel the way, had returned with the intelligence that the man-of-war was getting out her boat to capture them. The negro further informed Mr. Jackson, that the very dug-out in which he sat had been used as the pioneer of the blockade-runner, and that he himself had held the paddle. The mate of the steamer was with him ; and, after he had put him on board, he had cast off again, and had been paddling about for an hour in search of the man-of-war, or one of her boats.

His statement seemed to be very consistent, and as his case was that of thousands of his kind in bondage, he was readily accepted as a truthful witness.

" What did the steamer do when the mate returned on board ? " asked Mr. Jackson, after he had fully satisfied himself in regard to the character of his informant.

" She put back, massa. Dat schooner down dar got a big gun ; blow de steamer all to squash, if she git a rap at her."

" That's so," answered Mr. Jackson.

" Yes, sar."

" Then she has given up the attempt to run the schooner out to-night."

" No, sar ; she's gwine to wait till all tings is still again ; den she's gwine down. Dat's what I hear the nable ossifer say."

" The what ? "

" De nable ossifer — de man like you is, dat come from Sabannah to git de schooners out."

" Who is the naval officer ? "

" Dunno, massa."

" Do you know where the steamer is now ? "

" Well, sar, dis nigger dunno edzactly whar she is, but I reckon she done runned inter de creek," replied the contraband.

" What creek? "

" Tea-kettle Creek, massa."

" Give way, Dixon ! " said Mr. Jackson.

" Golly, massa ! Dis child ain't goin up dar, no how," said the negro, with something like a shudder.

" We will take care of you.   Come into the boat."

" Dis nigger's afeerd ob his life to go up dar, sar. Spose dey done cotch dis chile ! Golly, dey put him in de furnaces for bringin de Yankees up dar."

The contraband's fears were proof against the eloquence of the second lieutenant for a time ; but at last he compromised, by agreeing to follow in the dug-out.

" Give way ! " said Dixon ; and the boat darted through the fog, in the direction of the creek where the steamer and her companion were reported to be.

" We shall not go back empty-handed, after all," said Mr. Jackson, whose hopes had again risen to the highest pitch.

" No, sir ; I hope not," answered Somers.

" The chances are all in our favor, at any rate," added the lieutenant ; " that is, if the darky's statement is correct."

" I believe a darky was never yet known wilfully to give false information."

" No, I think not."

The boat continued on her course till, in the opinion of the officers, she had made four miles from the schooner's anchorage, which was the distance to the creek. All the officers of the Rosalie had diligently studied the chart, and calculated the distances between various points in the sound, in anticipation of occasions like the present. At this point she ran in towards the northerly shore of the sound. They did not strike the creek, for the calculations of distances were necessarily very imperfect; but they persevered until they accomplished the object, and the noise of escaping steam, half a mile distant, guided them to their prey.

" Stand by your cutlasses, my men," said Mr. Jackson, in a low tone, when the boat had approached near enough to the steamer to enable them to hear the voices of the men on her deck.

" Ay, ay, sir," replied the ready blue-jackets.

At that instant the roar of a gun saluted them, and a twelve-pound shot struck the cutter amidships, tearing open her side, while the water poured into her with the velocity of a mill-stream. From that moment of excitement and eager expectation, the officers and crew of the cutter passed to one of anxiety for their own safety.

CHAPTER XIX.

THE FIRST CUTTER IN TROUBLE.

HE shot had struck the cutter near her water-line, and she was no longer capable of bearing up her gallant crew. The groans of some of the men assured the officers that the effects of the shot were not confined to the boat. It was evident that the expedition had fallen into a snare of some kind; but it was impossible to ascertain the further purposes of the rebels.

"Jump overboard and hang on at the rail of the boat," said Mr. Jackson, who fortunately had the presence of mind to do what the desperate condition of the boat would permit.

"Ay, ay, sir," responded the men, cheerfully; for our sailors never give way to despair as long as there is a voice to direct them.

The order was promptly obeyed; and in a moment the crew were in the water, supporting themselves by holding on at the rail of the cutter. She had no ballast or other heavy matter on board which would cause her to

19

sink; on the contrary, when the weight of the men was removed, she rose so that the hole in her side was above the water. There were two men of the party who were unable to obey the order, and still remained in the boat. One of them was quite dead; the other was severely wounded.

Mr. Jackson directed the cockswain to examine into the nature and extent of the damage done to the boat; and he soon reported a ragged hole in her side about a foot in diameter. It was also found that she would support two or three men, without sinking so deep as to cause the water to flow in. Two of the lightest of the men were directed to get in on the opposite side and bale her out.

The sound was quite smooth at this distance from the sea, and there was no difficulty in carrying out the various orders which had been given. When the boat had been baled out, five more men got in, including Mr. Jackson, who had already devised a plan for stopping the leak.

"Where is Mr. Somers?" demanded the lieutenant, now for the first time noticing the absence of our middy.

"Mr. Somers," repeated the cockswain and several of the men.

The word passed around the circle of men clinging to the boat; but Somers was not there to answer to his name.

"Where is he?" demanded the lieutenant, almost paralyzed in his efforts to save the boat, by this sad discovery.

No one could tell where he was. In the excitement which had followed the discharge of the gun and the staving of the boat, no one could tell, in the gloom of the terrible moment, what his neighbor had done to secure his own safety. Dixon had seen some one go overboard before the order was given, but he did not know who it was.

"He could not have been killed by the shot," said Mr. Jackson, with a shudder.

"Perhaps he was hit by a splinter, sir," suggested one of the men, who proved to be the stroke-oarsman; "one of them struck me on the shoulder."

Several shots followed the first one; but it was evident that they were fired at random, and that it had been a chance shot which struck the boat. The tide had now begun to run in, and the shattered boat was drifting up the sound. The shots were directed farther down the inlet. It was evident, therefore, that the rebels did not know where they were, and had no idea of the mischief they had done.

Mr. Jackson, after the wounded man had been as comfortably disposed of as the circumstances would permit, ordered the sail, which had been placed in the bottom of the boat, to be hauled under her keel, and carefully secured to the gunwales. This work was successfully accomplished, in spite of all the disadvantages under which the men labored. No one was permitted to speak above a whisper, and all noise was carefully avoided, so that the rebels could not obtain any information to direct them in pointing their guns.

The men were all ordered into the boat again. Of course the leak could be only partially stopped, and two men were detailed to bale the water out, and two more to stand by the hole and keep the canvas in its place. The boat was not in condition for active service; and all that could be expected of her was, that she would enable the crew to reach the Rosalie in safety. Under these discouraging circumstances Mr. Jackson gave the order to return.

The dug-out, with the contraband, had disappeared about the time the shot was fired. The negro's worst fears seem to have been realized; and he had probably paddled away from the scene of strife in mortal terror. The lieutenant did not concern himself about the dug-out or its timid occupant; his thoughts dwelt only on the disappearance of Somers. He had not abandoned all hope of picking him up on his return. The middy was a powerful swimmer, and an oar or a log would enable him to support himself for a long period on the water.

At the risk of drawing the fire of the rebels, he called his name as the boat proceeded on her course towards the Rosalie, but without success. Everything was done which the circumstances would admit to recover the lost officer; and Mr. Jackson came to the conclusion that he had swum ashore, and, if not captured by the enemy, had concealed himself where he could return to his vessel the next day. While he was thus considering the fate of his young companion, the splash of the steamer's paddle-wheels was distinctly heard by the crew of the cutter.

"She is ahead of us, sir, and going down the sound," said Dixon.

"I am afraid we have made a bad night's work of it," replied Mr. Jackson. "Those guns were not on board of the steamer, as I supposed; for they are still firing them. They have got an artillery company there to protect the cotton. We can't catch the steamer if we chase."

But there was a remote possibility that something might be done to compensate for the mishaps of the night, and Mr. Jackson ordered the men to give way with all their might, hoping that something might occur to the steamer to delay or stop her. The men pulled a vigorous stroke; but using two less than her complement of oars, with the drag of the sail under her keel, she made but poor time through the water. Then, to add to these disadvantages, and cover the attempt with disaster, the canvas was drawn from its place, and the

19 *

water began to flow into the boat again. The chase was abandoned; and when the canvas had been restored to its former position, the boat proceeded slowly on her course.

The steamer was gaining rapidly on the boat, and was now at least ,a mile from her. The lieutenant chafed and fretted under the difficulties of his situation, and groaned in despair as he heard the steamer speeding on her way down the sound. He could not help thinking of the miserable report he should be obliged to give the captain, on his return, of the failure of the expedition, the staving of the boat, and, worse than all, of the loss of Somers.

While he was thus indulging in unpleasant reflections, he was suddenly startled by the report of a heavy gun, which he was satisfied was that of the Rosalie. A lively cannonading was heard for a few moments; but it soon ceased, and the lieutenant ventured to hope that the schooner had accomplished what he had failed to perform. This hope, like its predecessor, was soon dissipated by the nearer approach of the steamer; and it was rendered evident that she had again put about, and was seeking safety by a return to her former position.

" "Now is our time!" said Mr. Jackson, with energy. "We will board her, boat or no boat."

"Ay, ay, sir!" replied the stroke-oarsman, who did the speech-making for the crew.

"Have your cutlasses ready, my lads!" added he. "Stand by to lay on your oars!"

When the boat stopped, Mr. Jackson listened attentively to determine the position of the steamer. She was approaching her, and it was only necessary to be quiet till she came up. In a short time he could hear her close aboard; but when almost up with the boat, she shifted her helm, and stood away towards the northern shore.

" Give way, Dixon ! " said Mr. Jackson.

The men bent on their oars, just as the dark form of the schooner came in sight through the fog.

" Pull ! pull ! " shouted Dixon, with a zeal which promised good results.

The boat dashed up to the schooner : as she came abreast of her, the bowman made fast to her side, and the hopeful tars sprang into her chains.

" Lay aboard of her ! " shouted Mr. Jackson, as he followed them up, and leaped on the deck.

But there was no resistance. Only half a dozen men appeared on the deck, and they submitted without striking a blow. As soon as the steamer realized the situation of affairs on board of her consort, she cast off her tow-lines, and, thus relieved of her heavy burden, darted forward, and disappeared in the fog. It was useless to pursue her, and Mr. Jackson ordered his men to let go the anchor, for the prize, having no sail on her, was liable to drift ashore.

While the men were engaged in this manœuvre, the

second cutter of the Rosalie, with Mr. Greene in charge, dashed up to the schooner, and a dozen of her crew leaped on board.

" You are too late, Mr. Greene," said the second lieutenant. " The prize is ours."

" I am glad to hear it," replied the third lieutenant. " We began to be troubled about you when we heard the firing above. What was it all about ? "

" We are all right," replied Mr. Jackson, who felt that he had saved his credit by the capture of the schooner ; " that is, most of us are. The first cutter had a shot go through her, and we have lost Mr. Somers, missing, and one man killed, and one wounded."

" Somers missing ! " exclaimed Mr. Greene. " That's bad news."

" I have strong hopes that he is all right. I am pretty well satisfied that he was not killed, and we may pick him up in the course of the day. I dread to tell the captain of this part of our mishap."

" I was sent out to assist you as soon as we heard the firing ; but when I found the steamer was coming down, I went on board to report, and was then ordered to make sure she did not run by us in the fog," continued Mr. Greene.

" I will go on board and report with the second cutter," said Mr. Jackson ; " for I hope the captain will move the vessel up, and look after the company of artillery which I think is stationed up the sound. You must keep your weather eye open, Mr. Greene, for I should not be surprised if an attempt was made to recapture this schooner."

" I have not a gun to defend her, if the steamer should return with the artillery company."

" You shall hear from me before she can do that," replied Mr. Jackson, as he went over the side into the second cutter.

" Ah, Mr. Jackson," said the captain, as the second lieutenant reported on board the Rosalie, " I began to be very much alarmed about you when I heard the firing."

" We were somewhat alarmed about ourselves, sir, at one time ; and I regret to report the loss of one officer missing, one man killed, and one wounded."

" One officer missing, Mr. Jackson ! " exclaimed the captain.

" It is hardly necessary for me to add that it is Mr. Somers ; but I hope for the best in regard to him."

Mr. Jackson briefly reported the events which had occurred during his absence, concluding with the capture of the cotton schooner, and suggesting that she was in danger of being retaken by the rebels. The wind and the tide would permit the Rosalie to be moved up the sound, though she was powerless to chase a steamer in the opposite direction. Orders were immediately given to slip and buoy the cable, and in a few moments she was moving up the bay.

"What became of the contraband who gave you your information?" asked Captain Waldron, when the vessel was under way.

"He disappeared, I hardly know when. I heard the dug-out's paddle a moment before the shot was fired. I presume he made the best of his way from the danger, but in what direction, I don't know."

"Perhaps Mr. Somers was picked up by this contraband," suggested the captain.

"That is utterly impossible, sir," replied the lieutenant, shaking his head.

"Why impossible?"

"Because, if Mr. Somers had got into the dug-out, he would immediately have made his way to our relief, for he knew that the boat had a hole knocked in her side. He is not a man to look out for himself when his comrades are in danger."

"You are right, Mr. Jackson," said the captain, sadly.

After considerable difficulty in the fog and darkness, the Rosalie was moored near the blockade-runner. in readiness to repel any attack which might be made by the rebels.

CHAPTER XX.

SOMERS KEEPS HIS EARS WIDE OPEN AGAIN.

HEN the cannon shot struck the first cutter, Somers realized, as soon as any other person in the boat, that the expedition must prove to be a failure. He heard the water pouring in at the fractured side, and there was nothing to think of at that tremendous moment but the safety of the officers and crew. As we have before shown, our middy was not deficient in self-possession; and the question of what should be done came to his mind with all the force which such an event could require.

It so happened that he had noticed the position of the dug-out only a moment before the catastrophe occurred. The contraband, apparently frightened out of his wits, when the shot struck the boat, was paddling away from the spot as fast as he could; and when Somers looked for it, it was just disappearing in the dense fog. There was only an instant for reflection; and before the full extent of the mischief was known, Somers had leaped into the water, and was swimming with all his might towards the retreating skiff.

There would have been but a slight chance of over-taking it, if the contraband, attracted by his voice, had not suspended his labors, and waited for him to come up. The water was smooth, and Somers made good time ; but the negro did not offer to shorten the distance between them by paddling towards him.

" Why don't you pull up to the boat and help save the men ? " demanded Somers, incensed at the stupid course of the negro.

" Golly ! dis chile's afeerd he be shot by de cannon balls," replied the contraband, as he helped Somers into the boat.

" Paddle over to the boat as fast as you can," said Somers, fiercely, as he sat down on the bottom of the dug-out, out of breath from the violence of his exertions.

The contraband raised his paddle, as if he intended to comply with this reasonable demand ; but instead of applying the implement to its legitimate use, he sprang towards his exhausted passenger, and brought it down with tremendous force upon the top of his head. Somers sank back in the boat, unconscious of what followed. The boatman, having accomplished this treacherous deed, paddled up the creek a short distance to escape the flying shots, and then made for the shore, along which he rowed till his boat reached the steamer.

Probably the wretch believed he had killed his victim ; for without devoting any further attention to him, he fastened the boat, and stepped upon the deck. He passed half a dozen persons, but he did not stop till he had reached the bow, where he found the man of whom he had been in search.

"Now's your time !" said the black man. "You haven't a moment to spare."

"Where is the boat?"

"Smashed by a shot, and one half her crew killed."

"Are you sure of that?"

"Am I sure of it? I saw it with my own eyes," answered the black man. "I picked up one of them."

"But the firing must have alarmed the people on board of the schooner below," replied the cautious captain of the steamer — for he was the person who spoke.

"What of that? She will depend upon her own boat, which has just been smashed, to head you off, and will not get out another. Turn your wheels before it is too late."

"Well, I will make the attempt," said the captain.

The black man returned to the dug-out, jumped in, and paddled round the steamer to a point of land on which the guns were posted. Somers still lay perfectly quiet, and his captor seemed to be of the opinion that he never would move again, for he stepped on shore and walked up to an officer who stood in the rear of the guns. Somers was worth half a dozen dead men. The blow he had received was given with the flat of the paddle; and though it produced very great confusion of ideas, — indeed, a total suspension of all ideas for a time, — it was far from a fatal one. He had begun to have a tolerably clear idea that he was still in the land of the living, when the black man went on shore; and before he had been gone fifteen minutes, he was quite certain that he was not dead.

Having fully established this fact to his own satisfaction, he very naturally turned his attention to the circumstances which surrounded him. He first heard, then saw, the steamer, with the schooner in tow, moving away from the landing. He could not prevent her from going; and this fact filled him with regret. He was thankful to God that his life had been twice spared within an hour, and how much shorter time he knew not.

Somers sat in the boat a few moments, thinking over the events which had just happened. Some of the poor fellows who had been in the boat with him had " lost the number of their mess," and the others were in imminent danger of being captured by the rebels while in their helpless condition, if such an event had not already happened. Again his heart glowed with gratitude to God for his own preservation.

With this thought — and not only this thought, but this feeling — present in his mind and heart, he rose from his recumbent posture in the bottom of the boat. The guns on the shore had ceased firing, but he could hcar the voices of persons on the point of land. It was evident to him that he had been expected to lie still a much longer time than had actually been the case, for there appeared to be no person in charge of him. Taking advantage of this fact, he cast off the painter of the dug-out, and pushed her off a little way from the shore.

Unfortunately for him, as he then thought, the rising tide forced the boat back to the shore. He was in the act of repeating the operation, when he heard voices close by him. Hoping the last push would send the boat far enough from the land to permit him to use the paddle without exposing himself, he again lay down in the bottom of the dug-out. The voices of the men came nearer, and he did not deem it prudent to show himself.

" Now, Biggs, you have told me what I ought to do, and I want to know what you have done," said one of the persons on shore, in a voice which sounded strangely familiar to our middy.

" I told you I had smashed the boat, and killed half the crew. More than that, I have taken one prisoner; and I suppose he is dead by this time."

" Why dead? "

" Because I was obliged, in order to keep him quiet, to knock his brains out with the paddle."

" He won't miss them," replied the first speaker, facetiously, whose tones had already caused the heart of Somers to beat wildly with wonder.

He listened with the most intense eagerness — not to hear what the speaker said, but to compare the sound of his voice with the familiar one which he recalled. He could not believe the evidence of his senses, and he rejected the conclusion to which he was tending, as an illusion of his own imagination.

"If you had taken the guns on board the steamer, Mr. Kennedy — "

Somers could hear no more, for that name confirmed what he had rejected as utterly and absurdly impossible. Mr. Kennedy! This was the name by which Biggs had called him; and this evidence, added to that of the tones of his voice, left him no margin to doubt that one of the parties on the shore was Mr. Phil Kennedy. This gentleman had certainly been committed to Fort Lafayette before he left New York; and he was, within four weeks of that time, doing rebel work on the coast of Georgia. It was strange and unaccountable, and nothing but the most positive evidence would have justified him in believing what was now undoubtedly a fact.

" I tell you my orders would not permit me to take the guns on board of the steamer," replied Mr. Phil. Kennedy, in the same impatient tone which the listener had so often heard before. "Besides, I didn't believe in it myself."

" It is the most amazingly stupid plan I ever heard of. You might have put your guns on board, and blowed the schooner all to pieces, if she had given you any trouble," replied Biggs, highly excited by what he deemed the mismanagement of affairs on the sound.

" You have a right to your opinion, Biggs, and you can be as blind as you please. What sort of a chance should I have against the Rosalie, with her rifled fifty-pounder, and her four twenty-fours. I tell you I will capture the schooner, and go on a cruise in her within two weeks."

" Perhaps you. will," thought Somers.

" I have done all that has been done so far."

" Pray, what have you done, Biggs?"

" I have got that schooner out to-night, for one thing."

" If I had been near enough at the time, I should have prevented her from getting under way."

" I dare say you would," sneered Biggs.

" She will be captured, and the steamer with her, very likely."

" What was I sent out in that dug-out for?" demanded Biggs.

" To give you a little more practice in nigger talk," laughed Kennedy.

" Then I made a blunder, and did the enemy more damage than you will in six months."

" What damage have you done?"

" I put your guns in the way of killing half that boat's crew by luring them in shore."

20 *

" That was a chance shot which hit the boat. It looks
to me just as though you brought it in there to enable
her to capture the steamer and the schooner. If we hit
the boat, it was an accident, for we could not see or hear
the first thing to aim at. I don't think much of your
strategy, Biggs."

And he was doomed to think still less of it, when the
steamer returned with intelligence of the schooner's capture. Mr. Phil Kennedy and Mr. Biggs continued to
argue the point for some time longer; and Somers
listened, as he had done at Newport, with the most
intense interest. It was remarkable that he should find
himself overhearing Kennedy's plots and plans a second
time, though it was not half so remarkable as that Kennedy should be there, when he ought to have been a close
prisoner in Fort Lafayette.

From all that he heard, and all that followed as a
matter of course, Somers derived some valuable information, which may be summed up in briefer terms than
the conversation from which it was deduced. Biggs was
the black man, — a counterfeit contraband, — who, relying
on the Yankee's faith in the negro, had lured the boat
within range of the guns on the point. This fact our
middy could have argued out without any direct statement to that effect.

Mr. Phil Kennedy was there to assist in running
sundry schooners through the blockade; but the great

object he had in view was the capture of the Rosalie, iu which he intended to go on a cruise under the Confederate flag. Much to Somers's disappointment, he did not indicate the means by which he intended to accomplish this job ; and the listener was inclined to agree with the critical Mr. Biggs, that he never would do it.

" There comes the steamer ! " exclaimed Kennedy, when he had wrung all the information out of the counterfeit contraband which that clever actor contained, or would impart.

" Then she is not captured," replied Biggs, trium phantly.

" No ; but she has not had time to tow the schooner even down to the Chimney Spit, much less over the bars."

" I don't think she has, but she can speak for herself," replied Biggs, disgusted with this unpleasant conclusion.

" I'll bet you my year's pay she has lost the schooner."

" No, she hasn't ; she is towing her back, as she did before. The captain of that steamer hasn't pluck enough to look an alligator baby out of countenance."

" He is a prudent man, and I presume he has obeyed my orders."

" Very likely," sneered Biggs. " But I must look after my prisoner ; he may come to life."

" Who is he ? " asked Kennedy, carelessly.

" I don't know ; but I reckon he's an officer," replied Biggs, as he walked towards the boat in which Somers lay.

CHAPTER XXI.

SOMERS UNDER GUARD.

THE critical moment in Mr. Midshipman Somers's affairs appeared to have arrived. He had kept very quiet in the boat, hoping that something would occur to call Biggs and his dangerous companion away from the spot, and enable him to move to a place of safety. The return of the steamer promised at one time to afford him this relief. The noise of her escape-pipe could be heard at no great distance, but the prudence of Mr. Biggs was likely to defeat his expectation.

His captor was approaching the boat; indeed, he was on the point of stepping into it, and it was "now or never" with Mr. Somers, for the presence of Mr. Phil Kennedy complicated his affairs in this quarter. As he lay in the bottom of the boat, he had considered what chances he had to make a forward movement. He had a revolver in his belt, but it was embedded in his wet clothes, and he had some doubts about its present fitness for use. The paddle was in the boat, just where Biggs had left it, and Somers had one hand on the implement while he listened to the remarks of the gentlemen on shore.

Having arrived at the conclusion that the paddle was a more reliable instrument, for the present, than the pistol, he clung to it, and stood ready to use it when the critical moment should arrive. It had come now ; and when Mr. Biggs was on the point of putting his foot into the dug-out, he rose, and, with a couple of energetic strokes with the paddle, propelled the clumsy craft out into the fog and darkness.

Half a dozen pistol shots were promptly discharged at him ; but Somers was careful enough to lie down in his boat, as soon as he had escaped from the first and more immediate peril. The balls whistled over his head ; and again he had good reason to thank God for his preservation. Not deeming it safe to use the paddle yet, lest the noise of it should inform his enemies where he was, and thus bring another volley of pistol balls down upon him, he lay still in the dug-out. He was cool and self-possessed enough to do this ; if he had not been, in all probability his life would have paid the penalty of his nervousness.

" Your prisoner is gone ! " said Phil Kennedy, whose derisive tones were distinctly heard by Somers.

" He won't go far. I will have him again," replied Biggs.

" Perhaps you will. Did you say he was an officer ? "

" I did — a midshipman, I think."

" A midshipman? "

" I think he was. He appeared to be on excellent terms with the officer in command of the boat."

" Did you hear his name? " asked Kennedy, with more interest than he had before manifested in his companion's prisoner.

" I did not."

" There is a midshipman on board of that steamer whom I want very much. He and I have an old account that must be settled," continued Mr. Phil Kennedy ; and he was evidently the " nable ossifer " alluded to by the contraband, who appeared to have told more truth than the nature of his business required.

" You have got a grudge against him — have you? "

" I have. I lost the Snowden by his operations ; but that isn't the worst thing I have against him."

" What's the other? "

" Never mind the other ; it is a private matter. But why don't you take care of your prisoner, if you intend to recapture him? "

" There's time enough. I have no boat now, but the steamer will be here in a moment more."

She was now within a few rods of the place where the dug-out lay, and Somers found it necessary to change his position, to avoid being run down by her. But he was too much interested in the movements of his friends on shore to move a great distance, especially as the fog and darkness effectually concealed him from the view of the rebels. The steamer moved slowly up to the point : she had a man on her forward deck who constantly reported the soundings, as she felt her way through the fog. She had returned without the schooner, which gave Somers a hope and a fear — a hope that the Rosalie had captured the cotton vessel, and a fear that she had escaped and gone to sea.

" Hallo !" shouted Kennedy from the shore. " Where's the schooner ? "

" We lost her," replied some person at the bow of the steamer.

" What do you mean ? Did you get aground ? "

" No ; the Yanks boarded her, and we had to cut away from her," replied the captain of the steamer ; for he was the person who answered the question.

" Glory, Hallelujah ! " exclaimed Somers, in an emphatic whisper, as he listened to the volley of oaths which came from the shore.

" She is two miles from the man-of-war ; and if you will put your men and guns on board, we can take her again, with the boat's crew in charge of her."

The steamer now touched the bank, and the conversation between the captain and the men on shore was so low that Somers could not hear it ; but he waited with the most intense interest for further developments. Success had crowned the operations of the Rosalie, in spite of the destruction of the first cutter. It was plain that Captain Waldron and his officers had been wide awake; but our middy was disgusted with the idea that the rebels might recapture the schooner.

Somers was suffering from a severe headache, produced by the blow he had received; but while he lay in the dug-out, what he heard made him feel, with uncommon force, that he was an officer of the United States navy, and that he had no right to think of his own aches and pains, when there was an opportunity to serve the cause in which he had enlisted. He was but a few rods from the steamer, and in great peril of being captured when the search should be made for him. Yet he could not leave what he regarded as a very interesting and promising field of labor.

Further developments soon convinced him that the advice of the captain of the steamer was to be adopted; and he soon heard the orders given for taking on board the guns, and the soldiers or sailors — whatever they were — who manned them. In the excitement of the hour he hoped that Biggs would forget his prisoner, or that the exigencies of the moment would not permit him to make the expected search.

The steamer lay within a few rods of him; and he cautiously paddled the dug-out to a position near her stern, that he might obtain a better idea of the preparations for the capture of the schooner. The men were running out planks upon which to roll the guns on deck. Everybody seemed to be in earnest, and he could plainly hear the voice of Phil Kennedy, as he delivered his orders from the deck. Somers trembled for the safety of the prize, and wished his own feeble hands could be multiplied a hundred, or even ten fold, that he might be enabled to defeat the purposes of the rebels.

To obtain a nearer view of the operations, he rowed the dug-out up to the stern, where he discovered the steamer's boat, which had been towed behind her in readiness for immediate use, if occasion should require. Somers was a thoughtful young man, and he considered that anything which could be serviceable to the rebels would, in the same proportion, be injurious to the loyal cause. With this thought in his mind, he cast off the boat's painter, and pushed it out into the gloom, where the tide presently took it in charge, and started it off on a cruise up the sound or up the creek. Our middy had hardly carried out this suggestion before he heard persons approaching the stern.

" Are your oars in the boat?" demanded one of them, in the familiar tones of Biggs.

" Yes, sir ; all ready," replied one of his companions.

Somers pushed his dug-out away from the steamer, and lay as still as a mouse, under cover of the fog and gloom.

" Where is the boat?" continued Biggs.

" Made fast to the stern, sir," replied the other.

21

" Where ? "

But the man could give him no further information. The boat was not there, and Biggs was so angry that he indulged in some big words, which were neither pretty nor polite.

" All right, my dear fellow ! " said Somers to himself, as pleasantly as his aching head would permit.

He was safe for the present, at least ; for there was no other boat, as he had heard Biggs acknowledge ; besides, that worthy must have felt that he had delayed the pursuit so long as to render it almost hopeless. Somers felt secure in his present situation, and would have felt so even if there had been a boat to pursue him, for the fog and darkness were his best friends that side of the Rosalie.

Biggs swore, and ordered the men with him to search for the boat. They did so, but of course they could not find it. While the party were thus engaged, Somers heard the voice of Phil Kennedy at the stern of the steamer.

" The boat is gone," said the discomfited Mr. Biggs.

" Gone ! " exclaimed Kennedy. " We can't go without a boat."

" You don't want a boat to capture the schooner. You will get two or three when you take her."

" Very true ; but suppose we fail. Suppose a shot from a boat howitzer should plump into the engine of the steamer and disable her. What should we do then? No, sir; I have no idea of being a prisoner of the Yankees, if we fail."

" You are very prudent, Mr. Kennedy."

" It is fortunate that I am. You have lost one schooner for me to-night by your rashness, and I can't afford to lose myself. My boat lies on the other side of the point."

" I didn't know you had one," answered Biggs.

" If you had known it, probably I should not have had one by this time; it would have been added to your contributions to the Yankees. Take Wythe with you; he knows where it is. She pulls four oars."

" Good! I shall catch that Yankee yet."

" Perhaps you will."

" We can pull four miles to his one in the dug-out."

" The fog is in his favor."

" He will paddle with all his might down the sound, and we shall find him, you may depend upon it.'

Biggs, confident as ever, hastened away to carry out his purpose, leaving Somers to meditate upon his beclouded prospects. Of course it would not be safe for him to move down the bay, for the four-oar boat would soon overhaul him. It would be better to pull to the other side of the creek, and go on shore; but the banks of the sound, he had reason to believe, were occupied by rebels, whose business it was to watch the Rosalie, and report her movements to the blockade-runners above.

The steamer which Mr. Phil Kennedy employed to assist him in getting the cotton vessels to sea, was an ordinary river boat. Her guards, as is usual in these craft, extended over the water nearly the whole length of her. Somers knew all about these river steamers; and while he was considering his proper course under the trying emergency, it occurred to him that he might save a deal of hard paddling against wind and tide by permitting the rebel steamer to tow him down to the scene of action. She was high enough out of water to permit him to run the dug-out under her guard.

This suggestion of his inventive genius, daring as it was, he promptly adopted. Passing the painter through one of the braces, far enough aft to avoid destruction by the water from the surging wheels, and far enough forward to conceal the dug-out from the observation of any on board, he hauled her under the guard.

" Now I am under guard," said he to himself, facetiously, " aud I am perfectly safe."

After washing his aching head in cold water again, he lay down in the bottom of the dug-out to await the next move of his anxious friends on board. The operation of transferring the guns from the shore to the steamer was a difficult oue, on account of the depth of the mud on the land; and it began to be light in the morning before she was ready to move off. Somers saw nothing of the boat in which Biggs was to pursue the dug-out;

and he concluded that she had gone down the sound upon this errand.

The steamer backed out from the shore, and commenced her third trip in the direction of the Rosalie. As soon as the boat began to move, Somers found his situation very uncomfortable. As the steamer came about, she heeled over so far that the dug-out barely escaped being swamped, as the sinking guard forced her deep down into the water. The alarmed occupant grasped the painter, in readiness to let go; but as the steamer righted up in a moment, he decided to hold on for a time longer. While she went on an even keel he did very well, though his position was by no means a comfortable one. Unpleasant as it was, he remembered that he had a mission to perform; and he soon forgot the perils of his situation in the consideration of an exciting question.

21 *

CHAPTER XXII.

SOMERS MEETS WITH AN ACCIDENT.

SOMERS had been seeing, hearing, and inferring what the rebels intended to do; and the most important information he had obtained was, that they purposed to recapture the schooner, now in possession of a boat's crew from the Rosalie. On board of the steamer were at least two guns, and not less than twenty men. The man-of-war was two miles below the cotton vessel, and out of supporting distance.

The fear that the rebels would recapture the prize was very trying to Somers. He was not aware of the fact that the Rosalie had run up the sound, and lay within a few fathoms of the schooner. The force on the steamer was equal, if not superior, to that in charge of the prize; and he saw no reason why the rebels, with tolerably good management, should not accomplish their purpose. It was his duty to prevent so undesirable an occurrence, if possible; and the important question which he was engaged in considering was, whether he could do anything to defeat the rebels, either in whole or in part.

He was a single man against an armed host; therefore he could not fight under present circumstances. But the little mouse gnawed away the net that confined the majestic lion; and Somers looked about him for some means by which he might disable the steamer. If he could get at the engine, the removal of a bolt or a pin might render it useless; but it would be fatal to expose himself on the deck.

As he lay in the dug-out, he heard the creaking of the ropes and chains by which the rudder was connected to the wheel on the hurricane deck. They were within reach of his hand, and he immediately commenced an examination of them. If he could break this rope or chain, the steamer would at once become unmanageable, at least for a time. But the connections were all of iron near his locality, and it was impossible to sever them. He pursued his investigations as far as he could; but the steamboat law requiring iron " tiller ropes " had been complied with, so far as he could discover.

The steamer was rapidly approaching the cotton vessel, and if anything was to be accomplished, there was no time to be lost. Somers was nervous and uneasy, made so by his desire to do something to defeat the intentions of the rebels. Letting out the painter of his boat, he followed the rudder-chains aft, in the hope of finding a point where he could break the connection, but without success.

There was yet another practicable expedient, which afforded him some hope of stopping the course of the steamer. He tried to "jam" the chain where it passed through a bracket; but in this, also, he failed. If he could follow the chain farther, it was still possible that he might find a weak place, where it could be separated; but the rapid motion of the steamer prevented him from doing this, for if he cast off the painter, the dug-out would go adrift in spite of him.

While he was mourning over his weakness and inability to do the work he had resolved to do, the wheels of the steamer stopped. Without pausing to consider the object of the stoppage, he cast off the painter, and handed the dug-out round to the stern of the steamer. Here he found a ring, through which he passed the painter, and, without losing a second of his valuable time, he proceeded to make a further examination of the chain. To his great satisfaction, he found a place, near the rudder, where the chain had been "toggled;" that is, one link had been passed through another, and secured with an iron bolt. When the chain was slack, he pulled out the bolt, and the two ends dropped down into the water.

Having performed this work, he felt that his mission was finished, and that the steamer could go no farther down the sound. Having no other business to transact with the rebels, he concluded to push off, especially as it was now nearly daylight, and make the best of his way down to the cotton schooner, which could not be far off.

" I have done it," said he to himself, as he pulled the painter through the ring, and shoved off the dug-out from the steamer. "Your pipe is out for the present, Mr. Phil Kennedy."

The dug-out shot off into the fog ; and Mr. Somers, almost stunned by the noise of the escaping steam, of which the engineer relieved the boilers when the boat stopped, did not hear certain sounds which would have warned him of approaching danger.   Indeed, he was too well satisfied with himself, after the important job he had done, to think of anything except the fact that he had defeated another of Mr. Phil Kennedy's enterprising schemes.   As the dug-out darted away from the steamer, Mr. Somers's ideas were suddenly thrown into confusion by an unexpected crash.   Some object, moving rapidly through the water, had struck his frail craft on the broadside.   It was borne under, and our middy was " spilled into the drink."

But Somers immediately rescued his ideas from the confusion into which they had been thrown, and without stopping to consider how the catastrophe had happened, he struck out for the steamer, which was not three fathoms distant from him.

The crash had been caused by the four-oar boat, in which Biggs had been in search of the dug-out and his prisoner. The steamer had stopped to permit him to come on board, for he had given up all hope of recovering the prize he had lost. Just as Somers backed out from the stern of the steamer, the four-oar boat was rounding in under her quarter. It was still very foggy, and there was not light enough to enable Mr. Biggs at once to decide what had happened. He was looking at the steamer as he rounded in under her stern; and the men, sitting with their backs to the bow, had not seen the dug-out.

"What's that?" demanded Biggs, with an oath, as he grasped the gunwale to recover his balance; for the collision had given the larger boat a very sensible shock.

"A boat, sir," replied the bowman.

By this time Somers was perched on one of the braces under the guard of the steamer, engaged in relieving his throat and nasal organs of an uncomfortable quantity of salt water, which the suddenness of the accident had surprised him into swallowing.

"It's the dug-out, sir," added another of the men, whose eyes were better than those of his companion.

"Was there any one in her?" demanded Mr. Biggs.

"I think I heard a man swimming and puffing in the water," said Wythe, who pulled the stroke oar.

"We have blundered on him then. He can't be far off," added Biggs, with no little excitement at the prospect of recapturing his prisoner.

The blood of Somers ran cold in his veins at the imminent danger of his position. He could hardly escape being taken now, and handed over to Mr. Phil Kennedy, whose inveterate hatred would subject him to every discomfort, if not to death itself. He trembled with apprehension as he saw, at one glance, the fate that impended. There was hardly the shadow of a hope left; but he climbed in as far as he could under the guard, and wedged himself under a brace.

The boat pulled up to the steamer's stern, on which the captain and Phil Kennedy were now standing. Biggs was awfully in earnest, and he commenced a vigorous search for his prisoner. In answer to a question from Kennedy, he stated what had happened, and his own conviction that the Yankee was on board of the steamer. But Mr. Biggs could not find his prisoner. He searched under the guard and over the guard; but the middy's compact form was too closely stowed away to be seen in the darkness.

" He has swum ashore," said the captain.

" I don't believe it," replied Biggs.

" Of course he has, or you would have found him before now. Come on board, Biggs; we shall have the whole of them in a few days," said Phil Kennedy.

" I know he is about here somewhere," added the confident Biggs.

" Come on board, Biggs; we can't stop here all day.

We have something better to do," continued Kennedy, impatiently.

" I know he must be under the guard; send me a lantern, captain, and I will soon find him."

" Nonsense, Biggs ; I tell you he isn't there. He has swum ashore before this time. Come here," added Kennedy, in a tone so low that Somers could not hear him.

" I'll bet my life he is here," answered the obdurate contraband, that was ; but he stepped on board the steamer, as Kennedy had requested.

The two talked together for a few moments, during which the naval officer occasionally pointed to the boat. Biggs seemed to understand him, and to acquiesce in his decision ; for the men were ordered on board, and the painter made fast.

Somers could hardly believe his senses ; and, still shivering with cold and with apprehension, he audibly whispered his prayer of thanksgiving that he had again been preserved from capture. But he had lost the dug-out, and he had no means of reaching the captured schooner when the steamer abandoned her purpose, as he believed she would. The prospect was not as encouraging as it had been ; yet he had the consolation of knowing that he had delayed, if not prevented by the delay, the recapture of the Rosalie's prize. Then it occurred to him that the boat in which Biggs had been searching for him was at the stern of the steamer ; and he decided to get into it as soon as practicable, and bid a final adieu to his dangerous locality.

He heard the bell ring for the engine to start; and it did start. The wheels began to turn, and Somers was nearly drowned by the surging waters which they heaped upon him. Presently he heard the rudder chain rattling above him; then the bells were rung to stop and back her; and it was evident that the helmsman had discovered the mischief which had been done.

" Now's my time!" thought Somers; and he began to move from brace to brace aft.

It was not his time yet, and he soon discovered his mistake; for men were sent to the stern to repair the damage done to the rudder chain. The precise nature of the mischief was soon ascertained; but it required nearly an hour to overhaul the chain, and "toggle" it again. It was now broad daylight, though the fog was as dense as ever. Somers crawled as far aft as he dared. He saw the boat which he coveted, and had arranged the method by which he intended to get into her at the proper moment.

The steamer started again; but Somers was vexed to find that she was still headed down the sound — that the delay had not induced Kennedy to abandon his purpose. She continued on her course for a few minutes, and then stopped again. Our middy felt that he had done all he could for his country, and that it was time to do some-

22

thing for himself. He had delayed the steamer, and it was possible that this delay had favored his friends, though in what manner he was unable to tell.

He felt that the present was his own; and as soon as the wheels ceased to turn, he worked his way aft, and seizing the painter of the boat, drew it up so that he could jump into it. He then tried to unfasten the painter where it was attached to the boat; but finding this impossible, he stood up in the bow, and reached over the transom of the steamer to untie it at the ring.

At that moment, a man, who had been lying on the deck, sprang forward, and seizing the venturesome middy by the collar of his coat, jerked him on the deck, as he would have whipped a codfish from the water.

" I've got you, my little Yank!" exclaimed the burly fellow who had done this unkind act for him.

" Have you got him?" shouted Biggs, who had stationed himself near the stern, apparently for the purpose of witnessing the performance which had just taken place.

" Yes, sir," replied the man.

" Tell the captain to go ahead again," said Biggs, hastening aft to witness the discomfiture of his troublesome prisoner. " Hold on tight, Wythe!"

There was no need of this latter caution, for Wythe held our unfortunate middy in a grip of iron; and it was utterly impossible for him to make any resistance.

" How does your head feel, my little fellow?" de

manded Biggs, in mocking tones. "I thought I struck heavy enough; but I declare you have got the thickest skull, even for a Yankee, that ever I saw."

Somers made no reply. He was very much out of spirits, and did not feel a bit like giving or taking a joke. Biggs ordered Wythe to tie him hand and foot, and make him fast to a stanchion, which was done in the most faithful manner.

CHAPTER XXIII.

A SHOT FROM THE ROSALIE.

SOMERS had fallen into a snare which had been set for him. Mr. Biggs had not for one moment abandoned his hope of recovering his prisoner. The conversation which had taken place between him and Kennedy, and which was in so low a tone that the intended victim could not hear it, was the one thing needful to enable Somers to keep out of the hands of his enemy.

When Biggs went on board of the steamer, Kennedy had suggested to him that the Yankee would make his way into the boat and cast off at the first favorable opportunity. It was only necessary to watch the boat, and the game, if there was any game there, could be quietly bagged in a few minutes. Biggs assented to the plan, and the boat started; but the broken steering apparatus had produced a long detention, and Somers gave himself up for lost half a dozen times, when the men who were overhauling the chain came within a few feet of his perch on the brace.

When the steamer started, the man had been placed on the deck so that he could not be seen, to watch him and the boat. As Somers did not hurry out from his concealment, it was believed that the motion of the boat prevented his operations ; and she was stopped for a moment, to afford him an opportunity to be caught. Unfortunately for him, he had improved this opportunity, though it was his last chance of escape, and had been captured. He was now a prisoner, and bound hard and fast to a stanchion. The worst fate, in his own opinion, that could possibly befall him, had overtaken him. He was not only a prisoner, which was certainly appalling enough as the rebels treated their prisoners, but he was in the power of Phil Kennedy.

The clouds hung dark and black over him. His personal misfortune was not the only nor even the worst side of the picture ; for if he had succeeded in saving the cotton schooner from capture, he would have been compensated, in a great measure, for the mishap of being captured. But even this comfort was denied him ; for the rebel steamer, with two guns and a squad of trained artillerists, was hastening down to undo what the Rosalie's people had done. It was useless to fret, and he tried to make the best of the circumstances which surrounded him ; but it was hard work, with his aching head and disappointed heart, to submit cheerfully to his destiny.

Somers thought over the matter for a time, and his

22 *

sublime philosophy soon got the better of his vexation. It was useless to repine ; it would not improve his condition, and therefore he wisely determined not to repine. He had done the best he could, both for his country and himself, and unavailing regrets did not tend to promote his comfort nor his happiness.

The steamer must now be very near to the captured schooner, and the great event of the morning must soon take place. It was evident to the prisoner that he must soon be joined by some of his shipmates, who were to be captured ; but he did not look forward with any satisfaction to the meeting. If he could have blown up the boat on which he was confined, he would have been content to go to the bottom in her, if he could thereby have saved his friends in the Rosalie from capture, and prevented the rebels from recovering the cotton vessel. Somers indulged this reflection ; but we are forced to believe that it was a sentimental idea, and that, when he came to a decision, he would have chosen to remain above water.

While he was deliberating upon his unpleasant prospects, and was passing from the depths of despondency to the sublime heights of philosophical submission, he heard the voice of Mr. Biggs, as he walked aft. That gentleman had made several blunders during the night ; he had given the advice which had caused the capture of the schooner ; he had criticised the naval officer's policy ;

and it was no little satisfaction for him to be able to exhibit even a single Yankee prisoner, especially as that one was an officer. He was disposed to make some display of his prowess, and he was now conducting Mr. Phil Kennedy aft to show him his prize.

" If your prisoner has not escaped again, you have done one thing to-night, Biggs," laughed Kennedy, as they approached the place where Somers was tied to the stanchion.

" That's more than you can show for your night's work," growled Biggs, who, by this time, had washed off most of the burnt cork which had transformed him into a contraband.

" You are sharp, Biggs. What is the rank of your prisoner? "

" A midshipman ; but he is a smart fellow, and if we had half a dozen like him in the Confederate navy, we should have done something before this time."

" Thank you ! " thought Somers, who could not help acknowledging this handsome compliment.

" No doubt of it ; half a dozen men with your ideas would have ruined the Confederate States before this time. Where is your prisoner? "

" Here he is," replied Biggs, as he walked up to the stanchion with a lantern in his hand, which he held up so that the naval officer could see our middy.

" Ah, my dear Mr. Somers ! " exclaimed Kennedy, as he recognized the features of the prisoner.

It was plain that the meeting was entirely unexpected to him, for he started back, at first, in the utmost astonishment.

"No doubt you are better pleased to see me than I am to see you," replied Somers, pleasantly, for he knew how much satisfaction it would give Kennedy to see him despondent and depressed.

"Well, my dear fellow, I am exceedingly rejoiced to meet you; and if you are not glad to see me, of course that is not my fault. Circumstances have slightly changed since we met last," continued the traitor.

"Accidents will happen," replied Somers, coolly.

"Then I was your prisoner. Now you are mine."

"Mine, if you please," interposed Biggs, unwilling to be deprived of his hard-earned honors.

"Well, it's all the same. As your prisoner is a particular friend of mine, a young gentleman to whom I have taken a great liking, I am going to ask you, as a special favor, to turn him over to me. I want to use him."

"Certainly, lieutenant — with the greatest pleasure."

"Mr. Somers, I can't help commending my friend, Mr. Biggs, for his ability, when I consider that he has captured Miss Portington's prodigy. He is smart, Mr. Somers."

"I recommend him to join the first band of negro minstrels he can find, for he has a very decided talent in that direction," said Somers.

" Good !" added Kennedy. " You are as witty as ever."

" Thank you, Mr. Kennedy. That reminds me that your wits have served you better on this than on a former occasion, which you will readily recall. I think I left you locked up in Fort Lafayette."

" You did, my dear Somers ; but of course you did not expect me to remain there any great length of time."

" How did you get out?" asked Somers, who was burning with curiosity to know how he happened to be in Georgia at that particular time, though he did not very confidently expect an answer.

" I walked out, my sympathizing friend."

" I didn't know but the traitors there were ashamed of you, and kicked you out," answered Somers, with an unpardonable want of politeness.

" Excellent, Somers. Miss Kate Portington would have given you a crown of roses for that brilliant remark."

" Schooner in sight, sir," said an officer, who had been sent aft to inform Kennedy of the fact.

" I must leave you for a time, my dear Somers," said the rebel naval officer, in mocking tones. " When I have captured your ship's prize, I will do myself the honor to meet you again."

" Thank you, sir."

Somers was glad to have him go, not only because he disliked the man, after what had happened, but because he felt vexed at the idea of a rebel success, and he was afraid he might betray his feelings. As soon as Kennedy had gone forward, where the guns were placed, the steamer " slowed down," and cautiously approached her expected victim. Somers was disturbed by the most painful emotions ; for he felt that he was doomed to be a spectator to one of the navy's reverses, which had been so few and far between, that our gallant tars have not become at all accustomed to them, and have not learned to look upon them with anything like toleration.

Everybody was busy forward, now, either in watching the progress of the exciting event, or in making preparations for it. Somers could catch an occasional glimpse of the cotton steamer, just visible in the dense fog, as he gazed eagerly through the vista of men, guns, and machinery which lay between him and the vessel. He could now see that Kennedy's force were sailors, and that there were as many as thirty of them. There seemed to be no chance for the people of the Rosalie, in charge of the schooner, to make a successful resistance, and with a sinking heart Somers saw that the steamer was bearing down upon her prey, already — as the rebels viewed it — within her grasp.

Suddenly, however, a change came over the spirit of their dreams ; for, as the steamer advanced, the graceful outline of the Rosalie was discovered, moored a short distance from the cotton vessel. This was more than

they had bargained for, and more than they were prepared to meet; and the rebels were at once filled with
consternation.

"Hard-a-port the helm!" shouted Kennedy, with
energy.

"What's the matter now?" demanded Biggs.

"Don't you see that man-of-war?" said Kennedy,
nervously.

"Are you going off without giving or taking a shot?"
added Biggs, in disgust.

But this valiant gentleman was not to be entirely disappointed; for, as the steamer swung round, the thunder
of the Rosalie's big gun broke on the quiet of the dark
morning, and the shot crushed through the upper works
of the boat. At the same moment, and while the pine
wood was still cracking around him, Somers found himself lying flat on the deck, with the stanchion still clinging to him; but he was quite certain that he had not
been killed.

The shot had struck the steamer just abaft the port
paddle-box, and passed diagonally through her upper
works. It had torn away a portion of the cabin floor,
striking the stanchion to which Somers had been fastened,
and as it had fallen, the prisoner went down with it.
When he had satisfied himself that he was not killed, or
even materially injured, the truth dawned upon him that
the Rosalie had moved up the bay, and was in position to
defend her prize.

" Hail, Columbia ! " shouted Somers, as the gratifying fact became evident to his understanding.

As the rebels had received a shot, though they had not given one, Mr. Biggs was probably satisfied ; at any rate, the crashing of pine boards prevented him from making any further suggestions to the naval officer, and he walked aft to ascertain the extent of the damage, possibly in search of a safer place than the open deck afforded. The exclamation of his prisoner caught his ear, and he saw that the stanchion had been shot away. From prudential or other motives he went forward again, to call Wythe's attention to the matter, instead of examining into it himself.

Somers could not help thinking that the shot had been a godsend to him, and he used his best endeavors to shake off the stanchion, which still clung to him ; but, as his feet, as well as his hands, were tied, he met with but indifferent success. While he was wriggling and twisting to disengage himself from his encumbrance, another shot struck the steamer, and smashed through her upper works. Unfortunately for him, the machinery of the boat was not struck, and she still sped on her way from her dangerous situation.

While the prisoner was still exercising his inventive genius over the stanchion, Wythe came aft, and relieved him from all further exertion by removing the broken stanchion, and making him fast to another. The hope,

which Somers had cherished, of escaping during the confusion, was lost to him, and he submitted, with the best
grace he could command, to whatever doom his foes had
in store for him. Shot after shot from the heavy gun of
the Rosalie followed the retreating steamer; but as she
was now under the protecting mantle of the fog, she was
not hit again, and continued on her way up the sound.
This time she did not stop at the point of land where the
guns had been posted, but proceeded up one of the rivers,
where the shallow water would not permit the formidable
man-of-war to follow her. At a safe point, she was
moored to a tree on the bank.

While Somers was carefully watching the movements
of the steamer, Wythe came aft, unloosed him, and conducted him to the cabin above the main deck, where he
found Kennedy seated at a table.

23

CHAPTER XXIV.

IN THE CABIN OF THE VIOLA.

ENNEDY, disappointed by the failure of the expedition down the bay, was morose and even savage; but he knew the humor of his prisoner well enough to understand that any exhibition of ill nature on his part would subject him to a storm of taunts and sarcasms which were more unwholesome to him than even the screaming of shells and the hissing of cannon shot. There was on his face an expression of triumph, as he glanced at Somers — an expression which boded no good to the unfortunate young man.

" My dear Mr. Somers," Kennedy began, intent upon making the captivity of his prisoner as bitter as possible, " I am at liberty now to bestow further attention upon you."

" Thank you," replied Somers, with a low bow.

" You are in my power now," added Kennedy, as his compressed lips indicated an intention to use his advantage.

" I am; and my hands are tied behind me, so that

you need not fear to say and do anything which your amiable nature may suggest."

The lieutenant bit his lips, for he did not like the imputation on his courage which the remark conveyed. He was tempted to fly into a passion ; but he feared that his prisoner would keep cool, and sting him with his tongue beyond what he could endure.

"You are my prisoner, Mr. Somers," he repeated. "You have eluded my grasp several times before ; but I have you sure, now."

"There can be no possible doubt of the fact, Mr. Kennedy. I have no intention of denying or refuting your position. I await your pleasure."

"You carry a very bold face upon the matter. I think you don't quite understand your situation," sneered Kennedy.

"Perfectly."

"I think not. The circumstances under which you were captured justify me in regarding you, not as a prisoner of war, but as a spy."

"Anything you please, Mr. Kennedy," replied Somers, with apparent indifference ; but it is useless to deny that he was appalled at the announcement.

"The court-martial which · I have summoned will make all that plain to you."

"I am ready for anything that may come, while I am in your power," said Somers.

" Have you no favor to ask of an old friend?"

" None."

" I wish to save you, Mr. Somers, from the consequences of your own folly."

" Then of course you will do so."

" I cannot do so without some acknowledgment on your part."

" Of what?"

" Of the error of your ways."

" I am not conscious of any errors, such as you indicate. I have done my duty to my country as well as I could," replied Somers, firmly.

" That's all nonsense," said Kennedy, impatiently. " We will not talk politics. You have upset all my calculations several times."

" That was your fault, not mine. You should not have engaged in such calculations."

" You need not give me any good advice. I don't propose to hear it."

" I think it would be wasted if I did."

" You have been a stumbling-block in my path since the first time I saw you. You are aware that you have crossed me in that wherein no man will brook any interference. Before I left Newport I found myself less welcome at the house of Commodore Portington than before you went there."

" And I fancy that you will be still less welcome

whenever you go there again," added Somers, very impudently.

"Very likely. You own your guilt, and seem to pride yourself in it."

"I own no guilt. I refer wholly to your treasonable conduct. Miss Portington — for I will not affect to misunderstand you, Mr. Kennedy — will never smile upon a traitor to his country."

"You use hard terms, Mr. Somers, and wrong ones. I am a native of Maryland. I go with the South; and I am as true to her as you are to the North. There is a difference of opinion between us; and it would be wiser and safer for you, sir, not to use hard words when milder ones will suit the case better," replied Kennedy, his brow darkening with anger.

"Miss Portington is also a native of Maryland; but she sticks to her colors."

"Simply because her father does; but we will not discuss that question, for it has nothing to do with either of us at present. By some means, best known to yourself, you caused Miss Portington to dislike me. Of course you used your tongue to my prejudice."

"I never uttered a syllable to her in disparagement of you or any other person," replied Somers, warmly. "On the contrary, I had a very high regard for you until your treasonable practices opened my eyes; and I always expressed myself so to her, and to others. Since

23 *

that I have never spoken to her of you in any other than respectful terms."

" Your apology is well drawn up," sneered Kennedy.

" I make no apology. I only wished to say that I never presumed to look upon Miss Portington as anything but a friend. I never made any pretensions in that direction."

" Are you willing to promise me that you will never see her again?"

" No!"

" Consider your situation, Mr. Somers," said Kennedy, in mocking tones. " You are in my power, charged with being a spy."

" If you are afraid of me, in your Newport relations — "

" Nothing of the sort," replied the lieutenant, proudly. " I wish you to confess for your own sake, not mine."

" I shall not do it, either for your sake or mine. All I have to say about Miss Portington is, that you have ruined all your hopes with her, if you ever had any. The Snowden affair was quite enough to satisfy her, I presume."

" By the way, Mr. Somers, you managed that affair very well."

" I didn't manage it at all. It managed itself."

" You put Coles in the fort, and brought poor Tubbs to grief."

" My agency in those affairs was very small. Mr. Tubbs exposed himself."

" Exactly so ; Mr. Tubbs was a fool, and that is the reason why I employed him. Coles was no fool, and you used him up, and finally you brought me to the ring."

Somers tried to fathom the purpose of his inquisitor. It was evident that he had some object to gain, for he could not be making all these mortifying acknowledgments for nothing.

" Nothing of this kind could have happened, if you and your friends had not been engaged in a bad speculation," replied Somers.

" More good advice. I suppose you think that those who do their duty, as you understand it, never come to grief," sneered Kennedy.

" The fact that I am here now shows that I don't believe any such thing. Misfortunes overtake all men ; but those who are faithful to duty have the courage to endure them."

" That's a pious thought. I suppose you think you have the courage to endure whatever comes of this affair."

" I trust in God, and intend to do my duty. If it is his will that I should suffer, I will be as firm as I can."

" We shall see about that pretty soon, for the rope by which you will hang is waiting you now."

" Hang ! " exclaimed Somers, startled by the word.

" Certainly ; that is what you will come to within a few hours, unless you are less haughty than you have been yet," replied Kennedy.

" Do you hang your prisoners ? " demanded Somers, — a cold chill creeping through his veins as he considered how probable such a fate was in the hands of so inveterate a foe.

" Spies are hung on both sides, as you are aware. In few words, Mr. Somers, you have been in my camp, and on board my steamer, listening to all we said, counting our guns and men, and doing us what mischief you could while in our midst. This morning you untoggled the tiller chains of the Viola, and prevented me from capturing the schooner. This I call being a spy; for you conducted all your operations within my lines."

" But I was captured by one of your men — by Mr. Biggs," replied Somers, discouraged by the appalling array of facts which his persecutor alleged against him ; not that they would, before any fair tribunal, convict him as a spy, but because he knew that his enemy was malicious enough to draw any conclusion from these facts.

" I grant it."

" Mr. Biggs left me for dead in the dug-out."

" But you were not dead ; and instead of making your escape, as you could have done, you went on board of the steamer ; you went into your enemy's premises. If you had escaped when it was in your power, and then been recaptured, you could not have been held as a spy."

Somers was forced to acknowledge that there was an appearance of justice in the conclusion of Kennedy, and he already felt the rope of the hangman pressing against his neck. If his implacable foe wanted to hang him, there was no difficulty in procuring the charge, and the testimony upon which the deed could be perpetrated.

" You understand the matter, I perceive, Mr. Somers," said Kennedy, when the prisoner relapsed into silence, and contemplated the disgraceful death to which he had already been doomed, in advance of a court-martial's decision.

" I do, sir," replied Somers, in a sad and subdued tone; " if you choose to hang me, you can do so. I have no power to prevent it."

" You will perceive that your conduct justly entitles us to regard you as a spy; and as my operations here permit of no delay, I have summoned a court-martial to sit upon your case forthwith."

" Then you are determined to sacrifice me?"

" On the contrary, I desire to save you."

" Mr. Kennedy, if you have any proposition to make to me, I beg you to make it at once," said Somers, disgusted with the conduct of the inquisitor. " I will not deny that I don't wish to be hung."

" You are beginning to be quite sensible, Mr. Somers.

I have no proposition to make.   If you have any, I am willing to hear it."

Kennedy was too proud to offer terms; they must be proposed by Somers.   Our middy was perplexed.   Life was sweet to him, and he was completely in the power of the villain, who had plainly announced his intention to hang him as a spy, without even consulting his supe· rior.   It was possible that Kennedy was only trying to frighten him into something — what, he did not know; but he determined to find out, if he could.

" Shall I pledge myself never to see Miss Portington again ? " asked he.

" Yes; that would be a decent reparation for the wrong you have done me," replied Kennedy, with appar- ent indifference.

" Shall I beg your pardon for causing the capture of the Snowden and the Theban, and for bringing Mr. Coles and Mr. Tubbs to justice ? "

" That would do no good; you can do better than that," added Kennedy, with a smile, as though he had at last come to a result.

" What can I do ? "

" You can inform me where you obtained your infor- mation in regard to the Snowden."

" Truly, I can inform you," answered Somers, musing.

" Very good, Mr. Somers; if you agree to these two things — "

" What two things ? "

" Never to see Miss Portington again, and to tell me where you obtained your information in regard to the Snowden and the other vessel. If you will agree to these two things, I will promise to use my utmost endeavors to save your life."

" I will consider the matter," replied Somers, thoughtfully. "I see no objection to telling you where I got my information. It can harm no one now."

" I wish to know who the traitor was that betrayed me ; thus shifting the responsibility from you to him."

" You will not have to go a great way to find him."

" Who was he ? "

" It was you, yourself."

" Are you trifling with me ? " said Kennedy, sternly.

" I speak the truth. How long will you give me to consider the terms ? " asked Somers.

" While I eat my breakfast."

" What will be done with me in case I accept the terms ? "

" Your life will be spared, and you will be sent to Savannah as a prisoner of war."

" I will think of it."

" Take your prisoner down to the main deck again," added Kennedy, after he had called in Wythe, who had been sent out of the cabin at the beginning of the interview.

Somers had already decided not to accept the degrading and humiliating terms; at least not till the sham court-martial had convicted him. He had never made any pretensions in respect to Kate Portington; but the idea of being pledged never to see her again was so repulsive that he could not entertain the thought. He had no right to do so, he felt; for even if he did not wish to see her, she might wish to see him; and if such a bargain was to be made, she ought to be a party to it.

We are disposed to believe that Somers intended to decline the arrangement because he did not think Phil Kennedy would dare to execute his infernal threat — because he thought the whole thing was a plot to humbug and deceive him.

While he was still considering the matter, Wythe came for him again.

CHAPTER XXV.

THE COURT-MARTIAL AND ITS SENTENCE.

ELL, Mr. Somers, what is your decision?" asked Kennedy, as he was again ushered into the cabin. "Have you concluded to accept the terms?"

"I have concluded not to accept them," replied Somers, firmly.

Kennedy looked disconcerted and angry. It was some time before he spoke.

"Why so?" he demanded. "I thought you had concluded to do so before we parted."

"No, sir."

"You saw no objection to informing me where you obtained your information."

"I see none now."

"Then the other point is the one to which you object?"

"It is."

"You say you have no pretensions."

"None, Mr. Kennedy; but if ever I am near Miss

24

Portington again, I want the right to caution her against one who would make her the victim of a heartless speculation."

Undoubtedly this declaration was a very impudent one ; and if Mr. Kennedy had not before made up his mind to hang his victim, this would have been sufficient to induce him to carry out his barbarous threat. Somers did not believe that his captors, in the face of public sentiment and the recognized laws of war, would have the hardihood to perpetrate such an atrocious crime. It must be confessed, in the light of previous and subsequent revelations, that he failed to understand and appreciate the diabolical spirit of the rebellion.

Kennedy's stock of patience was exhausted, and he could no longer express himself in the assumed tones of politeness which he had before labored to use. He was angry and morose ; and the dark scowl on his brow was a witness of the darker purpose which brooded in his soul.

" Mr. Somers, you beard the lion in his den. I will waste no more words upon you," replied he, furiously ; and he sent the servants to summon certain officers whom he named.

" I think it my duty to say exactly what I mean," replied Somers.

The officers who had been sent for presently appeared. The number included Biggs and the captain of the steamer, neither of whom was competent to sit on a court-martial. Two naval officers, apparently masters or midshipmen, completed the quorum, aud the trial proceeded at once. The charges were written out in due form, and there was an appearance of fairness used, though the whole proceeding was simply a pretext to sacrifice the life of the prisoner. Fifteen minutes completed the business of the session; and Somers, after a consultation of fifteen minutes more, was sentenced to be hung as a spy forthwith.

By this time the prisoner had come to a painful realization of the fact that his enemies were in earnest. Hé was doomed to an ignominious death, and the sentence was to be immediately executed. He was taken to the main deck again by Wythe, who acted as master-at-arms. Over the hatchway a cord had been suspended from a deck beam above, and a board placed over the aperture, on which the culprit was to stand.

Somers saw these preparations, and the blood seemed to be frozen in his veins. He felt that he was about to die — that he was on the threshold of eternity. It was a solemn and awful thought, though he had often contemplated the possibility, and even the probability, on the eve of battle, of passing away from the scenes of earth. But now, it was more real than ever before; for there, before him, was the rope, and there the drop from which he was to be ushered into the world beyond the grave.

" Are you all ready, Wythe?" demanded Kennedy.

" All ready, sir," replied the master-at-arms.

" Then bring forward your prisoner."

Somers was conducted to the hatchway. He was conscious that he was still a living being—that his brain was still active ; but his body seemed to be detached from the thinking and feeling part of him. Everything looked misty and confused to him.

" Adjust the rope," said Kennedy, mechanically, for he seemed to be hardly less moved than his victim.

The command was obeyed ; but even Wythe's hand trembled as he placed the knot under the ear of the prisoner. Everything contributed to assure Somers that the rebels were in earnest—that it was no farce in which they were engaged. Even his executioner trembled, which would not have been the case if he had been engaged in an attempt to deceive him. There was no hope, and Somers breathed his silent prayer to God in that awful hour that his sins might be forgiven ; that the loved ones at home might be happy when he was gone ; and that his death might not be in vain, but be an acceptable sacrifice to the holy cause to which he had devoted himself.

His prayer gave him hope and strength ; his body and his brain seemed to be reunited ; and he looked his murderers full in the face. He was determined to die like a man and a Christian, and to permit his enemies to derive no strength from his weakness.

" Are you ready, Mr. Somers?" asked Kennedy, in tones so full of emotion as to betray his terror to his companions.

" I am," replied Somers, calmly and gently as one who can almost see the glories of the invisible world.

" Have you nothing to say?"

" Nothing."

" No message to leave?"

" None that I can intrust to you. You would defile it."

" Proceed, Wythe!" said Kennedy, fiercely; for the words of the victim roused anew the hatred which the solemn event had for the moment softened.

Somers was led out upon the board over the hatchway, which was so placed that it could be easily slipped, and thus precipitate the prisoner into the hold.

" If you ever say prayers, say them now, for you have but a moment left," said Kennedy, in sneering tones.

Somers prayed as he had never prayed before, for God was nearer to him, and he was speaking in the presence of the Infinite.

" Again I ask you, Mr. Somers, if you have anything to say, or any message to leave. If you can speak without insulting me, I assure you your last request shall be fulfilled," said Kennedy, again mollified by the awful circumstances of the hour.

" I thank you, Mr. Kennedy, and I forgive you for

24 *

the murder which you are committing. If you ever meet any friend of mine, say that I died like a Christain," replied Somers.

" Do you still adhere to your determination — "

As Kennedy reached this point in the sentence, a twenty-four pound shot struck in the upper works of the steamer, making terrible havoc among boards and beams, and sending confusion into the midst of the group that gathered around the victim of the intended murder. The cabin floor above them was torn away for the space of ten feet, and the wreck dropped down upon the heads of the men, who were completely absorbed in the barbarous scene which was transpiring there.

The first shot was followed by a second, whose effects were hardly less destructive. The beam to which the hangman's cord had been attached was shivered, but it still hung in its place, and Somers's situation was not improved by the event. The shots produced a panic among the rebels, and all eyes were turned from the prisoner in the direction from which the shots had come. Right over the bow of the steamer they saw two of the Rosalie's boats, each of which had a howitzer mounted in the fore-sheets.

" Give way, my lads!" shouted Mr. Jackson, who was in command of the expedition. " Lay 'em aboard!"

The cutters' crews bent on their oars, and the boats struck the bow of the rebel craft at the same instant.

Tom Longstone was in the bow of one, and in spite of his years, he leaped on the deck like a cat, followed by the boarding party. The other boat poured her men upon the deck at the same instant.

The rebels, who had been so intent upon the barbarous spectacle at the hatchway that they had neglected to keep a lookout on the bow and stern, were completely paralyzed by the suddenness of the onslaught. As the crews of the boats boarded the steamer over the bow, they fled to the stern, and leaped into the water, or made their way to the shore as best they could, leaving the assailants in complete possession of the steamer.

The attention of the rebels had been instantly withdrawn from Somers when the first shot struck the steamer. They had not a thought for him now ; and, as the men from the boats leaped up, they fled as though the avenging angel were already at their heels. Their guilty consciences gave wings to their flight, and there was no chance for the boarders to strike a single blow.

Tom Longstone was the first man to put his feet on the deck of the Viola. As he rushed forward, he discovered Somers, still standing on the board over the hatchway. He recognized him at a glance, and saw the rope extending from his neck to the broken beam above.

" My blessed ! " exclaimed he, in trembling tones, as he sprang out upon the board, and grasping the cord in one hand, he severed it with his cutlass.

Throwing the weapon on the deck, he placed his brawny arms around the middy, and raising him as though he had been a baby, he bore him over the bending board to the firm planking of the main deck.

" My blessed boy ! " exclaimed he, bursting into tears, as he pressed him to his beating heart. " What have they been doing to you? "

Tom Longstone stammered out the words, and then sobbed like a child. He was completely overcome, and for a moment he gave vent to emotions which were too strong for utterance.

" Thank you, Tom," said Somers, in a gentle tone, hardly above a whisper ; and the tears coursed down his cheeks almost as freely as down the weather-stained face of the boatswain.

The officers and crew stood in silence, but with hearts swelling with emotion, while Tom held his young friend. There was no enemy for them to strike, and they were chained to the spot by the affecting scene.

" The — the — infernal — villains ! " gasped Tom, struggling with his feelings, which would hardly permit him to utter a word.

" Be calm, Tom ; I am safe now," said Somers, in the soft tones of one who had just come from the embrace of death, and whose soul had been sanctified by his communion with his God, and with the great destroyer of man.

"Calm? Would the cutthroats hang you?" roared Tom, as he detached himself from the embrace of the middy, and seizing his cutlass, brandished it with a desperation which fired the souls of the crew.

They shouted in unison with him, breathing vengeance upon the wretches who had meditated so heinous a crime. The officers came forward and grasped the hand of Somers. They congratulated him on his miraculous escape ; but their words were few, for their mission was not yet accomplished. Mr. Jackson gave his orders in a spirited tone, and the men dashed on shore in pursuit of the flying foe.

A few of them were captured, but only a few, for the rebels had every advantage over their pursuers. They knew the country, and they had a choice of the paths, which, in that swampy region, was equivalent to a victory. Unfortunately, none of the officers were taken. It was well for them that they were not, for their lives would have paid the penalty of their barbarous conduct, and it was difficult for the officers to prevent the men from wreaking their vengeance upon the few who did fall into their hands.

The expedition, which had thus fortunately saved the life of Somers, had been organized as soon as the Viola turned her bow up the sound. It had gone up Tea-kettle Creek, choosing this course because the battery had been planted at the mouth of it, apparently to defend its waters from an approach in that direction. From the creek they had heard the noise of escaping steam, which guided them to their prey. By a cut-off they had reached Mud River, above the Viola. The dense fog protected them from discovery, and as soon as the boats came within sight of the steamer, Mr. Jackson gave the order for each to fire a single shot, and then board, in the confusion which a couple of twenty-four pound balls would be likely to create.

The Viola was not a valuable prize, for there was little on board of her except the two howitzers and the ammunition. Upon examination it was found that the second shot had passed through one of her wheels, and twisted it so that it could not be made to turn. Under these circumstances the two guns were transferred to the boats, and she was set on fire.

At meridian the boats reached the Rosalie, and Mr. Somers reported himself to the executive officer.

CHAPTER XXVI.

SOMERS was received on board the Rosalie as one who had come from the jaws of death. He told his story, which was listened to with breathless eagerness; for the perils through which he had passed won for him an attentive audience. He was highly commended for his fidelity in attempting to stop the steamer, and in obtaining information which would be valuable to the loyal cause.

"You probably saved the cotton schooner from being recaptured, Mr. Somers," said the captain, when he had finished his story; "if you had not delayed the steamer, the Rosalie would not have been near the prize."

"I am very glad, then, that I did not work for nothing," replied Somers. "I wanted to do something, and if I failed it was not because I did not try."

"You have done exceedingly well, Mr. Somers; and in my report of this affair, I shall take pleasure in mentioning your name."

"Thank you, sir," added Somers, touching his cap.

At the close of the interview, Somers went down to the steerage, and being alone, thought over the events of the morning. He had been nearer to death's embrace than ever before; and, from the depths of his grateful heart, he poured forth his thanksgiving to Him who had saved his life in that trying hour.

He could not help feeling that he had done something worth telling to Kate, and he wrote quite a long letter, detailing the events we have narrated; but he deemed it best to suppress the name of Phil Kennedy. She must some time know that he was little better than a fiend — that he was a rebel of the darkest dye; but he preferred that some other person than himself should give her the information. In the letter he confined himself strictly to the events which had occurred during the Rosalie's stay at Doboy Sound, and hardly introduced a personal allusion.

In the afternoon the fog cleared off, and the Rosalie went down to her former anchorage. Thompson was sent up to Port Royal as prize-master of the captured schooner, taking with him the prisoners and the mail. For a week the officers and crew were doomed to another quiet time. If there were any more schooners up the sound, as the counterfeit contraband had declared, they did not deem it safe to come out; for the Rosalie had proved herself to be a faithful sentinel at the mouth of the inlet.

Mr. Phil Kennedy had not yet done " a big thing" for

the Southern Confederacy in helping along the cotton loan ; nor had he yet secured a suitable vessel in which to make a cruise at sea. This seemed to be a favorite aspiration with him, and Somers had already reported to the captain his intention to capture the Rosalie, and make her the bearer of his fortunes on the broad ocean.

Shortly after the departure of. Thompson in the cotton schooner, a supply steamer came on the station, and with other good things, left a mail and a quantity of newspapers. Somers had several letters from home ; and while he was below, reading the news from Pinchbrook, which included the promotion and furlough of his brother Tom, the captain sent for him.

" Mr. Somers, the mystery is solved," said Captain Waldron.

" What mystery, sir?" asked Somers, somewhat surprised at the announcement.

" In regard to Mr. Phil Kennedy. The newspapers give us full particulars. It seems that General Portington died of the illness we heard of, and Kennedy was paroled to allow him to attend the funeral of his foster-father. He did attend it, but instead of returning to. New York, he went south."

" He is bad enough to do that, though he pretends to be a gentleman, and to value his honor as the apple of his eye," added Somers. " But it is rather singular that he should turn up just where we happen to be."

" Not very singular. The sending of a blockader here created the necessity for some action on the part of the rebels, and Kennedy, happening to report about the time we came, was sent here ; but he hasn't done them much good," laughed the captain.

"He means to capture this vessel. Perhaps that is what he is down here for."

" Perhaps it is ; but if he keeps on as he has begun, he will not get her very soon. He has lost two vessels now, instead of capturing one."

" I think he intends to make the attempt."

"I hope he will ; and the sooner the better," replied the captain, confidently.

" Did you see anything in the papers about General Portington's will, sir ? "

" Not a word ; but I presume Kennedy has been neglected ; for if half the fortune had been left to him, he would hardly have gone south — at least not before he had come into possession of his inheritance."

Somers returned to the mess-room to finish the reading of his letters, and to muse upon what the captain had told him. Mr. Phil Kennedy certainly did not improve on further acquaintance ; and, for his own part, he desired nothing better than to forget him. Events were not calculated to enable him to do this ; for that very night, our middy and the only personal enemy he had in the world were doomed to meet again, face to face, on the deck of the Rosalie.

It was early in the evening; eight bells had just struck, and the first watch piped on deck, when the lookout reported a steamer, apparently loaded with cotton, approaching the schooner. She was at least double the size of the Viola, which had been burned, and as she was a river steamer, it could not be supposed that she intended to go to sea.

The Rosalie immediately beat to quarters, and the captain leaped into the fore-rigging to examine the approaching monster; for such she was, with the cotton bales piled up to her hurricane deck. There were no guns to be seen, nor any men, for that matter, as even the wheel-house was encased in bales of cotton.

Captain Waldron looked very anxious when he came down from the fore-rigging, for the steamer was no blockade-runner, and the sad experience of our vessels in Galveston Bay was a sufficient warning to him, as well as an explanation of the character of the approaching steamer.

" She is a cotton-clad," said he to the first lieutenant. " She has come down to capture our vessel."

" So I perceive," replied Mr. Layard.

" Open upon her with the rifled gun," added the captain. " Aim low, and knock a hole in her hull if you can."

The fire was instantly opened from the pivot gun amidships; but the present contingency seemed to have been provided for by the rebels, for the shot appeared to have no serious effect upon her. The cotton monster continued on her course apparently unharmed, headed directly towards the Rosalie. There were still no signs of any guns.

' "Your friend, Phil Kennedy, has come at last," said the captain, as Somers passed him in the discharge of his duty.

"Yes, sir. I suppose he is on board that craft," replied Somers.

The captain watched the cotton-clad with an anxiety which he could not wholly conceal, especially after the pivot gun had been discharged several times without arresting her course. There was hardly a breath of wind, or he would have slipped his moorings, which would have enabled him to make choice of his own position, even if he could not run away from the dangerous craft. The Rosalie had kept a spring on her cable, while at anchor, to enable her to swing round, if necessary, so as to bring her broadside guns to bear on any passing vessel.

By the aid of this device, she was able to work two broadside guns as well as the pivot. But all her efforts with shot and shell were failures, and the monster was within speaking distance of the Rosalie, now apparently doomed to certain capture. The cotton-clad came up, bow on, and stopped her wheels at the distance of thirty or forty fathoms from her intended victim. If she was provided with guns, the present was the time to use them; but she was still as silent as though she were on a peaceful errand.

"Pipe below, Mr. Layard!" said the captain, suddenly. "All hands below!"

This remarkable order was promptly executed, and even the officers were ordered down upon the berth deck.

"There is only one way to fight that fellow," said Captain Waldron.

A volley of least a hundred muskets presently explained the wisdom of the captain's order, and proved that he had rightly comprehended the tactics of the enemy. The balls were heard rattling on the deck above, but not a man was injured. The captain's precaution had saved a fearful havoc among his officers and men. The volley was repeated several times, but there was not a soul on the deck of the Rosalie to be injured by the fire.

By this time the rebels probably concluded that they had killed half the crew of the schooner, and her wheels were started again.

"Stand by your cutlasses, my lads," said the captain. "They are going to board us."

"Ay, ay, sir!" responded the ready tars.

The cotton-clad came up with her head on the port bow of the Rosalie. No doubt the rebels were surprised, when they came near enough to overlook the deck, to find

25 *

it deserted.   Probably they were filled with exultation when they realized the fact, for they began to pour in like bees over the bow of the schooner.

" Repel boarders ! " shouted the captain ; and all hands sprang to the deck, and rushed upon the over-confident assailants.

" Down with them," shouted Somers, always among the foremost in such a scene.

No formidable resistance had been expected by the rebels, and Mr. Phil Kennedy was in the front rank of the boarding party.   Somers saw him, and rushed at him with his cutlass.   Kennedy discharged a pistol at him, but it failed, and he stood his ground with the sword for a moment, when, finding his impetuous foe was too much for him, he retreated.   His example was followed by the rest of the rebels, though most of them had fought with skill and energy.

" Lay 'em aboard ! " shouted the intrepid Mr. Layard, as he pressed the retreating rebels ou board the cotton-clad.

" Ay, ay, sir ! " roared the excited seamen, as they followed close upon the heels of their brave lieutenant.

But the rebels had all retired from the deck of the Rosalie, and the riflemen behind the cotton bales poured a volley into the daring sailors who were driving the boarders back.   Mr. Layard fell, and the captain ordered the men back.   They obeyed, bearing the wounded officer

On the Deck of the Rosalie.   Page 294.

with them. He was conveyed to his state-room, and breathed his last before the surgeon could find his wound.

The plan of the rebels was evidently a safe one, for they intended to remain behind their cotton bales, and shoot down every man who showed himself above the deck. Already half a dozen of the Rosalie's crew were killed or wounded. They had retired to the berth deck again, and the rebels had learned by experience that it was not prudent to board her. Behind the cotton, where no harm could reach them, they continued to fire into the hatch of the schooner; but the men had been so placed that no more of them suffered from the fire.

The cotton-clad still hugged the Rosalie, turning her wheels just enough to keep her in position. It looked like a "dead lock," and each party was impatiently waiting for the other to make the next move. If the schooner's people would only appear on deck, the rebels could shoot them down without exposing themselves to harm. If the steamer's people would only board, the brave tars of the Rosalie felt able to whip them, in whatever numbers they might appear, for then the riflemen could not fire without killing their own men.

The cotton-clad had at least double the number of men belonging to the Rosalie; and Kennedy, who commanded her, perhaps ashamed of his own timidity, ordered another assault. The boarding party was permitted to advance as far as the main hatch, when a dozen men rushed up the companion-way from the ward-room, and discharged the two swivels, which had been loaded with grape during the first onslaught.

The remainder of the men followed, and with stunning cheers rushed on the rebels, who had been terribly cut up by the grape from the swivels. They broke and fled to the shelter of the cotton bales again, while the captain instantly ordered his crew below, before another volley from the riflemen should be delivered.

CHAPTER XXVII.

AN ENTERPRISE WHICH ENDS IN AN EXPLOSION.

THE situation of the Rosalie, if not absolutely alarming, was calculated to excite a reasonable doubt in the minds of her officers in regard to the final result. It was in the highest degree galling to a man of Captain Waldron's temperament to be driven below, and be held in abeyance there, by his powerful enemy; but the safety of his officers and crew, and consequently of his vessel, depended on his prudence as well as his bravery.

For two hours the two vessels remained in the same relative positions, each waiting for the other to make the next move. In the mean time a breeze from the southeast had sprung up; but the Rosalie's crew, confined below, were unable to take advantage of it. If Captain Waldron was impatient under the perilous circumstances which surrounded him, the enemy were even more so; for they had come down the bay with the confident assurance of a speedy victory. Behind the cotton bales they could shoot down every man who offered any resistance, and in a short time compel the vessel to surrender. If Captain Waldron had insisted on fighting his ship according to the traditions of the navy, Mr. Phil Kennedy's calculations would have been correct, and he might have gone to sea in the Rosalie without any provoking delay.

Two hours were a long time to wait in the presence of death or capture ; and when Captain Waldron heard the fresh breeze piping merrily through the rigging of his vessel, he chafed still more under the restraint which prudence imposed upon him ; but there appeared to be no hope of immediate relief, unless the wind increased to a gale, and thus rendered the unwieldy cotton-clad unmanageable. It was quite certain that the wind was increasing in force, but it might be hours before it amounted to a gale.

The wind, though it did not blow hard enough to endanger the cotton-clad, now produced a change in the position of the vessels. The monster lying athwart the channel was no longer able to keep her head up to the bow of the Rosalie, for the vast pile of cotton exposed an immense surface to be acted upon by the freshening breeze, and she was compelled to retire for a time, in order to bring her bows up to the wind. Her movement was instantly perceived on board the Rosalie.

" Pipe all hands on deck, Mr. Jackson," said the captain, promptly, when the cotton-clad had retreated a short distance. "Slip the cable, and make sail in, stantly."

The acting first lieutenant obeyed the order; and the officers and crew, animated by a new hope, performed their duty with even more than usual alacrity. Before the steamer could assume her intended position, the Rosalie, close-hauled, was standing across the sound. The crew were beat to quarters, and she opened on the enemy again with everything that could be brought to bear, yet without any visible effect upon her mailed opponent.

"Ready, about!" shouted the first lieutenant, when she had gone as far as it was safe to go on the "short leg" of the tack.

Round came the schooner; but pressing forward with all her speed, the steamer immediately intercepted her, and poured a murderous volley upon her decks. Among those who fell was Mr. Brown, the sailing-master, now acting as third lieutenant. He was borne to his cabin, and the Rosalie sped on her way, out of gun-shot reach of the steamer. But on the long tack she ran a few fathoms too far, and, as if to crown the misfortunes of the night, she struck on the Chimney Spit, and was hard and fast aground.

This unhappy event promised to be fatal to the poor Rosalie, and the men looked aghast at each other. But the captain did not lose his presence of mind. The cotton-clad was standing on her course down the bay to intercept the schooner as she came up on the long tack. The useless sails were now furled, and nothing but the steadiness of the officers saved the men from despondency. As long as the leaders are firm, and have a voice, the seamen will never give up the ship.

The captain and his remaining officers could not conceal from themselves, if they could from the men, the fact that the situation of the ship was utterly desperate. Mr. Layard was dead, Mr. Brown was severely wounded, and ten of the crew had been killed or disabled. The cotton-clad would soon be down upon the disabled schooner, and her capture, so far as human wisdom could discern the future, was only a question of a few hours, more or less.

Under these desperate circumstances, therefore, the captain summoned a council of the officers. They met in hurried conference on the quarter-deck; but as fate seemed already to have fastened its seal on the ship, there was little that could be said. Mr. Jackson proposed to board the steamer, as a last resort; Mr. Greene was in favor of taking shelter below, and repelling any attack, hoping for a change in the circumstances.

"What do you say, Mr. Somers?" said the captain to our middy, who was now, by virtue of his rank, the acting third lieutenant.

"If you will give me two men and six kegs of powder, I will make an attempt to disable the steamer," replied Somers, who proceeded, without waiting to hear the comments of the officers, to detail the plan he had conceived.

Although the scheme did not look like a very hopeful one, the zeal and determination of the young officer did much to recommend it. He was familiar with the construction of these river steamers, and had had some experience with cotton-clads on the Suwanee River. As a desperate venture it was adopted, and Somers was ordered to select his companions for the perilous enterprise.

"Tom Longstone and the gunner's mate," he promptly replied. "I will take the dingy, and I recommend that the first and second cutters be in readiness for immediate service."

"With howitzers?" asked Mr. Jackson.

"No, sir; the men will need only their pistols, pikes, and cutlasses."

"Don't be rash, Mr. Somers," added the captain. "I would not tolerate the enterprise if our situation were only a little less desperate."

"I will be prudent, sir; but I assure you, I had rather be blown up at the post of duty, than be hung by the fiend who commands that steamer, for that will be my fate if we are captured."

"God be with you, Mr. Somers!" ejaculated the captain, fervently. "Remember that we have the boats

26

left, and can run for the shore if the worst comes ; so don': be rash."

By this time the gunner's mate had the powder for the enterprise on deck, and it was hurriedly transferred to the dingy, which Tom Longstone had hauled up to the gangway. It was not yet time to put the plan into execution ; and, as the cotton-clad was now approaching, having suspected the cause of the schooner's detention, all the crew were sent below, to escape the deadly fire of her riflemen. She drew but little water, compared with the Rosalie, and she swept round upon the spit, so as to bring her head to the wind, placing herself directly to leeward of her intended prize. Her bow overlapped that of the schooner, so that her men, concealed among the cotton bales, could fire down upon the deck of the Rosalie.

This time she carried her audacity a point farther, and made fast to the fore-chains of the schooner. It was quite dark, and nothing but the motions of the devoted tars could betray their presence to the enemy. Mr. Jackson stood in the shadow of the mainmast, while the captain was concealed behind the companion-hatch, on the quarter-deck, in readiness to summon the men when they should be needed to repel an attack.

Somers, with the acting boatswain and gunner, was in the dingy, waiting for the favorable moment to commence his desperate enterprise. The gunner was preparing the kegs of powder for use, agreeably to the directions of the officer.

" Well, my darling, are you going to send us all to heaven to-night?" asked Tom Longstone, in a whisper, as he glanced at the ominous powder kegs.

" I am going to do my duty to God and my country; and I cannot answer for the result to ourselves individually," replied Somers, cheerfully.

" Go ahead, my dear! I'm with you, ready to go up or down, which ever way the powder may send us."

" You and I have been engaged in an affair like this before, Tom."

" Yes, and you were shot in the leg, and left on shore."

" I intend to do better this time."

" I hope you will, my love. If you go up, I hope I shall go up with you."

" I hope none of us will go up. Now work the dingy along the side of the ship, but don't make a particle of noise."

The eyes of the rebels were too intently fixed on the deck of the Rosalie to see anything that transpired in the water. The dingy was concealed by the vessel from their sight till it passed the cutwater; and then the enemy were too far behind their breastwork to obtain a sight of it, even if they had been on the watch.

Tom Longstone, guided by Somers's directions, shoved

the little boat under the guard of the steamer, and continued to work it along by her side till he reached a point on the opposite quarter, where the young officer began to search for a favorable place to operate. The rebels were all over on the side next to the Rosalie, not expecting any danger from the opposite direction. They were straining their eyes to see a man, and their ears to hear a sound, which would enable them to reduce the number of their foes by even a single one.

The cotton on the steamer was piled up to a level with the hurricane deck. The riflemen were on the top, and fired over the breastwork. The dingy had to go forward of the wheels before any aperture could be found which would admit the six kegs of powder. Just forward of the paddle-box, a space about eighteen inches in width had been left, so that any water which the steamer might take on board would run off.

Through this hole Somers could see the engineers, and others connected with the boat; but they were busily engaged in watching the progress of events on the other side. The gunner then placed his powder so that the whole mass should explode at once, and he managed his part of the work so carefully that no hint of his movements was given to the enemy.

"Are you all ready, sir?" asked the gunner, in a whisper, when he had completed his arrangements.

"All ready," replied Somers.

" Hand me the match-paper, Longstone," added the gunner, whose husky tones indicated his consciousness of the peril to which he exposed himself. " Shove off! " added he, as he placed the burning match where, in a moment, it would fire the mass of powder.

Tom Longstone grasped the side of the steamer, and handed the dingy along the guard, assisted by Somers, till it shot past the stern. The two men then grasped the oars, and rowed with all their might to reach a safe position.

They had pulled but a few strokes before the explosion took place, which seemed to shake the very waters beneath them, apparently rending the cotton-clad into a thousand pieces.

26 *

CHAPTER XXVIII.

"THAT takes her off the hinges!" exclaimed Tom Longstone, coolly, while the fragments of the wreck were falling around the boat.

" Ay, ay! That give it to her good!" added the gunner. " I'd give a sixpence to know what them rebels are thinking about jest now."

" I dare say they are rather confused in their minds," said Somers. " But, give way, my men! I hope we haven't blown up the Rosalie."

" I cal'late we have shook her up some," replied the gunner, who was proud of the work of his hands.

The veterans pulled for the Rosalie, and Somers could not conquer his fears in regard to her. As yet he could not fathom the extent of the mischief caused by the explosion. He had, by the flash of the burning powder, seen the mass of cotton bales lifted up, or precipitated into the water. The steamer now appeared to be on fire, though the flames had as yet made but little progress.

The dingy dashed up to the accommodation ladder of the Rosalie. The gallant little craft seemed to be uninjured by the explosion, and Somers leaped on her deck, anxious to take part in any proceedings that might follow.

" I have to report myself," said he to the first lieutenant, as he touched his cap, for no circumstances could make him forget the discipline of the navy.

" You have already reported, Mr. Somers," replied Mr. Jackson, grasping his hand, hurriedly. " We have all heard you."

" Is the Rosalie damaged, sir? "

" I think you have smashed all the dishes in the pantry. I don't know that any other damage has been done."

" Bravo, Mr. Somers! " exclaimed the captain, seizing the haud of our middy. " You have done it! Are you hurt?"

" No, sir — haven't a scratch."

" Thank God for that! " replied the captain. " But we have no time to spare. Does she surrender, Mr. Greene? " he shouted to the second lieutenant, who was forward.

" No, sir; she has just fired several shots into us."

" Open upon her, Mr. Jackson. Strike while the iron is hot! Boatswain, see how much water we have forward!"

The report of the pivot gun followed the captain's order, and was succeeded by the minor roar of the two twenty-four pounders on the broadside, and the swivels aft. The forecastle was so lumbered up with cotton bales from the wreck, that the forecastle gun could not be used. In the mean time, the fires on board of the steamer had been gathering way, and the Rosalie was in imminent danger of being destroyed in the conflagration which must soon envelop her assailant. The firing was suspended in ten minutes, to learn the intentions of the rebels.

"Do you surrender?" demanded Mr. Greene, whose station was forward.

"Never!" shouted the well-known voice of Phil Kennedy; and as he uttered the word, several muskets were discharged.

Mr. Greene reported the result, and at the same time suggested that it would be best to board the steamer. Captain Waldron examined the situation, and concurring with the advice, ordered Mr. Jackson to lead the attack. Somers grasped his cutlass, and made sure that his pistol was in good condition.

"Lay 'em aboard, my lads!" cried Mr. Jackson.

"Ay, ay, sir!" shouted the ready tars, adding a rousing cheer to emphasize their willingness.

"You are not going without me, my blessed little officer," said Tom Longstone, as he put himself alongside our middy.

He had just reported the depth of water forward. The tide was rising, and in a short time the Rosalie would be afloat, if she was not doomed to burn with the steamer. He had carried an anchor out to windward to warp her off when she floated, and to prevent her from driving on any farther.

The boarding party, headed by the first lieutenant, with Somers hardly a pace behind him, rushed over the piles of cotton, and leaped upon the shattered deck of the steamer. As they advanced, a dozen shots were fired from the riflemen, and a couple of their number fell ; but heedless of everything but victory, they pressed forward to the deadly conflict.

Most of the rebels were engaged in an attempt to keep down the flames, which threatened them in the rear; but at the call of Kennedy, they abandoned this occupation, and sprang to their arms. The Rosalie's intrepid blue-jackets were fully imbued with the spirit of their gallant leader, and they poured over the cotton bales so impetuously that nothing could resist them.

" Down with them ! " shouted Mr. Jackson.

" Ay, ay, sir ! " roared the sailors, with a will, as they plunged into the midst of the rebels.

A desperate hand-to-hand fight ensued, with varying results for a time, for the rebels still outnumbered the Rosalie's people. Kennedy, evidently conscious that the crisis had come, and that his own fortunes were now to be decided, fought with a zeal and energy which he had not before displayed. His own salvation, rather than that of the Southern Confederacy, was involved in the conflict, and he fought as a drowning man clings to a straw. If he failed, his credit as an officer, waning before, would be utterly lost.

" Show me the beggar that wanted to hang you, my dear," said Tom Longstone, when he had cleared a spot around him with his cutlass.

" Fight for your country, Tom — not for revenge," replied Somers, as he rushed into the thickest of the fight.

" Show me the beggar, and I will do my country all the good I can."

But Somers was gone. He was some distance in advance of his party, for the stalwart arm of Tom Longstone, added to his own, had forced back the rebels near the place where they stood. In this exposed position he was seen by Phil Kennedy, whose soul was still rankling with evil passions, and whose revenge was still unsated. He crowded through his men, and rushed upon Somers with a fury which promised instant destruction to his enemy.

" Now we will settle the old score," gasped he, as he brought down his cutlass in the direction of Somers's head.

The blow fell ringing on the blade of the middy, who, with a sudden spring, passed his weapon through the body of his revengeful enemy. He fell, and Somers pressed forward, with Tom at his side, to win the victory, not to satisfy his own malice. The fall of Kennedy, whose words and example had been the life of the conflict on the rebel side, discouraged his followers; and having fought desperately for a few moments, they gave way all at once, retreating to the stern of the steamer. They were closely pressed by the enthusiastic tars; but they cried for quarter, and surrendered at call.

The victory was won, and loud cheers rent the air. The disordered masses of cotton bales were covered with dead and wounded, most of whom had been the victims of the explosion. The fire had begun to gather headway again, since the rebels had ceased to combat it, and the Rosalie was in danger of perishing with her shattered prize in the devouring element which knows no friends nor foes.

Mr. Jackson, panting from the violence of his exertions, ordered the men to roll the burning bales overboard. The rebels were required to aid in this necessary toil; and the officers, with cutlass in hand, compelled the able ones to work. The buckets were manned, and in less than an hour the flames were subdued, though the task was not accomplished without the severest labor on the part of friends and enemies.

When this pressing work was accomplished, attention was bestowed upon the rebel wounded. The portion of the steamer's cabin abaft the paddle-boxes was still in condition to be occupied, and the sufferers were borne to the state-rooms, or laid upon beds on the cabin floor. There were about thirty of them, most of whom had been injured by the falling cotton bales, or the flying missiles of the explosion. Not less than twenty dead men lay on the main deck; and the sight on board was sickening, even to those who had been accustomed to the carnage and ruin of hard-fought battles.

Somers was as active in his care for the wounded and suffering as he had been in the excitement of the battle. Among the first he saw, in his humane labors, was Kennedy. He bent over him to ascertain if his wound had been fatal; and he found that he was still alive. He was borne to the saloon above, and was one of the first who received the attentions of the Rosalie's surgeon.

After all had been cared for, Somers went again to the cot of his enemy. The surgeon had done what he could, but the patient was now suffering severely from the pain of his wound.

"Water! Water!" said he, with a heavy groan, as Somers entered the state-room.

"How do you feel, Mr. Kennedy?" asked the visitor.

"Somers!" exclaimed he, "have you come to revel in my misery?"

"No; far from it," replied the young officer, shocked at the very thought.

" You have finished me, Somers, and you ought to be satisfied."

" I did not seek you in the fight and I am sorry that my duty compelled me to strike as I did."

" You have killed me ! Tell Kate Portington you have killed me," gasped the sufferer.

" Perhaps not ; you may recover."

" Will you do me a favor, Somers ?" added Kennedy, more gently.

" With pleasure."

" Then give me a glass of water. I am burning up."

Somers brought a tin cup full of water to him, and he drained it at a draught. Another was brought, of which he drank a part. The surgeon of the Rosalie now entered the room, for a moment, to learn the condition of the most important personage among the rebels.

" What do you think of him ? " asked Somers.

" Speak out plainly, doctor," added Kennedy, as the surgeon proceeded to examine him again.

" He cannot recover," he replied.

" Do you think so ? " cried the wounded man.

" It is a plain case, sir," said the doctor, shaking his head. " He may live till morning ; but I don't think he will," he added, turning to Somers.

" Then it is all up with me," groaned the sufferer, as the surgeon hastened away to attend to the pressing duties of the hour.

"The doctor says there is no hope for you," replied Somers.

For a moment he lay breathing heavily, and apparently musing upon the solemn truth which had just been spoken of him. He was about to pass away from the world in which he had sinned, and be ushered into another, "where the wicked cease from troubling, and the weary are at rest." It was an awful thought to him, for the memories of the past were not pleasant in his dying hour.

"I *can't* die, Somers!" exclaimed he, suddenly, as the full force of the thought impressed itself upon him.

"I fear you must, Mr. Kennedy; and I hope you will prepare yourself for the trying hour while you have the time. I must go now, and — "

"Don't leave me alone, Somers!" moaned Kennedy. "You will forgive me the wrong I have done you?"

"Freely! Here is my hand," said Somers, taking that of his late enemy.

"Thank you; now don't leave me."

"I must report to the executive officer on board the ship; but I will return in a few moments."

"Do, if you can."

Our hero was almost disgusted by the praise bestowed upon him by the captain and Mr. Jackson, for he had just come from the couch of the dying man. By his heroism he had saved the Rosalie; but with Kennedy's glazing eye still before his vision, he felt how vain was all human glory. He readily obtained permission to return to the bedside of the dying rebel, and hastened down into the steerage for the Testament which his mother had given him, and which had not been an unused companion in his leisure hours.

He found Kennedy was sinking fast, on his return, and, with the patient's ready permission, he read to him a chapter from his Testament.

" That's all very well, Somers ; but if you forgive me, I feel that God will," said the sufferer.

" I forgive you ; and from my heart I pray that God will forgive you — as I know he will if you are truly sorry."

" I am satisfied, Somers."

But it was plain that he was not satisfied ; that he did not possess that inward peace which alone can smooth a dying pillow.

" I have wronged you, Somers, more than any other man," he added, after Somers had given him another drink. " When I heard that your ship was ordered here, I asked to be appointed here, that I might be re. venged upon you."

" Never mind me, Mr. Kennedy ; you have wronged your country more than you have wronged me."

" I have done what I thought was right, and I am not sorry for it, except so far as you are concerned. If you see Kate, tell her you forgave me."

" I will."

A kind of spasm impaired the dying man's utterance, and Somers, though he felt his own weakness in the midst of such a scene, read another chapter, and tried to raise the sufferer's thoughts to higher things than those of earth. He felt that he had succeeded to some extent. Kennedy could not speak now. Somers bent over him, and uttered a short prayer ; but the patient did not speak nor move when he had finished.

He was dead.

CHAPTER XXIX.

SOMERS IN COMMAND.

SOMERS closed the eyes of the only enemy he had in the world, and returned to the Rosalie to report the event. For the first time since the battle, he had an opportunity to ascertain the extent of the loss which his ship had sustained. Poor Mr. Layard, as noble and brave an officer as ever walked a deck, lay dead in his state-room. Mr. Brown, the sailing-master, was severely wounded in the hip. Five of the crew, in-cluding the acting gunner, who had fired the train that shattered the steamer, were dead, and twelve were dis-abled by wounds, in addition to as many more still able to attend to duty.

It had been a hard-fought series of actions, and nothing but the indomitable gallantry of the crew had saved the Rosalie from being captured. The plan which had been devised and executed by Somers was the immediate sal-vation of the vessel; but if the officers had been less devoted, and the crew less determined, the schooner would have been taken early in the evening. Somers realized now what a desperate battle had been fought against greatly superior numbers.

Though victory had crowned the terrible work of the night, there was nothing but sadness about the vessel. Not an officer nor a man was seen to smile, now that the excitement of the battle was over, and the fearful results even of victory had been summed up. The death of that one brave man, who lay dead in the ward-room, would have cast a deep gloom through the ship ; but the poor gunner, who had risked his life without a murmur to save the ship, had fallen, aud there were four other cold forms shrouded in the banner for which they had fought and died.

In the ward-room lay the sailing-master, suffering untold agonies from his painful wound, and the sick-bay was crowded with gallant fellows, who scorned to utter a groan or a murmur in the midst of their sufferings. Truly the consequences of victory are hardly less terrible than those of defeat.

There was no sleep in the Rosalie that night, for there were hardly men enough left to keep watch on deck, and guard the horde of rebel prisoners on board the shattered steamer. When Somers had his watch below, he devoted himself to the care of Mr. Brown, as other officers and men had done by their wounded shipmates.

The Rosalie had been hauled off from her dangerous proximity to the Chimney Spit. Gloom and sadness pervaded every part of her; but the duty which she had been sent to perform was not neglected. While the dead slept on, and the wounded stifled their sighs of pain, the lookouts on deck still gazed fixedly into the gloom of the night, serving the cause of freedom and humanity as truly as the admirals who led the fleets, and the generals who marshalled the armies of the Union.

" Sail ho ! " shouted the lookout on the bowsprit; but the tone was less buoyant and joyful than usual, for the speaker had a heart which was with the dead and the dying below.

" Clear away the midship gun," said the officer of the deck, when he had made out the approaching sail, which was a brig coming down the sound.

The captain presently appeared, and a shot was dropped across the forefoot of the blockade-runner — for such she was without a doubt. Mr. Somers was ordered out in the second cutter to board the vessel, which was beating out with a fresh breeze. It was quite evident that those in charge of the vessel did not expect to find any obstacle to her passage out of the sound, for they would not have attempted to run by the Rosalie with a head wind. Phil Kennedy had probably been so certain of capturing the Rosalie, that he had ordered this brig to sail at high tide.

Somers directed his cockswain to lay on his oars, when the cutter had pulled a few strokes from the ship. He sat in the stern, coolly contemplating the movements of the brig, and appeared to be fully master of the situation. The blockade-runner was now approaching the spit, and must tack in a moment.

"Give way," said Somers, when he had carefully timed the movements of the brig.

The men, hardly excited, under the trying circumstances of the hour, by the prospect of a prize, gave way with the vigor of discipline, rather than of enthusiasm, and the boat came up with the vessel just as she went in stays. The bowman seized her bob-stay, and Somers, who had gone forward into the fore-sheets, sprang into her head rigging, and made his way to the deck. He was closely followed by a dozen of his brave tars.

"Who are you?" demanded the captain of the brig, with an oath.

"Your vessel is a prize to the United States schooner Rosalie, Captain Waldron. Stand by her fore-braces! Mainsail, haul!" shouted Somers, finding the crew had not completed the operation of tacking, and that the brig was in danger of misstaying.

The ready seamen sprang to their stations as though they had shipped in the brig, which, having a good full, came round handsomely, and stood off on the other tack. The captain was very much surprised to find his vessel captured, for he had been assured that, in a few hours, there would be no man-of-war in the sound to dispute his passage. After one more tack the brig came to anchor a short distance from the Rosalie, and Somers went on board to report the success of his undertaking.

Captain Waldrou was entirely satisfied with the manner in which Somers had discharged his duty; and he was sent back with orders to remain in charge of her as prize-master. The boatswain of the Rosalie, and four seamen, were detailed as his command; but the crew of the brig were all foreigners, and as willing to serve under one flag as another. They volunteered for duty, and a majority of them expressed a desire to ship in the navy.

Somers, burdened by the responsibility of his first command, did not dare to sleep; and he spent the remainder of the night on the quarter-deck of the brig, talking over the affairs of the past and present with his faithful friend, Tom Longstone. When the morning came, the men, fatigued and saddened by the events of the night, were called upon to perform the heavy labor of moving the cotton-clad to a more secure position. She still floated, though her port paddle-box and guard, and all her upper works forward of the wheels, had been shattered to pieces. She was towed up under the shelter of a point of land, and the Rosalie anchored near her.

All the prisoners were put under guard on board of her, including the officers of the captured brig. Nothing could be done with them at present, for it was necessary to keep the well ones to nurse the wounded. In the course of the forenoon, Somers was electrified at the receipt of an order, addressed to him, as acting third lieutenant of the Rosalie, to proceed to Port Royal in command of the brig. Mr. Walker and Tom Longstone were detailed as his first and second officers, and he was to be the bearer of the despatches to the admiral. The remains of the first lieutenant were conveyed on board, to be sent to his friends at the North.

Almost overwhelmed by the responsibility laid upon him, and the confidence reposed in him, Somers made sail, and proceeded on his voyage. The record of his cruise would be only a narrative of sleepless nights, without any incident worthy a place in these pages. The young commander could not make the cares of his new situation rest easily upon him. But the pleasant weather and the favor of divine Providence enabled him to reach his destined port in safety.

Blushing and stammering, he reported to the admiral, who happened to be there, and delivered his despatches. The papers told the story, and he was thrown into a terrible state of confusion by the admiral seizing his hand, and thanking him for the valuable service he had rendered.

"I have heard of you before, Mr. Somers, and you have been true to your record. You shall go to Boston in command of the brig you have captured."

"Thank you, sir," stammered Somers, unable to say another word.

Before the brig departed, a steamer was sent down with a reënforcement for the crew of the Rosalie, and at sundown, the Harwich, which was the name of Somers's vessel, was out of sight of land. Our middy soon became accustomed to his responsible position, and was able to sleep nights. The brig ran through a gale of eighteen hours' duration, but, being well handled, she reached Boston in safety.

CHAPTER XXX.

MISS KATE PORTINGTON.

HE Harwich came to anchor off the navy yard at Charlestown, and her young commander went on shore to deliver his despatches from the admiral. The necessary legal proceedings were immediately commenced, and Somers was required to remain as a witness until the prize had been condemned. At the earliest moment his duties would permit, he ran down to Pinchbrook, where, of course, he was warmly welcomed. It required an afternoon and evening for him to tell his adventures; and no soldier or sailor from the stirring scenes of the South ever had a more attentive audience.

At the conclusion of the legal business he was ordered to New York, there to take passage for the South, where he was to join his ship, together with the officers and sailors who had accompanied him. Having found that the vessel in which he was to return would not sail for several days, he obtained permission to spend a day in Newport. Mr. Revere, the commandant of midshipmen, received him like a brother, and the officers and members of the Academy gave him a very pleasant welcome.

"Well, Mr. Somers, I suppose you will not forget to go over to Commodore Portington's — will you?" asked the commandant, with a siguificant smile, when our middy had answered all the questions about the service which had been proposed.

"I don't know, sir," said Somers, whose telltale face betrayed the fact that he had been thinking of such a thing.

"You don't know!" exclaimed Mr. Revere; "yes, you do know."

"I suppose I shall call there."

"You more than suppose it, Mr. Somers. If I thought you had any doubt about going there, I would put you under arrest, and send you under guard of a file of marines."

"I will go, sir," laughed Somers.

And he did go. Though he was not willing to confess it, even to himself, the anticipated pleasure of that visit had been considerably more than half the inducement for him to visit Newport. Kate was not in the room when he entered, and he received a very motherly greeting from Mrs. Portington. But presently the daughter's step was heard in the adjoining apartment, and poor Somers's heart fluttered worse than it did when he had been appointed to the command of the Harwich. It was

28

ten times worse than repelling boarders to meet her face
to face, after so long an absence.

Somers felt very much like going by the board, as the
rustle of the silk dress fell upon his ears; but Kate
entered the room, and rushed forward, with both hands
extended, to welcome him. Her cheeks were suffused
with blushes, and it was quite evident that she was not
taking the matter so coolly as her manner and her subsequent remarks might have led one to suppose.

" Why, Prodigy, is it possible that you have returned?" exclaimed she, as he took her extended hands.

" For a brief period only," said Somers, hardly able
to articulate the words.

" Why couldn't you say for ' a short time,' instead of
' a brief period,' Mr. Somers?"

" Now, Kate, you shall not begin to make fun of Mr.
Somers," interposed Mrs. Portington.

" If I had known your pleasure, I should certainly
have said so," added Somers.

" My pleasure! Why can't you talk like a Christian,
and not use that stilted language? You are not an admiral yet. Now, sit down, and tell me where you have
been, and what wonders you have done."

" I haven't done any wonders, Miss Portington."

" Yes, you have. I read all about it in one of the Boston papers."

" Then there is no need that I should tell you."

"But I want to hear it from you."

"I will give you an abstract of the log-book of Rosalie."

"Fiddlesticks! I don't care for the log book of the Rosalie. I suppose you want to tell me the latitude and longitude of Doboy Sound. But what awful stories are told about poor Phil Kennedy!" added she, suddenly looking as grave as a matron of sixty. "Are they true?"

"I am sorry to say they are. Of course you have heard of his death?"

They had not heard of it; and Somers narrated the events which had terminated in the death of the mis guided young man, including the last scene which had transpired on board of the cotton-clad. Mrs. Portington and her daughter were both much moved as he described the sad event; but both of them condemned, in fitting terms, his treason and his treachery.

Somers spent the afternoon, and took tea with the family. Kate's cheerfulness was not much impaired by the intelligence of Kennedy's death, after the first shock had passed away. Neither she nor her mother was disposed to say much about him. Perhaps they felt that he had disgraced the family by his connection with it, and that silence was the only proper commentary on his conduct. Somers had learned that General Portington had destroyed the will in which Kennedy had been joint heir with Kate of his property, and that the commodore, as the next of kin, would succeed to his fortune. Delicacy, therefore, as well as policy, required them to speak lightly, or not at all, of Phil's infirmities.

"Now you are going off to do new wonders — are you?" said Kate, after tea.

"I am going to do my duty; though for your sake I could almost hope that I shall have nothing to do but my daily routine for a year," replied Somers.

"For my sake! I hope you will capture every blockade-runner at the South. Why, you are a prodigy, Mr. Somers; and I believe, if they would turn you loose on the Atlantic Ocean in a jolly-boat, with nothing but a broken ramrod, you would capture the Alabama within twenty-four hours."

"I protest," laughed Somers.

"Well, call it forty-eight, then," added the merry girl.

"Wouldn't you oblige me by making it a week?"

"No, not another hour. Two days are enough for you to sink or blow up the biggest ship that ever floated."

"Well, I don't know what I might do, under the inspiration of bright eyes at home," said Somers, looking archly into her beaming orbs.

"What bright eyes?" asked she, with the least possible agitation.

"Yours, to be sure," laughed the little naval hero.

" That's silly, Mr. Somers. Do you mean to say that you ever think of any one besides yourself, while you are away?"

" To be sure I do; I don't believe there is a single hour of my watch on deck in which I don't think of my mother and you."

" Well, I declare, Prodigy, you are improving wonderfully. Wouldn't you like to have me fall overboard, or do some other ridiculous thing, to afford you another opportunity to save me from a watery grave?"

" I hope you are not angry with me for thinking of you when I am away. You have amused me so much that I cannot help thinking of you."

" Pray, Mr. Somers, is that the particular reason why you think of your *mother* when you are on duty?"

" Certainly not."

" Then I will thank you not to think of me as the sport of your idle hours."

" How may I think of you, then?"

" As an esteemed and valued friend, who is always ready to give you good advice, and keep your vanity from eating you up."

" Then I will think of you as such. I suppose you forgot, during my absence, Miss Portington, that such a person as Mr. Midshipman Somers was in existence."

" You are not here to catechise me, Mr. Somers. You are a prodigy; but there are some things you cannot

28 *

do," replied Kate; but she answered the question much
more satisfactorily in her looks and manner.

"Pardon me," said he, rising to go; "I must leave
now."

"Tear yourself away, you ought to have said, to be
entirely consistent with your record. But go; and remember that your esteemed and valued acquaintance in
Newport will look with friendly interest for intelligence
from you — in other words, write to me."

"I will, with pleasure; but what may I hope for in
return?"

"For an answer, of course."

"With a letter from you in my pocket, I could capture
the whole Confederate navy."

"You shall have it, then," said she, with some confusion.

"Good by," he added, taking her hand.

"You mentioned me, just now, in the same breath
with your mother, Mr. Somers. What did you say to
her when you parted with her?"

"That I would try to be true to God and my country," replied he, earnestly.

"Those were good words to leave behind you."

"Then I will leave them with you; I will try to be
true to God and my country."

"I know you will be," replied Kate, seriously.

"And then — and then --"

" What then ? " asked Kate.

" I kissed my mother," he replied, as, with one of those tremendous mental efforts which had braced his nerves in the hour of battle, the audacious wretch actually kissed Miss Kate Portington !

Kate was astonished, but not half so much astonished as Somers himself, when he realized what he had done. Again he braced himself to receive the rebuke which he was conscious of deserving; but it did not come. She only blushed and smiled, thus assuring him that he had not committed an unpardonable sin; and the memory of that happy moment lingered with him for months and years. He pressed her hand, both said good by, and he was gone.

" I wish she was my sister ! " thought Somers, as he walked down the street.

Perhaps he did. If he did, it was only because he did not know any better.

In the evening he took the steamer for New York, where he embarked for the South, and in due time reported on board of the Rosalie again. His welcome was scarcely less enthusiastic than that which had greeted him at home. The vacancies had been filled, and again he was nothing but a Yankee middy.

The capture of two sailing vessels and the destruction of two steamers gave the rebels a sharp warning, and nearly spoiled the occupation of the Rosalie; for though she remained on the station till the following spring, she captured but one schooner.   It was a dry time; but Somers employed all his leisure hours, as he had done before, in pressing forward his studies.   In June he was examined, having the highest recommendations which his officers could give, and came off with flying colors. He was immediately promoted to the rank of ensign; and though Mr. Somers served with distinguished fidelity and success under that "brave old salt" who com- manded the West Gulf Squadron, here properly ends his career as the YANKEE MIDDY.

THE ARMY AND NAVY STORIES.

In Six Volumes.

A Library for Young and Old.

BY OLIVER OPTIC.

———————————

LIBRARY FOR YOUNG PEOPLE.

BY OLIVER OPTIC.

I.
THE BOAT CLUB;
OR, THE BUNKERS OF RIPPLETON.

II.
ALL ABOARD;
OR, LIFE ON THE LAKE.

III.
LITTLE BY LITTLE;
OR, THE CRUISE OF THE FLYAWAY.

IV.
TRY AGAIN;
OR, THE TRIALS AND TRIUMPHS OF HARRY WEST.

V.
NOW OR NEVER;
OR, THE ADVENTURES OF BOBBY BRIGHT

VI.
POOR AND PROUD;
OR, THE FORTUNES OF KATY REDBURN.

Six volumes, put up in a neat box.

LEE & SHEPARD, Publishers.

WOODVILLE STORIES.

BY OLIVER OPTIC.

———◦◦⋆◦◦———

I.
RICH AND HUMBLE;
Or, The Mission of Bertha Grant.

II.
IN SCHOOL AND OUT;
Or, The Conquest of Richard Grant.

III.
WATCH AND WAIT;
Or, The Young Fugitives.

IV.
WORK AND WIN;
Or, Noddy Newman on a Cruise.

V.
HOPE AND HAVE;
Or, Fanny Grant among the Indians.

VI.
HASTE AND WASTE;
Or, The Young Pilot of Lake Champlain.

———————

LEE & SHEPARD, Publishers.

www.ingramcontent.com/pod-product-compliance
Lightning Source LLC
Chambersburg PA
CBHW021803110726
47902CB00006B/1625